The False-Hearted Teddy

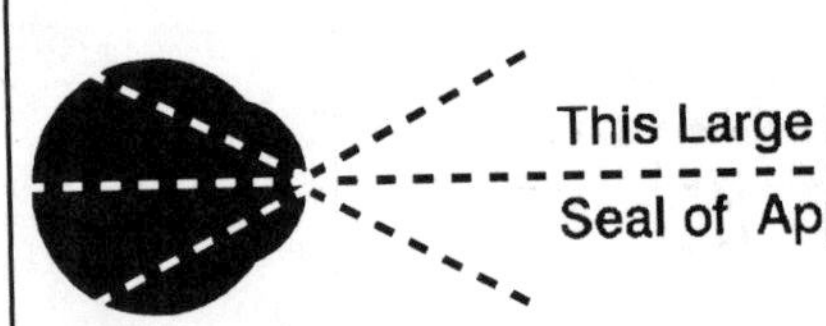

This Large Print Book carries the Seal of Approval of N.A.V.H.

The False-Hearted Teddy

John J. Lamb

WHEELER PUBLISHING
An imprint of Thomson Gale, a part of The Thomson Corporation

Detroit • New York • San Francisco • New Haven, Conn. • Waterville, Maine • London

A Bear Collector's Mystery.
Wheeler, an imprint of The Gale Group.

Wheeler Publishing Large Print Cozy Mystery.
The text of this Large Print edition is unabridged.
Other aspects of the book may vary from the original edition.
Set in 16 pt. Plantin.

LIBRARY OF CONGRESS CATALOGING-IN-PUBLICATION DATA

Lamb, John J., 1955–
The false-hearted teddy / by John J. Lamb.
p. cm. — (A bear collector's mystery) (Wheeler Publishing large print cozy mystery)
ISBN-13: 978-1-59722-616-5 (alk. paper)
ISBN-10: 1-59722-616-5 (alk. paper)
1. Teddy bear makers — Fiction. 2. Teddy bears — Fiction. 3. Baltimore (Md.) — Fiction. 4. Large type books. I. Title.
PS3612.A5457F35 2007
813'.6—dc22 2007022900

Published in 2007 by arrangement with The Berkley Publishing Group, a member of Penguin Group (USA) Inc.

Printed in the United States of America on permanent paper
10 9 8 7 6 5 4 3 2 1

With love to my father's sister,
Patricia Lamb Puffer,
my dear "Aunt Pat."

One

It was just after seven o'clock on a Friday morning on the last day of March. The sky overhead was the same brilliant hue as a London blue topaz, but slate gray snow-laden clouds were oozing over the top of Massanutten Mountain and the freshening breeze was as brisk and chilly as an audit notification letter from the Internal Revenue Service. Up on the crest there'd be snow, but down where we were on the valley floor, the moisture would come in the form of more cold and sullen rain. Although the calendar said that spring was eleven days old, the persistent ache coming from the reconstructed bones and titanium hardware that comprise what remains of my left shin proclaimed it was still winter. That crippling injury and the blackthorn cane I use to get around are mementos from my former career as a San Francisco PD homicide inspector. I'd have preferred a plaque or a gold watch.

Bradley Lyon is my name; however, there isn't anything leonine about my appearance. I'm five foot eleven when I don't slouch, I have blue eyes, and my drivers' license lists my weight as 220 pounds. I might look a little heavier, but hey, if the Commonwealth of Virginia says that's what I weigh, it must be true. I'll be forty-eight years old in July, but there's no denying the truth: I look much, much older. Getting shot has a way of aging you.

My wife, Ashleigh, and I had just left our Shenandoah Valley hometown of Remmelkemp Mill and were driving in our Nissan Xterra westbound on Coggins Spring Road through dormant and muddy pastureland when I squinted into the rearview mirror and sighed. A Massanutten County sheriff's cruiser was right behind us with its blue overhead emergency lights flashing and high-beam headlights wigwagging.

Although I was a cop for a quarter of a century, I have excellent reasons for being apprehensive about any encounters with the local gendarmes. Shortly after moving to the valley less than a year ago, Ash and I discovered that some of the county cops believed the motto "to protect and serve" meant looking after their own shady dealings. We'd had a series of harrowing experiences that culminated in one of them trying to murder us. Things are a little better now. However, there are some local folks — including a few that still wear badges — who view us as troublemaking interlopers from California, even though my wife grew up along the banks of the South Fork of the Shenandoah River and her family has owned and farmed the land here for over two hundred years.

When it became clear that the cruiser wasn't going to pass us, I said, "Don't panic but we're being pulled over."

Ash looked up from the nutmeg-colored mohair teddy bear she was grooming with a small brush and shot a glance into the passenger side mirror. "For what? You didn't break any traffic laws."

"And your point is? Sweetheart, you know as well as I do that we aren't going to win any popularity contests with some of the older deputies who were loyal to the former sheriff."

"But Tina —"

"Is doing a great job as sheriff and wouldn't allow this sort of crap. But she can't be everywhere at once and, as much as she wanted to, she couldn't fire deputies just because they liked their old boss."

"If they knew what he was up to and didn't do anything to stop him, they shouldn't be deputies. I'd fire them." Ash's normally warm blue eyes were as hard and cold as sapphires. Like me, she loathed corrupt cops.

"I agree, but who're you kidding, honey? You'd fire *at* them . . . with a twenty-gauge shotgun loaded with rock salt."

She smiled as if I'd paid her a compliment. "Mama used to say that the sharper the sting the better the lesson."

Come September, Ash and I will have been married twenty-seven years and although we spent over twenty-five years living in San Francisco before returning to rural Virginia, she remains a country girl at heart. Her creed is as simple as it is wholesome: be kind, work hard, be honest, always strive to do the right thing, and give other folks the benefit of the doubt — once. Cross the ethical line twice and the best you can hope for is that you cease to exist in her universe, which — believe me — is preferable to becoming her enemy.

The bottom line is that Ash is a fiery woman, strong and full of conviction and it's the main reason I adore her, although the fact she's strikingly beautiful, with long wavy golden blond hair and an exquisite full figure, doesn't hurt.

Behind us, the patrol car's siren sounded for a second.

"I guess I'd better stop before we get a warning shot across the bow."

I switched the turn indicator on, steered to the side of the road, and shut the engine off. Then I put my hands back on the steering wheel where they'd be in plain sight. The cruiser pulled in behind us, the blue lights were switched off, and the door swung open. A tall cop, wearing tan trousers and a brown car coat, climbed from the squad car.

I relaxed and said, "It's okay. It's Tina."

With her dark curly hair, soft brown eyes, and porcelain doll-like pretty features, Tina Barron didn't fit the conventional image of a county sheriff, yet we knew from personal experience that she was a brave and skilled cop. She'd assumed office as acting sheriff in October in the wake of our unofficial investigation and was elected by a landslide the following month. Since that time, she'd impressed everyone with her commitment to serve the community and repair the department's tarnished reputation. And if she was a good sheriff, she was an even better friend, to Ash in particular.

I rolled down the window and cranked up the heater a little to balance against the influx of cold air. Both Ash and I said, "Hi, Tina."

Tina bent over to look inside the SUV. "Hi, you guys! I wanted to say good-bye before you left for the bear show."

She was referring to the Baltimore Har-Bear Expo, one of the premier teddy bear conventions on the East Coast. It was being held at the Fell's Point Maritime Inn, a large hotel in a neighborhood just east of the inner harbor. We'd been preparing for it all winter and the back of the Xterra was packed with teddy bears and stuffed tigers.

"Wish us luck," Ash said.

"You won't need luck. I'll bet Hilda Honey Crisp takes top honors."

"I wish I was as certain as you are, but thank you."

Hilda was a fourteen-inch-tall, ivory-colored plush bear dressed up as a wedge of apple pie and was a member of Ash's new "Confection Collection," an assortment of teddies attired as decadent desserts. Don't ask me how she did it, but my wife designed and created costumes for the bears that looked exactly like pieces of pineapple upside-down cake, peach cobbler, and carrot cake. In fact, Brenda Brownie resembled the genuine article so much that I imagined I could smell the chocolate and that set my left shin throbbing — an extreme aversion to the scent of chocolate is one of the unpleasant psychosomatic side effects resulting from my having been shot in Ghirardelli Square back in San Francisco.

"And thanks for letting Kitch stay with you while we're gone," I said.

"It's our pleasure. The kids love having him around."

Kitchener is our Old English sheepdog. He usually stays in a big plastic crate while we're away from home, but since we'd be absent until Sunday evening, that wasn't an option this time. Fortunately, Tina had agreed to babysit him because there's no way we could put him in any of the local kennels. They looked far too much like doggie interment camps to me.

Tina continued, "And now I want to see it, Brad."

I assumed an expression of shock and embarrassment. "Jeez, that's a mighty personal request, especially with my wife here."

"Brad!" Ash sounded genuinely scandalized.

"And it's cold."

"You *know* I'm talking about your bear." Tina was blushing furiously.

"Oh, the bear! I thought you were talking

about, well, you know, something else."

"Brad." There was a warning note in Ash's voice now.

"Sorry, Tina. I'll be good. Let me get him."

I reached behind Ash's car seat and retrieved Dirty Beary, my fabric and polyester stuffing tribute to San Francisco's most famous cinema cop. I'd been working on the bear in utter secrecy throughout most of the winter, which was why Tina was so eager to see it. Beary was a lanky twenty-inch-tall, bronze-colored mohair teddy dressed in slacks, a brown tweed sports jacket, a dress shirt, and a little necktie. He also sported a small pair of sunglasses and wore a miniature seven-pointed SFPD gold star on his belt. I'd spent almost three weeks just working on the placement of his glass eyes and agonizing over the downward curve of the embroidered frown, trying to capture the essential spirit of Clint Eastwood.

I handed the bear to Tina and rasped out an altered version of the famous monologue from the film, *Dirty Harry:* "I know what you're thinking. Did he make five bears or six? Well, in all the excitement, I kind of lost track myself. But being that this is Dirty Beary, the most intimidating stuffed animal in the world, you've got to ask yourself, 'Am I feeling lucky?' Well, are you, Tina?"

She gaped in disbelief at the bear. "He's amazing."

"Thanks, but most of the credit belongs to Ash."

"Don't believe him, Tina. He made Beary all by himself," Ash said.

"Yeah, but you spent *how* many hours teaching me how to use the Bernina?" I asked, referring to our futuristic sewing machine which can do everything but sing the "Battle Hymn of the Republic," (although you *could* embroider the words to the song by simply pushing a combination of buttons).

"But he made the bear and the clothes himself," Ash said proudly.

Tina pulled one side of Beary's tiny sports jacket open. "Oh my gosh, he's wearing a leather shoulder holster with a tiny forty-four magnum!"

"I have a constitutional right to arm bears."

Ash and Tina groaned.

"Bad puns aside, do you like him?"

"I absolutely love him. Do you think you could make me one just like him? I'd pay you."

"Of course I'll make you a teddy bear, but

you aren't going to pay me."

"But —"

"No argument. You saved our lives. If you'd been a second or two later, Trent would have killed us."

"Sergei helped."

"Then I'll make him a nice little teddy bear, too."

While Ash and Tina chuckled at the absurd notion of Sergei Zubatov wanting a stuffed animal, I merely smiled, knowing that I'd come perilously close to revealing a secret about the retired Soviet military intelligence agent who owned the local barbecue restaurant. After seeing Dirty Beary the previous afternoon, Sergei had cautiously asked me if I'd consider making him a similar teddy bear dressed in the authentic dress uniform of a Red Army colonel. However, fearful of damaging his local reputation of being more cool and remote than the Ross Ice Shelf, he'd sworn me to silence about the project, with the understanding that that silence wouldn't include Ash. That was because I'd need her help with the uniform and, more importantly, I don't keep secrets from my wife — not that there's any chance I actually could if I were foolish enough to try.

Tina handed Dirty Beary back to me. "I

know you've been busy, but have you had the chance to give some thought to my offer?"

"I have, and I'm sorry but I still haven't made a decision."

"If it's the money . . ."

"No, that isn't it at all. There are just a couple of issues I'm trying to resolve. I promise I'll give you an answer soon."

"There's no rush."

Tina's offer was that I become a paid consultant to the Massanutten County Sheriff's Department. If I accepted, I'd provide training to the deputies on analyzing and investigating crime scenes, and would also be available for call out in the event of a murder or other major felony to provide expertise. Although it meant some extra income, which was always welcome, I was hesitant to accept because, to my shock, I wasn't certain I wanted to return to police work. I'd been away from the job for almost two years and enjoyed not having to gird myself in invisible armor to deal with the toxic environment cops operate in on a daily basis. Not attending horrific murder scenes or "grand openings" at the medical examiner's office, where business — because it's lying on stainless steel tables — is always looking up, was also a nice change. Besides,

I was enjoying my new career as Ash's partner in Lyon's Tigers and Bears.

Still, admittedly I missed some aspects of being a homicide inspector, but for bad and selfish reasons. I longed for the intellectual excitement of hunting a killer, the pleasure of outmaneuvering my prey, and the satisfaction of being thought of as the very best at what I did. So, can you see my Faustian dilemma? The egoist in me wanted back into cop work while the rational part of me knew that any return could be at a serious cost to my soul.

Then again, I wondered if I was imagining a crisis where none existed. The position would give me the opportunity to share some of my specialized knowledge with the local cops, and as there wasn't much violent crime in Massanutten County — the sole murder victim of the previous year was the guy who washed up in the river in front of our house — it wasn't likely I'd be called to many murder scenes. I'd discussed my misgivings with Ash, who made it clear that she'd support me in whatever decision I eventually made.

I said, "Actually Tina, I have decided and I'd like to accept."

Tina beamed and she patted my shoulder. "Thanks, Brad. We'll talk more about it when you come to pick up Kitch."

"Sounds great."

"You've got a long drive, so I'll let you get going now. Ash, good luck with the Confection Collection and maybe next year I can come, too."

"With your own artisan bears? We'd love it," said Ash.

"And Brad?"

"Yes, Tina?"

"There are times when you can be a real brat."

"Just times?" Ash and I said simultaneously.

Two

There are two ways to get to Baltimore from our house. The most direct route is also the longest drive because it means committing your immortal soul to Interstate 495, otherwise known as the Washington Beltway. With its shocking collection of bad drivers, omnipresent gridlock, and claustrophobia-inducing fleets of eighteen-wheelers, the Beltway is one of the *bolgias* of hell that Dante missed on his tour of the Inferno. The longer but prettier and less stressful route is to go northeastward along the Shenandoah Valley to Frederick, Maryland, and head for Baltimore from there. Guess which way we went.

A little more than three hours later we were off the interstate, passing through Baltimore's Little Italy and entering the neighborhood known as Fell's Point. The tourist industry makes a big deal about Baltimore's Inner Harbor, mostly because of the Camden Yards ballpark and the National Aquarium. But as far as I'm concerned, the rest of the district is one vast homogenized shopping center, mostly lacking in personality and featuring the same stores you can find in almost any mall throughout the county. Fell's Point, on the other hand, is loaded with character. The well-maintained buildings are a delightful melding of antebellum and Victorian architecture and the cobblestone streets and black wrought iron streetlights hearken back to an earlier and more elegant era. You won't find many national retailers in Fell's Point, but as we made our way through the neighborhood we saw upscale antique stores, art galleries, trendy clothing boutiques, and an interesting collection of pubs and restaurants.

Ash pointed to a store as we made the turn from Fleet Street onto South Ann Street. "Look, a mystery bookshop. Maybe we can come back later on and see if the new *Pam and Pom* mystery is out."

"Finally, a reason to go on living," I said, taking note of the shop's location.

My wife is a huge fan of mystery novels and her favorite books feature Pamela, a beautiful yoga instructor, and her cute talking Pomeranian dog, Bitsy. However, like almost every homicide detective I've ever known, I don't care for mystery novels.

Ash gave me a wry here-we-go-again smile. "Honey, I know you don't think they're very realistic."

"Really? You mean us dim-witted cops don't always arrest the wrong person?"

"I don't care, I still like them."

"Yeah, and I'm really sorry for being such a curmudgeon. We'll try to get back there this afternoon."

"And I want you to promise not to make any comments about how unrealistic you think the books are."

"You never let me have *any* fun."

"Oh? And how would you describe last night?" She ran her hand upward along the top of my right thigh and I could feel my pulse begin to accelerate.

"My love, the word 'fun' doesn't even begin to describe last night."

A minute later, we turned left onto Thames Street, which ran along the north side of the harbor. Off to the southeast, on the other side of the shipping channel, the brown angular walls of Fort McHenry — of the "Star-Spangled Banner" fame — were just barely visible and I hoped that we might get over there on Sunday before heading home. We followed the road until it dead-ended at the driveway entrance to the Fell's Point Maritime Inn.

The hotel was large and composed of dark brown brick. Its design was apparently intended to commemorate the clipper ships built long ago in Fell's Point because the eight-storied structure was shaped like an elongated almond, vaguely in the manner of a sailing vessel, and the roof was dominated by three tall white metal scalene triangle wedges, each larger than the next, which I assumed were supposed to recall an array of wind-filled jib sails. Personally, I thought the angular display looked as if a behemoth paper plane had landed on the top of the building.

We pulled up to the main entrance and had to wait a few moments until the traffic ahead cleared out. The Har-Bear Expo was a major show that routinely attracted over a hundred artisans from all over the U.S. and Canada and even some bear makers from Europe. It looked as if most of them had arrived just a few minutes before us. The temporary parking area was packed with minivans and SUVs in the process of emptying their cargoes of folding tables, display shelves, signage, and crates of stuffed animals. The first fat droplets of rain began to splatter on our windshield and everyone began to scramble to get their bears inside. I parked in a handicapped slot not far from the door and Ash and I shared our large umbrella until we'd reached the shelter of the covered portico. Then we went inside to register.

The lobby was decorated in an age-of-sail nautical theme — heavily varnished oaken floors, old naval flags hanging from the walls, and a wooden registration desk appointed in gleaming brass accents. A pair of painted and artificially weathered hand-carved mermaid figureheads were mounted on the wall flanking the desk, and thickly corded ship's rigging was strung overhead like giant spider webs. Although it was a little noisy in the lobby, I could faintly hear music from the hotel's PA system and it took a second before I realized it was an instrumental version of Pat Benatar's "Hit Me With Your Best Shot" being played with an unfretted guitar, tin whistle, and concertina as if it were a jolly whaling song. The place was seriously kitschy, but I still considered the atmosphere an improvement over the usual marble-appointed hotel lobby, which tends to be so cold and austere that I'm reminded of a mausoleum.

A four-foot-tall sandwich-board sign featuring an illustration of a bear wearing a

Cap'n Crunch–style old-time sea captain's uniform stood at the head of the corridor leading to the right, pointing the direction to the conference room where the Har-Bear Expo was being held. There was a continuous stream of people entering and leaving as they unloaded their bears. At last, we checked into the hotel, got our key cards, and as we headed back toward the door, saw that it was raining harder.

Ash said, "Why don't we drive the truck into the parking structure and unload it there?"

"I really need to stretch my leg, so if you don't mind, could you drive it in and I'll stand by here to grab one of those luggage carts?"

"Of course. How bad is your leg?"

"It isn't where I got shot that's hurting so much, but I end up holding my leg in a funny position —"

"And it causes the other muscles to ache. I'm so sorry, sweetheart."

"Actually, I shouldn't be complaining. I can still walk and there are people coming back from Iraq who are dealing with far more serious injuries and not singing the blues. Remind me of that the next time I snivel." I handed her the umbrella and the keys to the Xterra.

"You don't snivel." She leaned over to kiss me on the cheek. "I'll meet you in the parking structure."

Once Ash left, I snagged a freshly abandoned cart. I pushed it down a corridor, through two sets of heavy metal fire doors, and out into the concrete parking structure where I walked right into one of a cop's least favorite situations: a man and woman engaged in a domestic dispute. However, they were so involved in exchanging charming repartee that they didn't notice my appearance.

The couple stood next to the open side doors of a huge metallic salmon-colored Dodge van. There was a dolly near the open doors of the vehicle and it was loaded with plastic crates full of plush bears with golden halos, little wings, and wearing ivory gossamer angelic robes. A petite woman in her mid-thirties with curly russet hair, full lips taut with anger, and a slightly olive complexion that looked jaundiced in the bluish light cast by the naked fluorescent bulbs overhead stood behind the dolly, clearly trying to keep it between herself and a man I assumed was her husband.

The man was at least six foot two and pushing three hundred pounds, with short blond hair, bright porcine eyes, and a moustache-goatee combo that did nothing but serve to draw attention to a fleshy double chin that bordered on being a full-blown wattle. He wore tan khakis and a long-sleeved Stuart-plaid flannel shirt that wasn't tucked in because he erroneously thought it would conceal his huge gut.

She said, "Just for once, will you listen to me, Tony? I don't like it."

"Open your damn ears, we aren't breaking any laws."

My ears pricked up. Those are the words that corporate CEOs and politicians customarily use to describe unethical, dishonest, but technically legal behavior.

"I still don't like it."

"Yeah, and guess what? I don't give a shit what you don't like, Jennifer. You aren't going to screw this up for us."

"Us? I didn't see you making any of these frigging bears."

"But you *are* going to see me pound the snot out of you if you keep running that smart mouth of yours."

Jennifer jerked her right hand upward, extending her middle finger. "Sit on it and spin you lard-ass son of a bitch."

Tony moved fast for a big man. He grabbed her by the wrist and raised his meaty right hand as if to slap her. Up until that moment, I was going to let them bicker and not interfere. A verbal disagreement isn't a crime and all couples have arguments, even Ash and I on a very rare occasion, although we'd never used that sort of vile language toward each other and couldn't imagine ever doing so. However, I have absolutely no tolerance for even an iota of physical abuse. I'd investigated far too many spousal assaults that had suddenly escalated into homicide.

I rapped my cane loudly against the metal framework of the trolley and the clanging sound echoed off the cement walls. "Hey, pardon me for interrupting, but let go of the lady."

They both looked at me and Tony growled, "She's my wife."

"That's an even better reason not to manhandle her."

"Mind your own business." Tony tightened his grip and his wife winced.

"I'll be happy to . . . once you let her go."

"Are you deaf, Grandpa? I said, mind your own business. Go back inside the hotel."

The "grandpa" stung a little but I didn't let it show. The emotional rigors of all those years of police work and then getting shot had taken their physical toll on my appearance. My hair is completely gray and my face is beginning to show more tired lines than an episode of *Friends* in its final season. Ash says that I'm hypersensitive, but add the bum leg and the cane to the picture and I think my nickname should be Methuselah.

I flashed a disdainful grin. "Nah, I think I'll stay right here and watch the big brave man smack his wife."

Tony's jaw began to jut. "Yeah? How about I come over there and kick your ass first?"

I began to walk toward him, tapping the cane's tip deliberately on the cement floor. One of the first skills a successful cop masters is something called "command presence." That means exuding complete confidence and serenity in the face of disaster. I chuckled, fixed him with a cool stare, and said, "What is this, amateur night at the Laugh Factory? You? Kick my ass? Tony, I've arrested hundreds of blow-hard punks like you for domestic violence and there wasn't a one of them that ever wanted to fight someone who could really hurt them. You aren't any different."

"You're a cop?" There was a tiny flicker of doubt in Tony's eyes. Meanwhile, it looked like his wife was beginning to hyperventilate.

"Retired."

"So, you probably have a gun. That's why you're acting so brave."

I snorted in contemptuous amusement. "I don't need a gun to deal with a tub of pig manure like you."

"Oh, you've got me so scared."

"As a matter of fact you are. I can see it in your eyes. Now, let go of her."

We were only a few feet apart now and Tony suddenly released his grip on Jennifer's arm. He turned and stalked toward the fire doors, calling to his wife over his shoulder, "Get the rest of the crap and go to the conference hall."

I watched him until I was certain he was gone and then noticed that Jennifer's breathing had become very ragged and wheezy. She was searching her purse, frantically looking for something and at last produced a cylindrical-shaped asthma inhaler. Drawing deeply from the device, she held her breath for about ten seconds and then slowly exhaled. Meanwhile, a pair of vehicle headlights appeared at the opposite end of the parking structure and slowly headed in our direction. From the silhouette it looked like the Xterra.

The woman put the inhaler back into her purse and gave me a severe look. "What are you waiting for, a medal?"

"No, I just wanted to make sure you're all right."

"I'm fine and nobody asked you to interfere, so do me a big favor. Mind your own damn business." Jennifer shoved the dolly past me, headed toward the fire doors.

"You're welcome. And are those angel or anger bears? The difference is only one letter."

She flipped me off just before she entered the hotel.

Actually, I wasn't that surprised by her rudeness. I'd encountered similar responses from battered spouses — both husbands and wives — throughout my police career. Although it's difficult to understand, many of the victims genuinely love their abusive partners and often resent a stranger intruding, even to stop a savage assault. It's also possible that Jennifer viewed the relative ease with which I'd intimidated her husband as a silent indictment that she was allowing herself to be bullied by a coward.

Ash drove up in the rain-spattered Xterra and jerked her head in the direction of the fire doors. "Did she just do what I thought I saw her do?"

"The one finger salute? Yeah, but I'm pretty certain it was intended as an insult rather than an invitation."

"Why would she do that?"

"I walked into the middle of a four-fifteen that was about to go physical," I said, using the California penal code section for a disturbance of the peace. "She's annoyed because I stopped her husband from using her face as a tetherball."

"And they're teddy bear artisans? Did you catch their names?" Ash pressed the button that opened the rear hatch and climbed from the SUV.

"Jennifer and Tony, although they were using some rather more colorful expressions for each other."

"Jennifer Swift?" Ash stopped and stared at me. "Did you notice what kind of bears she had?"

"They were made from tipped plush fur with hockey-stick arms, little wings, and dressed as angels — probably of the fallen variety if they're any reflection of their creators. You sound as if you know her."

"I've never met her, but she makes the Cheery Cherub Bears. She's a very successful artisan —"

"If not a human being."

"And she won both a TOBY and a Golden Teddy last year."

Three years ago those names wouldn't

have meant anything to me, but now that I work with mohair instead of murder I was impressed. The Golden Teddy and the TOBY — a slightly out-of-sequence acronym for Teddy Bear Of the Year — rank above the prizes given out at local bear shows. They're prestigious annual awards given out by the two major American teddy bear magazines and it's an honor to merely be nominated for one because it's an international competition. Few artisans win even one of the prizes, much less both, and those who do are considered the aristocrats of the artisan teddy bear world.

I glanced back at the fire doors and then checked my watch. "Not bad. We've been here less than thirty minutes and I've already managed to piss off a VIP. What if she has some pull with the local show judges and screws you out of an award?"

Ash took my hand and squeezed it. "Sweetheart, you did the right thing and it's going to be fine. And besides, there's no guarantee that either of us is going to even be nominated for a prize. We won't know that until this evening."

"You, I can see nominated. The Confection Collection is great. But, me? A nominee? Ash honey, when did you start having hallucinations?"

"Right about the same time I fell in love with this wonderful man who became a San Francisco cop." She kissed me on the cheek. "Now let's get this stuff unloaded."

THREE

We went back into the hotel, Ash with the dolly loaded with bears, and me pushing our two folding tables and chairs in the luggage cart. As we entered the lobby, I caught a glimpse of Tony Swift as he emerged from the corridor leading to the conference hall and headed in the direction of the hotel restaurant. He didn't seem to notice me, but that's probably because he was lost in a daydream about a nice green salad with low-cal oil and vinegar dressing.

I nudged Ash and nodded in the big man's direction. "Jennifer's husband."

Ash's eyes narrowed. "My God, he's three times her size. Maybe you should have called the police."

"There'd have been no point. She'd simply deny it happened and with no physical injuries, it'd be my word against theirs."

"And now he's going to lunch."

"Hey, you can work up a real man-sized

appetite terrorizing your wife."

"How did you stop him from hitting her?"

"I think he was afraid I was going to clobber him with my cane."

"If you ever get another chance under similar circumstances, do it."

"Always happy to be of service."

We went down the hallway towards the conference room, checked in at the organizers' table, and after a short wait received our exhibitor IDs, pamphlets containing schedules of the special events and workshops, and a couple of commemorative magazines. Stopping briefly to show our event IDs to a sleepy-looking security guard, we went into the exhibit hall.

In contrast to the *H.M.S. Pinafore* atmosphere of the lobby, the conference hall was about as welcoming as a police interview room. It was a large stark rectangle with the walls and floor upholstered in beige industrial carpet and a ceiling of white acoustic tiles. There were only two items of decoration: an oversized crystal chandelier in the middle of the room with so many cobwebs on it that it looked as if it had been borrowed from the Haunted Mansion in Disneyland, and a long white banner attached to the far wall that read, THE 17TH ANNUAL HAR-BEAR EXPO WELCOMES YOU in red letters.

The room was a mass of activity and filled with the buzz of cheerful conversation. There was a series of nine aisles marked out with blue masking tape on the floor and along each row booths and display tables were being set up. Facing the main entrance at the head of an aisle, in the very best foot-traffic location in the room, was the slot assigned to the Cheery Cherub Bears. We both paused to examine the lavish booth with a mixture of awe and embarrassed amusement.

Like most artisans, we simply set our bears up on cloth-covered tables with a sign attached to the front. The Cheery Cherub Bears display, however, was housed behind a hinged, seven-foot-tall and sixteen-foot-long plywood barrier upon which was painted an exquisite fresco of a heavenly scene showing angel bears with harps sitting on fluffy white clouds and others flying above them. I looked through the arched doorway into the enclosure, which was brightly illuminated by several battery-operated halogen lamps, and saw Jennifer releasing her bears from plastic crate captivity. A man in his mid-thirties, with short brown hair and a friendly looking, clean-shaven round face, was assisting her by setting small books with brightly colored illustrations of cherub bears on the covers next to each stuffed animal. The man quietly said something to Jennifer, but her only response was a brusque shake of the head.

Behind me, I heard a woman call, "Ashleigh, is that really you?"

I turned and saw Ash embracing a middle-aged woman with curly brown hair. Ash said, "Oh my gosh, Karen, once we moved back to Virginia I didn't think we'd see you again! How are you?"

"Jet-lagged but wonderful."

"And you're doing this show?"

Karen tapped the handle of a dolly loaded with teddy bears. "It's my first trip to an eastern event in a few years and I was hoping to see you since I know you're making bears now."

"Yes, but they aren't as good as yours."

"Thanks, but that's not what I've been hearing. I saw the article about the Harrisonburg show in *Teddy Bear Review.* Congratulations on the award."

"Thank you." Ash grabbed my hand. "Brad, honey, you remember Karen, don't you?"

"Of course. It's really great to see you," I lied, shaking hands with her. Ash could have told me that the lady was the lost Romanov Princess Anastasia and I wouldn't have known any different.

"Is it all right if I ask what happened to your leg? When you took Molly Mae home . . ."

"I didn't have a cane. I got shot a couple of years ago and I'm retired from the PD."

"I'm so sorry."

"Thanks, but it's okay. Life is good."

"And he's making bears," Ash added proudly.

The teddy bear named Molly Mae refreshed my memory. The woman was Karen Rundlett, an artisan from Southern California whom we'd first met at the Nevada City Teddy Bear Convention back in 1999 when we were just avid collectors. Two years and several events later, at a San Diego show, we'd purchased a large and beautiful honey-colored bear from her named Molly Mae, which led to an unexpected bit of fame for me: after buying Molly, I carried her through the rest of the exhibit hall and attracted the attention of a professional photographer who was doing an article on the centennial anniversary of the teddy bear for *Smithsonian* magazine. He snapped a picture of me smiling and holding Molly, which subsequently appeared in the August

2002 issue.

I thought it was great until Detective Merv "The Perv" Bronsey, a creepy co-worker of mine in the homicide unit, saw the picture and decided it constituted excellent fodder for a practical joke. And if you want to ponder a *real* mystery, how did he find it? Merv's favorite magazines were purchased from adult bookshops and the only notion more outlandish than him reading *Smithsonian* is that reality TV programs are "real" and produce "stars." My guess is that he found the magazine in the waiting room of some doctor's office just before going in to get a shot of penicillin.

Anyway, cops can be cruel, especially to each other. Merv scanned the picture into his computer, digitally added a pair of handcuffs to my wrist and Molly Mae's paw, and attached a caption underneath that read, "The courageous Inspector Lyon captures another violent felon." Then he e-mailed the modified photo to every cop on the SFPD. That was bad enough, but when criminals were brought in for questioning and they saw the picture on display at detectives' desks it got worse — much worse. Soon almost every lowlife informant or crook I contacted chafed me over it. I eventually got my revenge on Merv, but I'll share that story once I'm absolutely certain that the statute of limitations has expired.

Karen nodded toward the Cheery Cherub Bears booth as the archway began to glow pink due to the young guy turning on a battery-powered strip of fiber optic lights. "Pretty impressive, huh? But then again, it paid off."

Ash raised her eyebrows. "How so?"

"I guess they haven't made it public yet, but the Swifts and Todd there are about to become relatively wealthy. I heard some other artisans talking about it."

"Who's Todd?"

"The young fellow helping Jennifer. If I recall correctly, his last name is Litten. Each of the bears comes with a children's book that he writes and illustrates. They're sweet little books on how to behave and the importance of being kind to others."

"Interesting. Have the Swifts actually ever read the books?"

Ash gave my hand a warning squeeze.

As we talked, I noticed a slightly plump woman pushing a cart loaded with very cute bears dressed as medieval knights, damsels, and one that looked like Robin Hood, complete with a longbow. She paused to shoot a brief but venomous glare at the Cheery Cherub Bears booth then quickly turned away. That caught my full attention. The woman looked to be in her mid-forties, with long dark brunette tresses gathered into a clear plastic hairclip, and she wore jeans, a burgundy pullover shirt, and a white Quacker Factory sweater decorated with hearts, angels, and topiaries. However, the cheerful clothing didn't match her expression. Her brown eyes looked sad and lonely and they scanned the room as if in search of a friend but not expecting to find one. Then she drifted casually in our direction, looking shyly interested in joining our conversation.

I turned to her and smiled. "Hi. How are you? This is only our second show, so it's good to meet you. I'm Brad Lyon, this is my wife, Ashleigh, and this is our friend Karen Rundlett."

The woman's face brightened a little and she held up her name tag. "Hi, I'm Donna Jordan and it's been awhile since I've been to any shows myself. Thanks for making me feel welcome."

Once everybody had shaken hands, I asked Karen, "So how are Litten and the Swifts about to become wealthy?"

"I'm old enough to remember when three hundred and fifty thousand dollars was a lot of money, so maybe 'wealthy' is an overstatement." Karen gave a wry chuckle. "Wintle Toys is going to buy the manufacturing rights to the cherub bears and books and the Swifts are also selling the television rights to some animation company so that they can make a cartoon series about the bears."

I thought: *During which they'll broadcast a half-dozen brainwashing commercials advertising the stuffed animals, a Cheery Cherub Bears' breakfast cereal, and inevitably, some sort of related video game. Talk about a license to print money.*

Karen continued, "Some of the other big manufacturers do a nice job on producing mass-market versions of artisan bears, but Wintle? You *know* the quality will go right down the drain. What a shame."

"It all sounds a little . . . mercenary. But maybe I'm only saying that because I'm jealous," said Ash.

Karen half-whispered, "No, you're right, it does seem mercenary, which is really surprising considering the wonderful reputation Jen has in the teddy bear community."

It was hard to tell with all the background conversation and the tinny synthesized version of "Spring" from Vivaldi's "Four Seasons" that began burbling from the speakers built into the Cheery Cherub Bears booth, but I thought I heard Donna quietly mutter, "Yeah, Jen's a frigging saint."

Karen sighed. "I guess I should get going. Are you guys going to the reception tonight?"

"We'll be there," said Ash.

"Good. I'm in space number forty-one. Drop by and say hello if you get the chance and I'll see you later at the reception."

"And we're in space twenty-three. See you tonight." Ash gave Karen a hug.

As Karen disappeared down one of the aisles, I turned to Donna. "Hey, I really like your Robin Hood–themed bears."

"Actually, they're characters from *Ivanhoe.* I used to read it to my son." She reached into a crate and pulled out a bear dressed in a long coat of silvery material that resembled iron chain mail. "Here's Sir Wilfred."

"This is amazing workmanship," said Ash.

"Thank you."

I pointed to another bear that was wearing gray fabric armor and a black sleeveless tunic embroidered with a crimson Latin cross. "Brian Bois-Guilbert?"

"Right, the evil Knight Templar. It's a pleasure to meet someone who's read Sir Walter Scott."

"And your son was lucky to have someone to read him *Ivanhoe.*"

Ash twisted my arm slightly to look at my watch. "Oh, my gosh, we'd better find our places and get set up. The judges will be making their way through the hall at two o'clock to pick out the finalists for the show awards and we haven't even set our table up yet."

"We'll see you at the reception tonight. Good to meet you." I shook Donna's hand and she disappeared into the crowd.

Meanwhile, we went up the second aisle to the left from the doors. Halfway up the row we found space twenty-three on the left-hand side. I began to set the tables up as Ash went back out to the parking structure to bring in another load of bears. Once the tables were up, I covered them with the fitted white cloths with lace ruffles that Ash had made and attached our LYON'S TIGERS AND BEARS sign to the front. But I didn't begin setting the bears up for display, because that's a talent I completely lack. The fact is, I'd just stand the bears up in a row like they were suspects in an ursine police lineup, but Ash possesses an artist's eye for positioning the stuffed animals and her arrangements never fail to attract foot traffic.

Picking up Dirty Beary and looking into his sunglasses, I said, "In the words of the immortal Clint in . . . I forget which cop movie: 'A man's got to know his limitations.' "

Ash returned about ten minutes later with the remainder of the bears and a wicker basket containing our lunch of turkey sandwiches, fiery jalapeno-flavored potato chips, slices of dried apple, and bottles of water. Hotel and restaurant food is expensive and we'd be eating out a lot over the next few days, so we were trying to save a few pennies. Besides we really didn't have time to sit down over a leisurely lunch.

Once we finished eating, Ash went to the restroom to wash her hands before arranging our wares. The first bear she picked up was Teri Tiramisu, who wore a rectangular-shaped costume of simulated ladyfinger cookies topped with a glossy layer of faux Mascarpone cheese bisected with a thin and irregular ribbon of brown fabric that looked exactly like a mixture of cocoa and espresso.

Ash scrutinized the bear with a furrowed brow. "I don't know. I still think this one is just kind of blah."

"She's wonderful."

"Honey, you say that about all my bears."

"And I mean it. But if you're worried, put

Teri next to a couple of the ones I made. She'll look great in comparison."

"There's nothing wrong with your bears —"

"That a skilled artist couldn't fix, given enough time," I added. I leaned over to give her a kiss on her forehead. "Hey, while you arrange the bears, why don't I take the dolly back to the Xterra and get our luggage up to our room?"

"That sounds good. Hurry back." Ash sounded a little distracted as she put Teri Tiramisu down and picked up Patty Pumpkin Pie, a bear wearing an orange wedge-shaped costume complete with golden brown crust and a dab of satin whipped cream.

I'd volunteered to do the grunt work because I knew that Ash found it easier to focus on posing the bears when I wasn't looking over her shoulder. It also gave me the opportunity to check out some of the other artists' displays. As always, I was profoundly impressed with the number, variety, and above all, the quality of bears on display. On our aisle alone, there were bears dressed as Teddy Roosevelt, Little Red Riding Hood, Long John Silver, Mia Hamm, and Neil Armstrong in an incredibly realistic looking spacesuit. The other thing I noticed was the atmosphere of good will and unfeigned joy pervading the room . . . right up until I limped past the Cheery Cherub Bears booth.

Tony was standing just outside the archway. However, this was a Tony from some alternate universe — a Tony that was seeking camouflage behind the popular myth that all fat men are jolly. He'd changed into a periwinkle-colored T-shirt with the message, I WUV CHEERY CHERUB BEARS printed in white three-inch tall block capital letters on the chest, and he wore one of those red-striped *Cat in the Hat* felt top hats they give as prizes at county fair game booths. Tony's toothy smile was as big as Michael Jackson's attorney's bills and the big man was calling out to friends while greeting and shaking hands with folks passing the booth. I'll give the guy this, Tony was an accomplished actor because when he saw me he only broke from character for a split-second to give me a hateful and challenging look that's known on the streets as a "mad dog." I met his gaze and laughed scornfully as I trudged by. As I went out the door, I heard him shouting out a cheerful hello to someone else.

I dropped our luggage off in our room on the fifth floor and returned about fifteen minutes later. Tony was gone — off pressing the flesh in another part of the hall — and Jennifer was inside the booth seated on a folding chair with her arms folded across her chest and eyes shut. Todd stood behind her, looking for something inside a brown shoulder bag while prattling away, even though the woman's posture clearly said that she wanted to be left alone. Meanwhile, "The March of the Gladiators" — the song played when a circus troupe makes its grand entrance into the arena — was blaring from the booth's music system while the fiber optic lights pulsed in time to the music. I paused and shook my head in bemusement. I'd never seen anything like it at the thirty or so bear shows we'd attended. It was like slowing down to look at a bad traffic accident. You know you shouldn't do it, but there's an unsavory fascination in looking at something awful.

Coming up our aisle, I saw that Ash had finished arranging the stuffed animals. The Confection Collection looked as delectable as a dessert tray and the centerpiece of the display was her amazingly realistic-looking Siberian snow tiger. It had articulated limbs and seemed to be prowling across the table. I was also pleased to see that Teri Tiramisu had made the cut and was on display with the other members of the Confection Collection. Then I noticed that Ash had attached Dirty Beary to a stand and placed him on one of the felt-covered cylindrical pedestals we'd refashioned from some old paint cans. Leaning against his legs was one of the small placards Ash had produced earlier in the week on the computer that bore the bear's name and that of the artisan.

I'll admit it; suddenly I was a little scared. It was only a few minutes until two o'clock and I wasn't eager to have teddy bear experts examining my work because I knew Beary and the four other stuffed animals I'd completed over the winter bore the unmistakable marks of being made by an amateur.

Slipping behind the table, I said, "Sweetheart, why don't you take him down and put up one of your bears? Where's Cheri Cherry Pie? Put her there."

"I'm proud of Dirty Beary, and you should be, too."

"He's just a bear wearing a sports jacket and sunglasses."

"No, he represents three months of hard work and a quarter-century of what you did very bravely for a living," Ash said quietly. "And he represents our new life together. So, do you still want to take him down?"

I took her hand. "No."

"Thank you."

"And you know what? When the judges visit our table and check Beary out, I'll just give them a steely-eyed look and say" — I paused to add a muted snarl to my voice — "Go ahead. Make my day."

Four

While we waited for the judges to appear, I told Ash about Tony's T-shirt, cheesy top hat, and unctuous carnival barker's performance.

She gaped in disbelief. "*Wuv?* It actually says, *wuv?* I think I'm going to be sick."

"The shirt wasn't half as nauseating as his hyperactive Barney the Dinosaur shtick."

"And I'm sorry, but the longer I think about that booth with its flashing lights . . ."

"The more words such as 'sell-out' and 'pimped' come to mind?"

Ash nodded and frowned. "But I keep wondering if we're just saying that because we're envious of their success."

"That isn't success. They're just a miserable couple who took a sweet concept like an angel teddy bear and distorted it for a little money. And the really pathetic part is that the cash will all be spent before the year is done — probably most of it on visits to Hardee's from the look of Tony."

"You're right, of course. So, why does everybody seem to like them so much?"

"The overwhelming majority of teddy bear artisans are nice people, and unfortunately, nice people always assume the best about other folks."

The trio of judges arrived shortly after 2:30 and, no, I didn't give them my Clint Eastwood impression because it's just like my left shin — pretty feeble. Besides, one of the unwritten rules of conduct is that you aren't supposed to chat with the judges during their inspection. The evaluation team consisted of two women — one in her sixties and the other in her forties — and a balding guy, all with clipboards, pens, and the stern facial expressions usually seen on department of motor vehicle driving test examiners. The man took a long look at Hilda Honey Crisp and made some muttering sounds of approval while the older woman picked up the Siberian snow tiger and experimentally moved its limbs. Meanwhile, the other lady bent over to read the information card and then picked up Dirty Beary. She opened the bear's sports coat and blinked in surprise at the shoulder holster and replica revolver.

She shot me a sly glance and in a solemn

yet droll voice said, "My, that's a big one."

It was my turn to be astonished. I nodded and gave her a tight-lipped smile. The reason for my shock was that the lady had just quoted the line from *Dirty Harry,* when the bad guy sees the detective's large .44-magnum revolver. I wasn't certain precisely what the comment signified, but suddenly I felt lucky. What were the odds that a female teddy bear judge would also be enough of a fan of Clint Eastwood's cop films to be able to cite some dialogue? She put Beary back on the pedestal and made several notes on the sheet in her clipboard.

As soon as the judges were gone, Ash showed me a pair of seriously raised eyebrows. "Do you mind telling me just what the heck that was all about?"

"It sounded pretty clear to me."

"Me, too, and she'd better have been referring to Dirty Beary, otherwise I'm going to go have a little chat with her."

"Why, whatever else do you think she could have meant?" I asked in an artificially earnest and puzzled tone.

"Brad."

"Relax, honey. What she said was a line from *Dirty Harry,* so it's possible it's a really good sign."

"Oh, well, that's all right then —"

"But we'll know for certain tonight at the reception, if Beary doesn't get nominated but she does start flirting with me."

"You are incorrigible."

"And insanely in love with you, so stop fretting." I leaned over to kiss her on the cheek. "They really seemed to like Hilda and the tiger. Hey, what's wrong?"

Ash suddenly looked a little downcast. "It's just that both Hilda and Beary are costumed and over fourteen inches tall."

"And?"

"Don't you see what that means? They're in competition with each other because they're in the same judging category. What if they nominate Hilda over Beary?"

"I'll be overjoyed and besides, how likely is that to happen? This is a major national show." I gestured with my hand toward the crowded exhibition hall. "There are more than a hundred artisans here — some of them TOBY and Golden Teddy winners — and every one of them has bears in the running. How many nominees are allowed for each award?"

"Just five."

I shrugged. "You can do the math. What are the odds of either of us being selected?"

"I see what you mean." However, Ash didn't sound convinced. "But Beary deserves to be nominated."

"I appreciate that, darling, but you're voting with your heart instead of your head. And you've completely overlooked the possibility that your tiger will be nominated in the soft-sculpture plush category." I was referring to a judging classification that was for stuffed animals other than bears.

"Not likely with artisans like Marsha Friesen and Cindy Malchoff here. Cindy's birds are amazing."

"I still think you have a chance and there's no point in worrying about it. So, now that the judges have finished with us, is there anything else we have to do here?"

"Not that I can think of."

"It's almost three. Then why don't we take a quick drive up to the bookshop so you can get that new mystery novel and then we can go back to our room?"

Ash grabbed her purse. "Okay, and that will leave us plenty of time to get ready. The reception doesn't begin until six-thirty."

"Yeah, we'll be back by four, you can get into the shower at five —"

"And what are we going to be doing between four and five?" Ash dimpled, reading my thoughts.

"Hey, I checked into a hotel with a beautiful woman who's so hot I need oven mitts.

What do you think we're going to be doing?"

Outside, the sky was cloudy but the rain had stopped for the moment. We drove up to Fleet Street and found a parking spot near the store, but took the umbrella with us because it looked as if another downpour could start at any moment. The bookshop had copies of the new *Pam and Pom* in hardcover, including autographed copies, one of which we bought. I behaved in an exemplary manner. When we returned to the hotel, Ash showed me how much she appreciated my good conduct, so my forbearance was richly rewarded.

Later, as Ash was blow-drying her hair, I sat in a chair near the window and leafed through the event program. There was a long list of all the participants and I found our business name listed. There were also paragraph-long bios on some of the more prominent artisans in the front section of the magazine and I looked up the entry for Cheery Cherub Bears. Atop the profile was a small black-and-white photo of Jennifer, Tony, and Todd standing in staggered profile as if it were a group mug shot. The text said that all three were from Basingstoke Township, near Lancaster, Pennsylvania, and — get this — that Tony and Jennifer spent "countless joyful hours" working together making the bears. Finally, almost as an afterthought, it mentioned that Todd Litten wrote and illustrated the books that accompanied the angel bears and also worked as an EMT with a local fire department.

Ash turned off the blow-drier and came out to get dressed. I sat for a moment to admire her golden hair and voluptuous figure and again reflected on just how lucky I was to be married to her. She'd been my pillar of strength during the awful days after I was shot and, having come so close to death, I was never going to take her for granted.

Finally, I went into the bathroom and showered and shaved. When I came out I paused to stare in awe. "You are absolutely beautiful."

"It's just my basic little black dress."

"Your little black seductive dress. It's been so long since we've been out, I'd forgotten how great it looks on you."

Made from silk, the dress was cut just above the knee, and had a V neckline that showed off the tiniest bit of cleavage. Her jewelry elegantly accented the outfit: gold pendant earrings with glittering quarter-carat diamonds, a gold San Marco-style bracelet on her right wrist, and her gold wedding band with dual ramps of pave diamonds flanking a brilliant-cut carat diamond. Ash doesn't have loads of jewelry, but the pieces she owns are timelessly stylish and of top quality — like her.

"Can you help me with this?" Ash held up the star-shaped diamond pendant on a gold chain that I'd given her on our fifteenth wedding anniversary.

"Happy to. Turn around." As I stepped closer and smelled her perfume, it took every ounce of self-control I possessed not to unzip her dress while I was behind her fiddling with that tiny lobster claw clasp.

Then I got dressed in tan slacks, a sage-colored turtleneck that Ash said went well with my eyes, and a sports coat. The jacket was new because all my old ones were hors de combat. Unless you've worn a shoulder holster everyday you have no idea of just how badly and quickly a pistol can tear up a coat lining. When I finished dressing, Ash inspected me, smoothed a couple of rogue hairs in my left eyebrow, and pronounced me the handsomest man in the hotel. The best part about the compliment is that I knew she really meant it. She handed me my cane and we headed down the hall to the elevator.

The reception was being held in a ballroom adjoining the exhibit hall and there were already seventy or so people present. Up at the front of the room was a wooden podium where the show's award nominees would be announced a little later in the evening. *Not too much later,* I hoped. I can only stand for so long before my leg begins to ache and I'd noticed that there were only a couple of tables and perhaps a dozen chairs set out for the guests.

While Ash stopped to chat with an artisan she'd met earlier in the day, I excused myself and went over to the bar to get us some drinks. A man in a suit who'd just been served by the bartender turned around and gave me a startled once-over. It was Todd; he held a glass of white wine in one hand and some sort of mixed drink made with cola in the other.

We locked gazes as if we were scenery-chewing actors in a bad Kung Fu film and at last I said, "Yeah, I'm the evil guy with the cane."

"I know and whatever you did this morning, thank you." Todd's voice was quiet and grave.

"Jennifer didn't tell you?"

"No, but I know Tony." Todd took a few steps as if to leave and then stopped. "I heard him say you used to be a cop, so you must have seen stuff like that a thousand times. Tell me something. Why do they stay when there might be someone who could give them a much happier life?"

Knowing he was referring to battered women in general and Jennifer in particular, I sighed and said, "I'm no psychologist, but I suspect it's because they've been beaten down so thoroughly that they no longer have a capacity to even imagine a life that doesn't involve routine assault, much less a genuine loving relationship."

Todd nodded glumly and moved on.

I ordered a gin and tonic on the rocks for Ash and Glenfiddich neat for me, even though the bartender seemed very confused and disturbed when I insisted that I didn't want any ice cubes with my whiskey. Ice completely ruins the intense flavor of fine single-malt Scotch, although Ash says that regardless of the temperature it's served, the stuff I drink tastes exactly the way she imagines kerosene would.

Tucking my cane beneath my arm and carrying drinks in both hands, I toddled back to Ash and handed her the G and T. I toasted her and then, sipping our drinks, we wandered aimlessly through the room, watching people and enjoying the convivial atmosphere. That is, up until we encountered Tony and Jennifer holding court for a small group of folks. Ash and I stopped to gape.

This being a dress-up event, Tony was, of course, attired in a tightly fitting triple-XL Hawaiian shirt from hell. It was the same obnoxious yellow as a school bus and there were five-by-seven-inch color photos of the Cheery Cherub Bears imprinted on the fabric and scattered all over the shirt. I'd heard about the photo-onto-cloth process, but I never thought I'd encounter it in the form of a wearable billboard for teddy bears. Jennifer, on the other hand, had gone with the Mother Superior look: a black pantsuit with a stark white blouse and a prim look of disapproval with the world in general. She held a glass of white wine and I wondered if it was one of the drinks I'd seen Todd carrying. I looked for Todd, but didn't see him; however, that could have been because of the blinding glare from Tony's shirt.

"Why can't you find shirts like that for me?" I murmured.

"Because I love you too much to allow you to be seen in public like that. Lord, that's so tacky."

I paid a little closer look at the people

chatting with the Swifts. Two of them were men wearing charcoal gray woolen business suits that screamed money and I wondered if they were execs from Wintle Toys here to close the rumored merchandising deal. I considered marching up and telling the businessmen that they were about to buy angel teddy bears from a wife-beater, but decided that bit of news probably wouldn't horrify people who were in the industry of mesmerizing a generation of children into buying crap.

As usual, Ash could read my thoughts and she gently tugged on my wrist to lead me away before I did something bullheaded.

Then, as we turned to do some more wandering I saw Todd again. He was in the back of the room — maybe sixty feet away — huddled in deep conversation with a thin woman wearing black slacks and a long black duster. Unless Todd was in the process of being jilted, I could tell the woman wasn't his wife or girlfriend because their postures showed no evidence of intimacy. The one thing I knew for sure was that the topic of conversation wasn't pleasant because Todd's shoulders were drooping and his chin was on his chest.

Ash and I mingled some more, chatted with several artisans, and a few minutes later I noticed that the woman I'd seen in conversation with Todd had joined the group surrounding the Swifts. Slightly curious, I scanned the room for Todd, but I was UTL, which is California cop speak for Unable To Locate.

We'd nearly finished our drinks and were waiting for the nomination announcements to begin so that we could go to dinner, when we found Donna Jordan sitting alone in a chair at a table in the far corner of the room. She was attired in a somber midnight blue dress and held a glass that looked about a third full of a blush Chardonnay. At first she didn't recognize us and then she smiled, but it looked as if it took a lot of effort to do it.

"Hi. Ashleigh and Brad, right?" Her speech bore the slightest trace of a slur and I wondered how many drinks she'd already had tonight.

"Hello, Donna. Are you okay?" Ash asked.

"Fine. Absolutely fine. You see them over there?" Donna took a swallow of wine and inclined her head slightly in the direction of the Swifts. "You don't like them, do you?"

"Not particularly," I said.

"That's only because you don't know them."

"Really?"

"Really. Because if you knew them you'd hate both their goddamn guts. She's a shameless thief and he is as rotten a son of a bitch as they come." The words were delivered with quiet malice, yet a nanosecond after they'd been uttered she looked up at us, wearing an expression of shock and profound mortification. "Oh my God, I'm so sorry. I don't know what got into me. It must have been the wine."

In vino veritas, I thought, while Ash soothingly touched Donna's shoulder and said, "It's all right."

"No, no, I'm so very sorry. Please excuse me." Donna put the wineglass on the table and scurried for the door.

As we watched her leave, Ash said, "What do you think she meant when she called Jennifer a thief?"

"I don't know, but her description of Tony was right on the mark."

However, we couldn't give the matter any further consideration for the moment because we heard a woman's throat being cleared over the public address system. The judge who'd examined Ash's Siberian snow tiger earlier today was at the podium and she announced that the award nominees were about to be revealed. We put our glasses on the table and joined the half-crescent crowd of people facing the front of the room. I tried to convince myself that my hands were damp as a consequence of the ballroom being warm and not because I was the least bit nervous.

It was a long process, as there were seven different award categories and after each name was read there was a smattering of polite applause. That is, up until Jennifer Swift was nominated for an award in the "Dressed / Accessorized, Over Five Inches and Under Fourteen Inches" group because Tony bellowed out that moronic sea-lion-like "ooh, ooh, ooh" sound so popular among the old *Jerry Springer Show* audiences and other gatherings of the Brain Trust. At last the judge came to the "Dressed / Accessorized, Fourteen Inches and Over" bracket and began reading the list of nominees. I was so absorbed in listening for Ash and Hilda's names that at first it didn't really register when I heard the woman say, "Dirty Beary made by Bradley Lyon of Lyon's Tigers and Bears."

Ash threw her arms around my neck and gave me a moist kiss. "Congratulations! Honey, I'm so proud of you!"

"Thanks, but Hilda wasn't nominated."

"That's not important."

"Wrong. You were robbed. Are those

people blind? Hilda is better than Beary."

"Brad, sweetheart, it's all right. Truly. I couldn't be happier." Ash's eyes were glistening.

Meanwhile, the judge began announcing the nominees for the final category, "Soft-Sculpture, Plush Animals." A moment later, it was my turn to hug and kiss Ash when we heard that her Siberian snow tiger was a finalist. At the conclusion of the event, the judge asked the chosen artisans to go into the exhibit hall, retrieve the nominated stuffed animals, and personally hand them to one of the selection team. We did so and were told that the prizes would be awarded the following afternoon.

After the reception, we hooked up with Karen Rundlett and some other artisans and went out to dinner at a seafood restaurant. The food was wonderful and the company even better but we didn't stay out late. We knew that tomorrow was going to be a very exciting day.

FIVE

We woke up early, got ready, and just after 7 a.m. returned to the ballroom to attend a special breakfast banquet for the artisans. The room was now full of large round tables, each covered with crisp white tablecloths and glittering with glassware, china, and silverware. I noticed a thus far empty VIP table near the podium where all the place settings were marked with folded cardboard placards that read RESERVED in the same bold script used for the signs warning people away from high voltage electric lines.

Up along the front wall, the finalist bears selected the previous evening were on display on a series of tables. We'd brought the digital camera along and took photos of each other standing next to our creations. Then I saw a couple of large coffee urns in the corner and made a beeline for them. The coffee wasn't bad — a little weak perhaps — but then again I still have a taste for the brown sludge I used to drink back in the SFPD homicide bureau.

Other people began to filter into the room and I wasn't surprised to see Jennifer, Tony, and Todd seated at the VIP table with the event organizers and judges. Interestingly, the suits I'd seen with the Swifts the previous evening were nowhere to be seen. Tony was again wearing the I WUV CHEERY CHERUB BEARS T-shirt but, thankfully, not the goofy top hat. He was talking loudly to some guy about how early he'd gotten up to go down to their booth and repair the base of a Plexiglas teddy bear stand, making the entire operation sound as challenging as a space-walk to fix something on the International Space Station. Jennifer actually seemed cheerful as she chatted with the woman beside her. Meanwhile, Todd stared straight ahead at the table's centerpiece, one of Jennifer's bears.

I refilled my coffee cup and we found a place at an adjoining table. A few minutes later, things got under way as the event organizer, an older woman in a cream-colored dress, went up to the podium. She greeted us and then delivered some announcements about the day's forthcoming activities. Several special workshops would convene at 8 a.m., the general public would be allowed entrance into the exhibit hall at 9 a.m., and the winners of the teddy bear competition would be announced at 5 p.m. As the lady spoke, a squad of waiters began circulating through the room carrying trays with glasses of various juices.

"And I have one final bit of wonderful news I'm very pleased to share because I know that everyone here will want to applaud their success." The organizer paused to glance and smile at the VIP table. "Yesterday, our good friends Jennifer and Tony Swift signed a licensing agreement with Wintle Toys and Dumollard Ani-Media. That means that those sweet Cheery Cherub Bears will soon be in stores nationwide and are also going to be featured in their own animated television series."

Tony grinned and raised his clasped hands like an old time prizefighter, while Jennifer smiled shyly in response to the applause. Todd merely looked up and grimaced. I thought his reaction was pretty strange and probably would have kept watching him if Ash hadn't tapped on my arm and discreetly pointed toward the back of the room. That's when I saw Donna marching up the aisle. Her fists were balled, her face was livid with rage, and she was headed for the VIP table.

Although she wasn't a large person, I don't think I'd have wanted to try to prevent Donna from reaching her destination. Visualize a charging two-thousand-pound African Cape buffalo or better yet, a sixty-eight-ton M-1 Abrams tank racing along at forty-five-miles-an-hour and you'll grasp some sense of her implacable demeanor.

When the Swifts noticed Donna, I was intrigued and entertained by their responses. Jennifer blanched and began blinking as if she were sending some sort of ocular semaphore SOS message while Tony looked down at the table, wearing an expression that up until that moment I hadn't imagined he was capable of: red-faced embarrassment. Meanwhile, Todd's lips seemed to be twitching. I couldn't be absolutely certain but it appeared as if he was struggling mightily not to smile.

Donna stopped before the table, pointed an accusing finger at the Swifts, and although she didn't shout, her icy words were audible throughout the now silent room. "I hope the pair of you burn forever in hell. Those cherub bears were *my* designs and you not only stole them, you turned them into something cheap and dirty."

Tony tried to square his shoulders. "Now, Donna —"

"Shut your mouth, fat boy, or I'll tell everyone here all about the time your thieving wife 'fell down the basement stairs' and was in the hospital for five days. Looking back at it, I wish you'd broken her damn neck."

The big man flinched as if he'd been snapped with a whip and was silent. Up behind the podium, the shocked old lady's mouth was opening and closing in a way that reminded me of a goldfish. Everybody was just sitting there taking in the impromptu breakfast theater and I looked at Ash to see if she wanted me to intervene before a food fight broke out. She nodded vigorously and I pushed myself to my feet. As I approached, I caught sight of the hotel security guard coming through the door.

Donna returned her baleful gaze to Jennifer. "And you, sitting there like a queen. Once these people know the truth about you they'll be so disgusted they'll want to vomit, just like I do every time I remember that you called me your best friend."

I touched Donna lightly on her upper left arm. Startled, she spun to face me. "I'm not done."

I kept my voice gentle. "Much as I'd like to hear the rest of the story, I think you are. You need to go before the guard ejects you from the building."

Why do most unarmed security guards behave with all the icy menace and swagger of an old-time Hollywood cowboy villain? Slouching slightly with his thumbs tucked into his belt, the rent-a-cop had clearly modeled his tough guy persona after Jack Palance's classic performance as the evil hired gunslinger in *Shane.* He inclined his head toward the door, flashed a humorless half-smile, and said, "C'mon lady. You're outta here."

As if awakening from a trance, Donna took in all the staring faces and her lower lip began to tremble. Her gaze fell to the floor and she shuffled toward the door as the guard escorted her. For a moment, there was utter silence and then the room erupted into hushed conversation that, unless I misread the tone, was tinged with disappointment. Clearly, I wasn't the only one curious to hear the end of the story.

Then I heard the sound of wheezing and looked at the VIP table. Jennifer was bent forward holding her right hand open over her upper chest and was clearly having great difficulties in catching her breath.

"What's wrong?" Ash asked as she joined me.

"She's got a long history of asthma." Todd

turned to Jennifer and placed a comforting hand on her lower left arm. "It's okay. Slow down and try to breathe a little more deeply, Jen. You're panicking."

It was good advice. Sometimes asthma attacks can be provoked by stress or emotional upheaval and when the victim becomes naturally frightened from being unable to breathe properly, the episode becomes a vicious cycle. She needed calm, but what she got was Tony, who'd just shifted into caveman mode.

"Get your hands off her!" Tony delivered the command at bullhorn volume about six inches from Jennifer's right ear as he pushed himself out of the chair.

"She needs help."

"You're the one that's gonna need help if you don't get away from her. You must think I'm stupid not to know."

"This is insane. Your wife can hardly breathe."

Jennifer wheezed and erupted into a long cadence of savage hacking coughs to emphasize the point. Meanwhile, there was a growing cacophony of agitated voices from the rest of the folks in attendance.

"That's right, she's *my* wife!"

"This crazy shit will cease immediately!" I barked in my best hands-up-or-get-ready-to-show-St.-Peter-two-forms-of-picture-ID voice, deliberately using the obscenity for shock value. Both men shut up instantly and the room became much quieter. I pointed to Todd. "You. Move away because Stupid there is going to continue his temper tantrum until you do. We'll take over."

"You?" Todd looked doubtful.

"Todd, I've been handling emergencies since you were probably still in third grade. We can handle this."

"But I'm an EMT."

"I know, but Tony is going to go into low earth orbit if you touch her. We'll take over."

"Fine." Todd spat the word. As he rose from his chair and stepped away, he quietly added, "I'm sorry, Jen."

Ash slid into the vacant chair and took the gasping woman's limp left hand. In the same tender and serene voice I'd heard her use so long ago to soothe our children when they were sick, she said, "Jennifer, pay attention to me: you're panicking, honey, and you need to calm down."

"I don't want you to touch her either," Tony snarled.

"I'm not exactly thrilled over it myself, considering whatever you two did to Donna, but we're out of options. Now, try to behave like an adult for just a couple of minutes. I assume she has an inhaler. Where is it?"

"Upstairs in our room."

"Then make yourself useful and go get it."

Tony glowered for a moment. Then he turned to jog toward the door and the elevator as Ash continued to urge Jennifer to breathe more slowly. I sat down on the other side of Jennifer and didn't interfere. Ash's voice was hypnotically tranquil and I could see the fear slowly receding from Jennifer's eyes as her breathing gradually became more normal. Jennifer was only wheezing slightly when Tony reappeared. His T-shirt was damp with sweat and he had the inhaler in his meaty hand. He handed the small cylindrical canister to his wife.

Jennifer put the device to her mouth, took a deep huff of the medication, and flinched in pain and alarm. She tried to cough and her eyes widened with terror as she realized that she couldn't catch her breath. The inhaler fell from her hands as Jennifer clutched at her chest with both hands and was wracked with powerful respiratory spasms as she attempted to breathe. With every exhalation, I could hear horrible gurgling sounds. This wasn't an asthma attack anymore and if we didn't do something immediately, Jennifer was going to find out if there really were Cheery Cherub Bears in heaven — provided of course, that was her final destination.

"What's wrong with her?" Tony sounded frightened and was dancing an anxious and clumsy jig, skipping from one foot to the other.

"I don't know. Go to the lobby and call nine-one-one, now! And wait out there to show them where we are."

I figured there were probably a dozen people calling for the paramedics on their cell phones at that very moment, but it would be best to give Tony some task to divert him while we tried to save his wife's life. Otherwise, he'd just get in the way. Tony took off for the door with the same speed, grace, and agility of a bull walrus trying to escape from a polar bear and I hoped this second session of light aerobic exercise didn't cause him to have a heart attack. Things were already going to hell in a handbasket.

"Ash, let's get her on the floor for CPR." Then I yelled over my shoulder to the circle of spectators that had closed around us, "Clear out and give us some room!"

The people moved back and Ash and I lowered the shuddering and gasping woman to the floor and laid her on her back. Her eyes were locked on Ash, silently begging for help, then her pupils rolled upward as she lost consciousness. The violent breathing convulsions continued for another couple of seconds and then her body suddenly went limp. I grabbed the woman's wrist and felt for her pulse and couldn't find one. Jennifer was in full cardiac arrest and death was imminent. For the briefest of instants I wondered why Todd hadn't come back to help and assumed it was because he'd left the ballroom. That meant it was up to us.

I told Ash, "No pulse. You do rescue breathing and I'll do the chest compressions . . . and be prepared for her to throw up."

"I'm ready."

As I interlaced my fingers over Jennifer's heart, Ash blew three rapid breaths into the woman's mouth and I saw her chest rise each time. That signified the airway was open. As she finished the sequence, Ash looked up at me and made a face as if she'd tasted something awful. However, there was no time to ask her about it, because it was now my turn. I'll spare you a full description of the unpleasant details, but suffice it to say that delivering real chest compressions isn't like what they show on television. If you're doing it right, more often than not you fracture some of your patient's ribs. I don't know how long we were at it, but at last I felt a gentle tap on my shoulder.

Looking up, I saw a Baltimore City paramedic. She said, "Any response?"

"Nothing."

"We'll take over now. Good job."

I pushed myself to my feet and someone handed me my cane. Ash moved out of the way as another paramedic slipped an oxygen mask over Jennifer's nose and mouth. Tony stood opposite us. His face was pale and his jaw slack, as he watched the paramedics attach the EKG sensor pads to his wife's motionless chest. The diagnostic device's tiny screen told the entire story: Jennifer was flatline. The medics tried to jump-start her once with the defibrillation paddles and when that didn't work, they quickly loaded her onto a gurney.

Tony yelled, "Where are you taking her?"

"Mercy Medical Center."

"I'm coming, too!"

"There's no room for you in the ambulance. You'll have to follow in your car," the woman paramedic called over her shoulder as they began to push the gurney rapidly toward the door.

"But my car keys are upstairs and I can't follow you! How do I get there? I don't know my way around Baltimore!"

I grabbed the big man's wrist and was surprised he didn't resist. I said, "They've got no time to talk. Go up and get your keys and I'm certain the hotel concierge can give you a map to the hospital."

Tony watched the paramedics and gurney disappear around the corner and nodded. Then, he seemed to suddenly realize who I was and shook his hand free as his face contorted with rage. "You didn't know what you were doing. If my wife dies, I'm going to sue you for every penny you own."

I was about to tell him what part of my anatomy he could kiss when Ash pushed past me, her eyes incandescent with wrath. "You're a *real* piece of manhood, Tony. Your wife could be dying and you're standing here trying to figure out a way to make some money from it? You have exactly five seconds to shut your cake-hole and get the hell out of this room before I do a clog dance on your skull. Now, git!"

Tony was about to deliver a spiteful reply when he saw something in Ash's gaze that obviously caused him to conclude that discretion was indeed the better part of valor. He turned and scuttled through the door. Meanwhile, the room was in an uproar and the old lady was at the podium frantically shouting into the microphone that everyone should calm down, but all she accomplished was adding one more amplified voice to the tumult.

Ash leaned close and whispered in a troubled voice, "This is going to sound crazy, but I think Jennifer was . . . oh, I don't know. Never mind."

"Does this have something to do with that face you made when you gave her the rescue breaths?"

Ash nodded. "I smelled the fumes of something coming out of her lungs and it definitely wasn't medication. Mama has asthma and I know what the inhaler stuff smells like."

"So, what *did* it smell like?"

"I don't know. It had a kind of weird chemical aroma . . . like solvent or something."

"So what you started to say was, that you think Jennifer may have been poisoned."

"Do I sound completely fifty-one fifty?" Ash asked, using the California cop slang she'd picked up from me over the years to describe someone crazy enough to be committed to a mental institution.

"No, and just to make certain, I think

we'd better find the inhaler."

We looked on the floor around the VIP table but couldn't find the cylinder. Then, speculating that someone might have kicked the inhaler, we expanded our search area but still met with negative results. The inhaler was gone.

I went up to the podium and asked the old lady to give me a shot at restoring order. She gestured helplessly at the microphone as if to say, "It's all yours." It's a paradox, but one of the ways to settle down a noisy crowd is to begin speaking in a low but authoritative tone, which is what I did. After only a few seconds, people began to quiet in order to hear what I had to say and once the room was silent, I said, "Folks, there's been a medical emergency and we need to help the paramedics. We can't find Jennifer's inhaler and they're going to need it at the hospital to figure out how best to treat her. Did anyone pick it up?"

I heard some scattered "no's" and saw people shaking their heads. From the back I heard a woman ask, "Is Jennifer going to be all right?"

"We don't know," I replied, which was crowding the truth a bit. The fact was that unless they had some sort of miraculous "Lazarus-come-forth" quality treatment at

Mercy Medical Center, Jennifer was going to be DOA. However, no good could come from telling the crowd that and we needed to find a vital piece of potential evidence. I continued, "That's why this is so important. Did anyone see someone pick up the inhaler?"

Again, no one knew anything. I handed the microphone to the old lady and said, "Thanks. You can take it from here."

The organizer told everyone to resume their seats so that breakfast could be served and many of the artisans complied. After all, as far as they knew, Jennifer had simply succumbed to a particularly violent asthma attack. However, Ash and I strongly suspected otherwise.

I noticed the security guard standing near the door and waved him over. When he arrived, I pointed at the wireless phone in the pouch on his belt. "Do you have the number for the Baltimore City police preprogrammed into that thing?"

"Yeah."

"Then press it and give me the phone."

Five minutes later, a uniformed Baltimore cop arrived. Showing him my SFPD "retired" badge and giving him a very brief synopsis of what had just happened, I quietly told the officer that he needed to get some homicide detectives to the hotel and Mercy Medical Center immediately.

Six

I swear I wasn't trying to get us involved in another murder investigation. The last time I'd done that, Ash and I had been almost killed twice in less than six hours, so I'd learned my lesson. I only wanted to discharge my citizen's duty to make the Baltimore cops aware that this incident might deserve closer scrutiny . . . but at the same time, I'll admit I was very intrigued by the possibility that Jennifer had been poisoned. It was only natural that I'd be interested; I'd spent most of my adult life investigating murders, and poisoning is an extremely unusual crime.

Most people are shot, stabbed, or bludgeoned to death. During my career I'd only worked one killing caused by the deliberate use of a toxin, a case where a disgruntled wife mixed a massive dose of arsenic-laced grain into her philandering husband's morning bowl of granola. His name was Jason and so, naturally, I christened the investigation, "Arsenic and Cold Jace."

Like most homicide detectives, I embraced gallows humor as an emotional defense mechanism to cope with the hideous things I saw on pretty much a daily basis. That's how I came to give my homicide cases droll and, some might even say, macabre names. It was a harmless pastime — none of the murder victims ever complained. That might sound like I'm about as cold and hard as that bag of spinach that sits forgotten on the bottom shelf of everyone's freezer, but I learned during my police career that it's far easier to be gloomy than cheerful. Cop angst — the entire woe-is-me-because-I've-seen-*so*-much-horror — is self-pity dressed in a blue uniform. The bottom line is that the cops that laugh the hardest, usually live the longest.

So, although it had been a couple of years since I'd nicknamed a case, it was just like riding a bicycle — you never forget how to do it. I was ready to suggest "Leaving in a Huff" or "Gone With Her Wind" to the Baltimore cops.

I hadn't been on scene much more than twenty-five minutes in that previous arsenic-poisoning case when it became clear to my old partner Gregg and me that the wife hadn't quite thought this entire unsolvable "perfect" murder thing through: we found the empty rat poison box in the trashcan outside. The killer later told us that she hadn't thought we'd look there.

However, if Jennifer had indeed been poisoned, this crime showed sophistication, knowledge of toxic chemicals, and more than a little advance planning. It also signified that there had to be a very compelling motive to kill her, because the suspect had taken a huge risk. Poisoning is one of those classifications of murder that usually leads to a sentence of death by lethal injection, which is kind of ironic or, if you're of an Eastern philosophic bent, karmic, since it's basically execution by poisoning.

Once the patrol officer called headquarters to pass along the information, he wrote down our names, address, and cell phone number, and asked where we could be found if it turned out that the detectives needed to talk to us. But from the bored and slightly amused tone of his voice, I could tell he didn't think that was likely. As far as he was concerned, I was a pathetic old former cop, grandstanding to recapture a couple of moments of glory.

"After we go upstairs and clean up, we'll be in there. Space number twenty-three." I pointed to the entrance of the Har-Bear Expo, where a group of about sixty teddy bear collectors, overwhelmingly composed of women, was already eagerly waiting for the doors to open in about forty-five minutes.

"You were really a San Francisco homicide dick?" he half-smirked.

"That's right."

"But now you make teddy bears."

"And I enjoy it, though I imagine that does sound pretty silly to someone like you. How long have you been a cop?"

"Seven years. Hey, I didn't mean —"

"Seven whole years, huh? Are you on your first, second, or third wife?" When he didn't reply, I continued, "I had twenty-five years on the job when I got shot and the city retired me. I'm more in love with this beautiful woman than the day I married her twenty-six years ago. We spend most of our free time together, and I take great pleasure in life, an important part of which includes making teddy bears. Do you think you'll be as happy as I am when you're my age?"

I'd touched a nerve, because he suddenly looked downcast. "Point taken, man. Sorry."

"Apology accepted. If the detectives need us, they know where to find us." Ash and I went across the corridor to the elevator and as we waited for it to arrive, I said, "You were magnificent back there with Jennifer."

"But it wasn't enough." Her eyes were red and brimming with tears. The fact that Jennifer had likely died in her arms was beginning to strike home.

I pulled her close and hugged her. "Honey, we did the best we could in an awful situation."

She took a deep breath. "I know, but it doesn't make me feel any better. And I have no idea how you coped with this sort of stuff for all those years. It was one thing for me to listen to you talk about your cases, but it's completely different when you actually experience it."

"That's true and I'm sorry you had to see it firsthand."

The elevator door slid open and Todd stood there looking pale and wild-eyed. Striding from the car, he paused to give us a glare. "Is it true?"

"Yeah, Jennifer is on her way to the hospital." I reached out to hold the elevator doors open.

"I could have helped her if you'd just let me treat her."

"Maybe. It was a little more complicated than a simple asthma attack."

"Then you should have left it to a medical

professional, you goddamn idiot."

Ash wiped at her eyes and her jaw got hard. "Look, I know you're distraught, but we did our best."

"Which obviously wasn't good enough. I hope you're *real* happy." Todd waved us away in disgust and started jogging toward the doors leading to the parking garage. I guided her into the empty car and pressed the button for the fifth floor.

Ash said, "Okay, I'm not upset any more, just mad. He had no right to behave that way."

"Agreed. If he's this upset and rude now, I wonder how he'll act when he finds out she's dead. Maybe Tony will tell him."

Ash looked skeptical. "If it turns out that she was poisoned by the inhaler, wouldn't that point directly to Tony as the prime suspect?"

"Yeah, but it's also at odds with what we know about him. Does he impress you as the Wile E. Coyote, super genius kind of guy who would take the time to cobble together some ingenious device to kill the roadrunner or, in this instance, his wife?"

"Well, no."

"I agree. He'd throw her down the stairs or crush her skull with a floor lamp." Then something occurred to me. "Unless . . ."

"Unless what?"

"What if Tony has a girlfriend? Would *that* be out of character?"

"No, but I can't imagine any woman that desperate."

"That's only because you're aware he abused Jennifer."

"That, and he's an ugly slob."

"An ugly slob about to pick up an extra three-hundred-and-fifty grand, which might make him a lot easier on the eyes to a certain type of woman. Assume you had really low standards and didn't know his history of violence. What would your opinion of Tony be?"

Ash looked thoughtful. "Jovial, bordering on manic and a bit of a blabbermouth, but basically harmless."

"Exactly and that's how he would appear to a new girlfriend during the courtship phase of their relationship. She wouldn't know that their future together was going to include being used as a punching bag."

"I see what you mean."

There was a chime from overhead and the door opened. We left the elevator and headed toward our room.

"So, what if Tony's found his sole mate — and I'm talking about someone new that he can wipe his feet on — and wants to be free of Jennifer? If the contracts with Wintle and that cartoon company are written in a certain way, and I'll bet they are because Jennifer was smart, divorce wouldn't be an option."

"But murder would be, if you made it look like a severe allergic reaction to medication." Ash shook her head, her expression reflecting both disgust and wonderment.

"Right. Maybe he was hoping that, due to Jennifer's past medical history, there wouldn't be an autopsy. And perhaps there wouldn't have been if you hadn't noticed that chemical smell," I said as we arrived at our room. "But it's time for a big reality check. We don't know if she's even dead, and if she did die, that she was murdered, and most importantly, I'm not a cop anymore. So there's really no point in any further speculation."

"Not that it's ever stopped you in the past," Ash said sweetly.

I unlocked the door with the card key and held it open for Ash. After I washed my hands, she went into the bathroom to clean her face, reapply her makeup, and fix her hair. Ten minutes later, she emerged looking perfect and we went back downstairs. The crowd was larger outside the exhibit room door and we paused to show our event

IDs to an organizer.

Inside the hall, we paused for a moment to look at the Cheery Cherub Bear booth. It was dark and the arched entrance was blocked with a couple of folding chairs. I noticed a single long-stemmed yellow rose lying on the seat of one of the chairs — evidence that either there was fresh news from the hospital or that at least one of the breakfast attendees hadn't believed my cautiously hopeful and fraudulent spin on the incident. The affectionate message embodied in the flower reminded me of Todd and I wondered if he'd heard the awful news yet.

As is so often the case, Ash was thinking along the same lines and said, "Where do you suppose Todd went?"

"Probably the hospital. Do you think there was any truth to the stuff Tony said?"

"That Todd and Jennifer were having an affair? Of course not." Ash sounded incredulous.

"How can you tell? From the brief conversation I had with him, it was pretty clear he was in love with her."

"He may have been, but she didn't feel the same way about him. Most women can tell when another woman is attracted to a man, even if the other woman is playing it completely cool."

"Really? Is that why —"

"Yes, that's why I reacted so strongly to the judge making the 'big one' crack. She'd better keep her distance from you. I've got one of the few good men on the planet and I'm not about to share."

"She was flirting with me? You're kidding."

"No, and for an otherwise extremely intelligent man, you're clueless when it comes to recognizing when a woman is hitting on you."

"Which should be very reassuring to you because it means that I'm not paying that sort of attention to any woman but you." I took her hand and kissed it. "Now, let's get to our table because I know that you want to rearrange everything before the collectors are allowed in."

I wasn't exaggerating. Ash is a perfectionist and the absence of the snow tiger and Dirty Beary had ruined her original eye-pleasing design. That meant starting over from scratch. I sat down and watched in fascination as she cleared the table and began carefully positioning the bears and tigers, pausing every so often to step back and assess the effect.

This time, Cindy Sundae took center

stage. She was a pink plush bear dressed in a costume of two big scoops of fabric strawberry ice cream inside a golden brown quilted waffle cone, with a dollop of satin whipped cream and an artificial cherry on her head. As Ash worked, she was briefly interrupted a couple of times by passing artisans who stopped to thank and commend us for our lifesaving efforts.

When we were alone again, I said, "And how do you think Donna reacted when she heard the news?"

"She was probably horrified."

"Or kicking herself because she missed the incident. That was big league-quality hate and it wasn't just caused by a stolen teddy bear design."

Ash looked up from straightening the French blue bow on a brown bear that I'd made from faux fur. "People say things when they're upset that they don't mean."

"That's true, but can you indulge me for a moment?"

"Sure. How?"

"If you can spare me for a minute or two, I think I'd like to limp on over to her booth and scope her out . . . just to satisfy my unsavory curiosity."

I grabbed the expo program from the top of the upside-down crate that constituted our clerical workspace and opened the booklet to the middle page where the event map was located. Donna was assigned to slot fifty-three, which was two rows over and near the back of the room.

"But I thought you'd decided this wasn't any of your business." Teasingly feigning surprise, Ash raised her hand to her mouth and her eyes widened.

"Oh, as if you aren't the least bit interested either."

She came over to kiss me on the forehead. "Of course, I'm interested. Just stay clear of that judge."

"I promise I'll be back in a couple of minutes with my virtue intact."

"It's not *your* virtue I'm worried about."

I walked to the end of our aisle, checking out the amazing collections of bears, and made a right turn. Two rows later, I turned right again and immediately saw Donna's booth, which was identified by a superbly hand-painted sign with metallic blue Gothic lettering that read, THE IVANHOE COLLECTION BY DONNA JORDAN. The single table was covered with bears cleverly arranged as if they were at a jousting tournament. All the classic book's characters were there: Sir Wilfred of Ivanhoe, Wamba the jester, Lady Rowena, Sir Cedric, Isaac and his daughter Rebecca, and King Richard the Lion Heart. Everyone was present but Donna, who was nowhere to be seen.

Glancing at a woman in the adjoining booth, I asked, "Excuse me, but have you seen Donna?"

The woman was tall, blond, and utterly focused on posing a brown German merino wool teddy bear boy wearing blue denim shorts, a shirt, and boots. Beside the bear was a framed eight-by-ten color photo of an exquisite shadow box diorama display of the scene from *Winnie the Pooh,* where the characters try to free Pooh, who's stuck in Rabbit's door. The tableau seemed vaguely familiar and I suddenly realized where I'd seen it before. It had been featured a few months ago in one of the teddy bear magazines we subscribe to. The display had won first prize in one of the judging categories at last year's Teddy Bear Artist Invitational, one of the most prestigious shows in North America. However, I couldn't remember the artisan's name.

At last, the woman looked up from her work and said, "Not since that scene at breakfast, although I don't blame her for being furious if Jennifer actually did steal her designs. I had it happen to me once, so I know how it feels. You and your wife are the ones who tried to help Jennifer, aren't you?"

"Yeah. Hi, I'm Bradley Lyon and my wife is Ashleigh." I extended my hand.

"It's nice to meet you. I'm Dolores Austin. Please tell your wife thanks for all you did."

"I will."

"Is there any news about Jennifer?"

"I haven't heard anything." I don't know if she noticed the oblique nature of my reply, but I figured it was better manners to profess ignorance than to tell her that Jennifer was probably dead. To further change the subject, I nodded in the direction of the photograph. "Congratulations on your win at TBAI. Your work is superb."

"Thank you for noticing."

"I guess I'd better get back to our booth. Take care and good luck."

"If I see Donna, should I tell her — oh, wait, there she is!"

I turned and saw Donna walking stiffly down the aisle toward us. Her face was pale and taut with stress. She marched past us and threw herself into the chair behind her display table, where she began to unconsciously wring her hands. Then she jammed them in her jacket pockets, while continuing to stare straight ahead.

I quietly said good-bye to Dolores and went back over to Donna's booth. "Are you okay?"

I startled her from an unpleasant reverie. "What do you want?"

"I just came to see if you were all right."

"You mean you just came by to see if I was gloating over what happened to Jennifer."

"Nah. I've run into hundreds of genuinely evil people in my time, but you aren't one of them."

"I don't feel bad that she's dead."

"For starters, we don't know for a fact that she is dead, and secondly, she hurt you very badly, so your attitude is understandable." I paused for a moment and then gently asked, "Would it help if you told me what she did?"

"I've got an idea. Why don't you leave me the hell alone? You wouldn't let me tell everyone, but now *you* want to know? Go away. I've got work to do." Donna pushed herself from the chair and turned her back on me to rearrange her bears.

"I'm sorry for intruding and I hope you do well with your bears today."

Donna shot a dirty glance over her shoulder.

Of course, I was intrigued that Donna was

so utterly certain that Jennifer had died, but I couldn't tell whether it was firsthand knowledge, something she'd heard in garbled form from another witness, or just wishful thinking. Furthermore, I wondered where she'd been for the past hour or so. However, it was none of my business and I hoped that if I just kept saying it, the simple concept that I wasn't a cop anymore would eventually sink into my thick skull.

As I walked back to our aisle, I could tell the doors had been opened because the room began to fill with enthusiastic collectors. A man and a woman were already standing in front of our booth talking to Ash and you didn't need to be a clairvoyant to know that they hadn't stopped to admire our teddy bears. Homicide detectives look the same all over the globe and their arrival at our booth meant that Jennifer was dead.

SEVEN

Ash said, "Honey, these are detectives from the Baltimore City Police and they'd like to speak with us."

I shook hands with the woman first because it was obvious that she was the ranking investigator. "So I take it Jennifer was DOA?"

"That's correct, Mr. Lyon. I'm Homicide Lieutenant Sarah Mulvaney and this is my partner, Sergeant Richard Delcambre." Mulvaney's voice was a pleasant yet mildly officious contralto.

"Any idea of what killed her?"

"Excuse me, but that's confidential information."

"Of course," I said, while thinking: *Give us a break, lady. We're the ones who called you to report that Jennifer was probably poisoned.* Still, I suppose I'd have said the same thing if I were in her place because you have to safeguard "case specific" facts

— things that only the killer and the detectives know. That knowledge can be invaluable in discerning whether you're dealing with a genuine suspect or some pathetic twit who falsely confesses to a murder hoping to achieve a few moments of fame on the television news. Still, she didn't need to make it sound as if I'd asked her to reveal the Strategic Air Command's ICBM launch codes.

I guessed Mulvaney's age as about fifty years old and she would have been reasonably attractive if it weren't for the fact that her cheeks were so immobilized with skin-paralyzing cosmetics that it called to mind Jack Nicholson as the frozen-faced Joker in the *Batman* film. Her hair was a dark brunette with barely discernable maroon highlights and her hazel eyes were as cold as the waters of San Francisco Bay in January. She wore brown, cuffed slacks with a tiny plaid pattern; a long-sleeved burgundy pullover knit top, and a camel-colored woolen blazer. The coat hung open enough for me to see the silver badge hooked to her belt and the auto-pistol in the cross-draw holster on her left hip.

Delcambre was more the archetypal burly veteran cop — big shoulders accentuated by the black leather jacket he wore, no waist, and alert brown eyes that moved constantly as he scanned the room and passersby for any signs of a threat. His face was round with a rich café-au-lait complexion, his short black curly hair was flecked with gray, and he wore a full salt-and-pepper moustache and wire-framed eyeglasses.

At last Delcambre's eyes settled on me and he stuck out his hand. "Your wife told us that you're a former San Francisco PD homicide inspector."

"Yeah, up until my shin got FUBAR-ed." The sanitized version of what the acronym FUBAR stands for is "Fouled Up Beyond All Recognition." However, cops usually employ a more expressive word than "fouled."

"How'd it happen?"

"Gun fight with a murder suspect."

"You mind if I ask if you're CCW now?" Mulvaney asked. The initials stood for carrying a concealed weapon.

"I haven't carried a gun in a couple of years and don't miss it either. So, how can we help you guys?"

Mulvaney said, "We came here from the hospital. The emergency room physician is almost certain that Jennifer died from a toxin that basically shut her lungs down.

However, we won't know what kind of poison it was until tissue samples are collected at the autopsy and the ME's office runs toxicological tests."

"And it usually takes five or six working days before we get the results from the lab," Delcambre added.

Mulvaney frowned slightly at what she clearly considered an interruption. "So naturally, we're interested in how you knew she'd been poisoned."

"That's because my wife smelled a strange chemical odor when she was giving Jennifer rescue breaths."

"Yes, she told us that."

"And before that, there was Jennifer's reaction when she took a huff from the inhaler. She wasn't expecting whatever it was that came out, because she looked shocked. Then there's the fact that the inhaler disappeared while we were doing CPR. Put it all together and I thought it looked suspicious."

Mulvaney nodded and looked thoughtful. "I strongly agree. That's why I'd like to have Sergeant Delcambre conduct a pat-down of you while I search your wife."

"Excuse me, but why would you want to search us?" I asked, attempting to keep my voice congenial.

"To eliminate the possibility that you might have the inhaler."

Ash recoiled slightly in surprise. "Why would we have it?"

"I've received certain information that I have to follow up on."

Suddenly, it began to make a little sense. The detectives had just arrived from the hospital, which meant that the only witness they'd had the opportunity to interview was Tony, who probably had a great deal to gain by shifting responsibility for Jennifer's death onto us. I said, "Tony told you that we were responsible for his wife's death, didn't he?"

"Mr. Swift provided me with a preliminary statement."

"What did he say?"

"As an ex-homicide detective, you know I won't tell you that."

"But whatever it was, the fact that you want to search us, tells me you believed him. Do you have any idea of how strange this is?"

"I have a sworn duty to follow all investigative leads . . . even if they point in the direction of a former cop and his wife."

"Let me get this straight: Are you actually looking at us as suspects in Jennifer's murder?"

Ash looked stunned and asked a more

pertinent question. "And are you utterly nuts?"

The atmosphere surrounding our small group had quickly grown very tense. I shot a quick glance at Delcambre, who wore a blank expression, but there was something in the slight downward tilt of his head and rigid set of his mouth that told me he didn't agree with his boss's conclusions or tactics. At the same, he didn't look very surprised, which told me that he'd seen this sort of ambush interview technique from her before.

Mulvaney threw her shoulders back authoritatively. "No, I'm not accusing you of murder . . . at this time. Nor am I nuts, Mrs. Lyon. But there are a number of things that puzzle me."

I wanted to say: *If you actually believe we had anything to do with the murder, I'll bet that things like printing your name and tying your shoes puzzle you.* Instead, I said, "Such as?"

"Isn't it true you had a violent confrontation with the Swifts yesterday morning in the hotel parking structure?"

"No. I interrupted them in the middle of a domestic dispute and stopped Tony from slapping his wife into low earth orbit."

"What were they arguing about?" Mulvaney sounded mildly interested.

"From the little I heard, Jennifer was concerned over some sort of situation and Tony got mad because he thought she was going to mess it up. There wasn't much talk before he went ballistic and I had to step in."

"What if I told you that we'd heard you threatened the Swifts with your cane?"

"Then I'd say Tony was talking out of his ass because his mouth knew better."

Delcambre chuckled and Mulvaney frowned. She said, "So, you're denying it."

I sighed. "Yes, I deny it."

"Were there any witnesses that can confirm your version of the incident?"

"No, and this is getting ridiculous."

"Not from where I stand. You say you allegedly witnessed this crime, yet our records indicate that you never called the police."

"Of course I didn't call. Why would I?" I began ticking the reasons off on my fingers and resisted the powerful urge to shift into "rant" mode. "*A,* there was no actual battery, so the crime was a very thin misdemeanor. *B,* like many domestic violence victims, Jennifer wasn't exactly thankful that I'd interceded and undoubtedly would have denied the incident ever happened. *C,* Tony threatened to kick *my* ass, but I wasn't interested in pressing charges. *D,* I had a truck full of stuffed animals and other stuff to unload and didn't feel like waiting for a patrol car to arrive and then wasting another half-hour giving information for a report that would never be investigated. And *E,* my cell phone probably wouldn't have worked in the parking structure."

As I spoke, Mulvaney pulled a small note-pad from her coat pocket and jotted down some information. Without looking up, she said in a thoughtful, yet slightly smug voice, "Huh. So, you essentially admit that you didn't want the police to know about your encounter with the Swifts."

"That's not what he said." Ash glowered at Mulvaney. "And lady, a word to the wise: Don't try to play word games with my husband, because you'll lose."

"Since it's obvious you've already bought Tony's version of the incident, did he also think to tell you why *he* didn't call the cops to report being assaulted by a cripple?" I asked.

"Anything that Mr. Swift may or may not have said to us is confidential." Mulvaney snapped the notepad shut and shoved it back into her coat pocket. "Moving on. Can you explain why you ordered a certified EMT to stop treating Mrs. Swift, so that you and your wife could take over?"

"Because Tony thought that the EMT — whose name is Todd Litten, by the way — was playing 'hide the kielbasa' with his wife. Tony was behaving like a complete fool and exacerbating the situation, so there wasn't any option but to have Todd step aside. But you don't have to take our word for it." I waved toward the crowded exhibit hall. "There were over a hundred witnesses."

"We'll get to them."

"And as long as you're on a fishing expedition for suspects, you might want to take a good look at Todd. The Good Samaritan was nowhere to be seen when things went south."

"That's because you told him to go and, for your information, Mr. Litten came to the hospital and was very helpful . . . unlike you."

"You want help? Here's an idea: you might want to spend a few moments figuring out just what our motive would be to kill a woman we didn't know."

"And then tried to save her life," said Ash.

"As I said earlier, I'm not accusing you of anything, yet. So, any speculation about your motive would be premature. Right now, I suspect everyone and no one."

The situation was becoming progressively

more surreal, because Mulvaney had just unwittingly quoted Inspector Clouseau from the old comedy film, *A Shot in the Dark,* and imagined she sounded profound.

I took a deep breath. "Listen carefully, Lieutenant. We didn't kill anybody and frankly, it amazes me that you didn't do a little digging into Tony's background before you came over here to roust us."

Delcambre cleared his throat. "Actually, we've confirmed that Mr. Swift has two prior convictions in Pennsylvania for spousal battery and that he just got off probation."

"That's confidential information," Mulvaney snapped.

"Thank you, Sergeant. I can't tell you how comforting it is to know that at least one of you thought to do something as basic as check and see if Tony had a criminal record." Turning back to Mulvaney, I continued, "If Tony has two priors for D.V., why isn't he at the top of your suspect list?"

"I'm not saying he isn't on my list, but with your background as a cop, you know as well as I do that wife-beaters tend to remain very MO constant. They punch, they kick, and they throw their spouses against walls because the motive is domination and terror. They almost never break from pattern to poison them."

"Okay, so he doesn't fit the profile. How come we do?"

"Look at it from my point of view. Out of all the people at this teddy bear show, who possesses the most knowledge about methods of committing and concealing murder?"

I thought for a second. "Me. But —"

"That's right, you — the same person who had a violent showdown with the victim and her husband yesterday and then prevented an EMT from helping the victim this morning."

"All of which he explained, if you'd been listening," Ash snapped.

"You, be quiet." Mulvaney pointed a warning finger at Ash.

"And if you speak that way to my wife one more time, I'll end this interview right now."

Mulvaney took a deep breath. "I apologize, but I don't know why you're making this so difficult."

"I don't know, maybe it has something to do with the fact that it looks like you're trying to frame us for murder. We're standing here answering pointed questions, while Tony the Tiger — the guy who brought Jennifer the inhaler, I might add — is probably at the breakfast buffet."

"That's not true. He's upstairs, standing by while another team of my detectives searches his room. So, we're not just 'rousting' *you,*" Mulvaney said testily.

"That was mighty fast work getting a search warrant."

"He gave us permission, and when we're done here, I want your consent to search your room."

"Why? You have no reason."

"If you're innocent, it'll help me eliminate you from consideration as a suspect."

"It seems to me that you're a little turned around on our system of law, Lieutenant. It's your job as cops to collect the evidence, investigate, and identify potential suspects. I, on the other hand, don't have any duty to prove my innocence to you."

Mulvaney's lips became compressed and pale. "Mr. Lyon, I'm very busy and I've tried to be nice. Now, I want your co-operation or you'll force me to pursue a more aggressive course."

"It isn't cooperation if I consent because you've threatened me. That's called coercion."

"I'm going to search your room."

"Then I think it would be best if you got a search warrant because I'm not giving you permission."

"Why, do you have something to hide?"

It took every ounce of restraint I possessed

not to answer: *Only my contempt for you.* I'd spoken with Mulvaney long enough to understand that she derived unsavory enjoyment from exercising power over other people and viewed any resistance to her agenda as a personal affront. The fact of the matter was that searching our room was no longer as important as satisfying her intense need to assert dominancy.

Finally, I said, "No, I have nothing to hide and you've exhausted my patience, so we have nothing further to say. You can refer any further inquiries to our attorney."

"Fine. You want to lawyer up? See if I care."

A woman walked up to our table and picked up Brenda Brownie. Smiling, she began to ask Ash something about the bear. Mulvaney pulled her coat open so that our prospective customer could see the gun and shield on her belt and said, "These people are busy with us right now. Come back later. They might still be here — that is, if I don't book them."

"Was that necessary?" I asked, watching the potential customer scurry away and knowing that it wouldn't be long before the word circulated throughout the exhibit hall that Ash and I were under investigation by the cops.

"You're the one that decided to play hardball and I'm not going to waste any more time on you. Put your hands behind your head and interlock your fingers, so that my partner can conduct a pat-down for that inhaler."

"Not happening."

"Pardon me?" Mulvaney's jaw jutted out.

"You aren't going to touch my wife, or me, because this isn't Nazi Germany and you don't have the right to search people at random. And, if you insist on trying to conduct a pat-down, I will resist, so you'd better be prepared to physically subdue me and take me into custody."

"Both of us," Ash added as she moved next to me.

Delcambre began, "Lieutenant, maybe we'd better —"

"I'm in charge here."

I said, "Then you — as the on-scene commander — should know better than anyone else that you have absolutely no evidence or valid information to establish the 'reasonable suspicion' necessary to conduct a cursory pat-down search for weapons. That's prehistoric case law — Mapp versus Ohio. So, if you proceed, you're in clear violation of the Fourth Amendment of the Constitution."

"Don't lecture me."

"*Somebody* should have, at some point in your career. What are your options? You can take us into custody for interfering with your investigation and search us incident to a 'lawful' arrest — except we all know it won't *be* a lawful arrest. So, that will put you in violation of the Fifth Amendment of the Constitution, too." I held my hands up in mock surrender. "But hey, if the Baltimore City Police Department has six or seven hundred grand to settle the ten-million-dollar false-arrest and violation of civil rights lawsuit we'll file — and you don't mind reading about your recklessly criminal behavior in the *Washington Post* — let's get this party started."

"He's right, Lieutenant," Delcambre said quietly. "Maybe we should back off a little and rethink this."

"I don't *back off* from anyone, especially not from some wise-ass gimp who thinks he's F. Lee Bailey," Mulvaney said as she reached behind her back and fumbled for something.

"This is insane!" said Ash.

"Close your eyes and hold onto my hand, honey."

I hoped Mulvaney was reaching for handcuffs, but had a feeling she was grabbing her pepper spray and I got ready for the sensation of having my eyes lit on fire with a road flare. I'd been accidentally sprayed with the stuff several times during my police career and I don't have the words to tell you how much it hurts. However, we'll never know what she was going to do, because we were interrupted.

"Lieutenant! We think we've found something important!" said a man as he jogged up the aisle carrying a brown-paper lunch sack. He wore blue coveralls, latex gloves, and a ball cap that bore the embroidered letters, BCPD CSI, which meant the guy was an evidence technician.

I heard Delcambre quietly sigh with relief as Mulvaney turned to the tech. "What do you have?"

"He did a great job of hiding it, but we found it hidden behind the ventilation duct grate in the bathroom," the tech said proudly as he carefully lifted an asthma inhaler from the bag. "Check this out. There was a tiny hole drilled in the canister and then he tried to reseal it, so that it wouldn't be noticed."

"But the repair didn't hold," said Delcambre, squinting at the inhaler.

"Exactly. We also found the drill — eighteen volt, battery-operated and a box of bits."

"What is that clear stuff oozing out?" asked Mulvaney.

"Not medicine, that's for sure. We'll obviously have to wait for the crime lab, but if I had to guess . . ."

"What do you think it is?" Mulvaney demanded.

"It could be superglue."

"If she inhaled enough of the fumes, what would happen?"

"It would likely immediately freeze the cilia of her lungs and she'd quickly drown in her own fluids," I interjected.

Everyone looked at me and Mulvaney asked, "How do you know that?"

"Back in the nineties, I knew an evidence tech that was doing the superglue process to raise prints from a gun. He got a big huff by accident and was in the hospital for two weeks. His lungs never completely healed."

Delcambre was shaking his head angrily. "Jesus, and remember that residue we noticed on Tony's hands? Now that I think about it, it might have been dried superglue."

"Where is Swift?" Mulvaney asked the tech.

"Still in the room with Detectives Oleszak

and Crawford."

"Does he know you found this?"

"I don't think so. I told Oleszak about it in the corridor because I figured you wouldn't want the guy to know."

"Good work. Did the detectives let Swift use the bathroom?"

"I . . . uh, I don't know."

"We've got to get up there before he cleans his hands. Come on, Delcambre." Mulvaney turned and jogged for the exit with her partner and the tech hard on her heels as they cut a path through the crowds of teddy bear collectors.

As Ash and I watched the cops leave, I shouted, "We accept your apology."

EIGHT

Can you please explain something to me? I was a cop most of my adult life, I've always been a law-abiding citizen, I'm crippled, I've never cut off one of those menacing DO NOT REMOVE UNDER PENALTY OF LAW tags from a new pillow, and I'm of a mature enough age to remember when Woody Allen's comedy films were funny. Add those elements together and I think it's pretty clear I don't fit the criminal profile. So why is it that over the past nine months, I've been threatened with jail so many times that you'd have thought I was Robert Downey Jr.?

And make no mistake; if that evidence tech hadn't shown up with the inhaler, Lieutenant Mulvaney would have arrested us for *something,* just to show us that she was the boss. The formal charge against us would probably have been that we'd interfered with a homicide investigation — which of course, we hadn't — but we *had* committed the grave and unofficial crime of "contempt of cop" by our refusal to grovel before the detective as if she were a demigod.

"What in the name of God is wrong with that woman?" Although the cops were gone, Ash continued to glare in the direction in which they'd departed.

"An acute case of being badge-heavy. She's in a hurry to pit someone for this homicide and viewed our lack of cooperation as a deliberate challenge to her authority."

"But how can she solve the case if she randomly accuses people of murder?"

"Unfortunately, it wasn't a random accusation. It's obvious that Tony did a first-rate job of twisting the circumstances to make it look as if I might have killed Jennifer."

"To cover his own guilt for the murder of his wife." Ash shook her head and sighed. "What a scumbag."

"Agreed, he's a scumbag, but I'm not so certain he killed Jennifer."

"Huh?" Ash turned to look at me. "Sweetheart, less than an hour ago you were explaining to me in detail why Tony was the prime suspect."

"I know, but something doesn't make

sense. Let's go sit down and I'll explain." I nodded in the direction of our table.

"Your leg is hurting, isn't it?"

"A little. I've been on my feet a lot this morning." I lowered myself onto a folding chair with a tiny moan.

Ash got the black leather satchel we use to carry our sales receipt books, business cards, sewing kit, and other miscellanies we need at a teddy bear show, which unfortunately also includes painkillers. Unzipping the bag, she said, "Ibuprofen?"

"Please."

She handed me three white pills and I took them with a swallow of bottled water. But before I could begin my explanation we had some potential customers visit the table. Ash chatted with the women, one of whom was admiring Suzy Cinnamon Streusel. Suzy was one of Ash's masterpieces: a bear wearing an amazing realistic coffee cake costume that included drizzled white icing made from melted silicon. After a few minutes of conversation, the lady put Suzy down and said she'd be back after she'd seen the rest of the show.

That meant one of two things: either the woman wasn't interested in Suzy and was lying to us to be courteous or she was a teddy bear show rookie and didn't yet understand that if a bear really calls to you, that you should buy it now instead of later. Wait, and the odds are good that the bear will be gone when you come back. Teddy bear shows are a lot like life and finding true love; you have to be a little adventurous.

Once the women were out of earshot, Ash said, "Okay, so why isn't Tony the killer?"

"I'm not completely eliminating him from consideration, but think about it: if he was smart and cunning enough to come up with the idea of using superglue as a toxin and altering the inhaler like that, then why was the inhaler found in his hotel room? That should have been the very last place on the planet we'd expect to find it."

Ash's eyes widened. "I see what you mean. He would have had a plan to dispose of it someplace else."

"Right. He had plenty of time and a thousand opportunities to ditch the thing in a restroom wastebasket, along the road as he drove to the hospital, or even in the bay. Yet it was found in his room."

"Maybe he wasn't expecting us to get involved and when we did, he panicked. I mean, what's the likelihood that there was going to be a retired homicide inspector attending a teddy bear artisan breakfast?"

"He knew I'd been a cop. I told him."

"But not a detective."

"I suppose . . . but hold it right there. Are you suggesting that manly-men don't attend teddy bear shows?" I pretended to be offended.

Ash leaned over to kiss my cheek. "My manly-man does, but not many others do. You being there could have derailed Tony's plans."

"Possibly, but it doesn't change the fact that he'd have known that once the cops realized Jennifer had been poisoned, they'd begin their search for evidence in his room."

"Why?"

"Because his priors for DV would make him an immediate and obvious suspect."

"True."

"Furthermore, it just doesn't make any sense that Tony would run the risk of being seen by a hundred witnesses as he picked the inhaler up from the floor, only to take it to his room. That's felony-stupid."

"I agree, but how do you explain the glue they said was on his hands?"

"Again, if he went to all the trouble of developing this James Bond-quality plan, don't you think he'd have worn gloves while sabotaging the inhaler? Besides, just before things went to hell, I overheard him telling someone that he'd repaired a broken plastic teddy bear stand earlier this morning."

"Convenient. Maybe he was trying to establish an alibi."

"Honey, I'm troubled by your distrustful view of your fellow creatures. Wherever could you have picked up such a deplorable tendency?"

Ash smiled sweetly. "Why, I have no idea."

"However, I like the fact you're thinking like a homicide detective. Mulvaney could take lessons from you."

"Thank you."

"But how he got glue on his hands isn't nearly as important as this question: would Tony give Mulvaney permission to search his room if he'd just hidden the inhaler there?"

"No. That would be suicidal."

"Exactly."

"So, he didn't know it was there?"

"And following the progression of logic, that means the real killer planted it in his room to frame him for first-degree murder. Considering he tried to do precisely the same thing to me, I find it deliciously ironic."

"But what are you going to do about it?"

"Nothing."

"What do you mean 'nothing'?"

"Just what I said, sweetheart. Nothing, *nada,* zilch, zip, not happening. I have no desire to see the inside of the Baltimore City Jail and if I start meddling in this investigation, and Lieutenant BOTOX finds out, that's exactly where I'll end up."

Ash frowned. "But an innocent man is going to jail for a murder he didn't commit."

"An innocent man who threatened to assault me yesterday, who's also a convicted felon, and who smashed his wife up so badly that she was in the hospital for a week. Sorry, honey, but I won't be real upset if Tony spends a couple of days in the slammer until the Baltimore cops decide he isn't the killer. Besides which, it's out of our control because I'm not a cop anymore."

"I suppose you're right." She pretended to watch the teddy bear aficionados as they strolled by, but only a second or two passed before she turned back to me and said, "So, who's the real killer?"

"Beats me."

"And you aren't even interested?"

"I won't go so far as to say that."

"And you don't think you'd enjoy identifying the real killer before Mulvaney even knows that she's arrested the wrong person?"

"Get thee behind me, Satan."

"You would. Don't deny it."

"Okay, I'll admit it would give me a great deal of unsavory pleasure to rub her nose in it by solving the case, if you'll explain to me why you're egging me on."

"Because she treated us like dirt in front of everyone and all but accused you of murder. That was flat wrong and I think she needs to be taken down a peg or two." You can always tell when Ash is genuinely angry because her normally dormant Shenandoah Valley accent becomes more pronounced.

"No argument it was wrong, but there's nothing we can do about it unless . . . no! You aren't suggesting I —"

"Conduct your own homicide investigation."

"Danger, danger, Will Robinson!" I waved my arms spasmodically like the robot from *Lost In Space.* "Honey, let me preface this by saying I love you more than life, but at what point this morning did you lose your mind? Just think of how many teddy bears you'd have to sell to post my bail."

"Mulvaney would have to catch you first and she won't even be here if she's at the police station questioning Tony."

"There'll still be a platoon of cops and evidence techs here."

"Looking in the wrong places."

I covered my ears. "La, la, la, la, la! I'm not listening."

"Think of the unhappy expression on Mulvaney's face when you solve the case."

"We wouldn't be able to tell what she felt, because her face is paralyzed."

Ash gave me a grave look. "Okay, what if I asked you to find the real killer because you and I both know it's the right thing to do?"

I was going to offer another feeble protest, but stifled it because she was absolutely correct. Whatever Jennifer Swift's faults were, she didn't deserve to be murdered, much less spend her final moments of life in a tortured gagging panic, trying to force her inoperative lungs to work. It was a hellish way to die. During my career as a homicide inspector I'd investigated over a thousand murders and this one belonged in the top tier — or bottom, depending on how you looked at it — for sheer, cool, premeditated cruelty. So, regardless of the fact I was no longer a peace officer, I felt I had a moral duty to help identify and capture the killer, especially if the police had arrested the wrong person for murder.

At the same time, my motivation wasn't entirely altruistic. I was fascinated by the prospect of investigating one of the most rare forms of homicide, a poisoning murder, and I craved the excitement of going monster hunting again. Furthermore, the murder had been committed in my presence and, rightly or wrongly, I viewed that as a personal challenge. Most of all, I wanted revenge on Mulvaney for abusing Ash and me in front of our teddy bear artisan peers. The best way to do that was to identify the killer and withhold the information from the egomaniacal lieutenant until she'd made a groveling apology. As you'll have gathered by now, "forgive and forget" isn't one of my maxims.

At last, I said, "Does it *ever* bother you that you're always right?"

She pretended to be lost in thought for a moment. "No, not really. So, where are you going to begin?"

"By trying to figure out all the angles associated with the inhaler. It tells us an awful lot about the murderer, such as it was someone that understood what the superglue fumes would do to Jennifer's lungs."

"And it also has to be someone that was well acquainted with Jennifer, since the suspect had to know she used an inhaler. That means Todd or Donna."

"As far as we know right now, although I'd have to imagine that some of the other teddy bear artists would have known Jennifer was an asthmatic."

"But how many of them would have wanted her dead?"

"None, and I can't figure Todd as the killer either. Yeah, he'd poison Tony, but not Jennifer."

"Then my money is on Donna. She knew Jennifer and obviously hated her." Ash inhaled sharply. "You don't think that confrontation this morning at breakfast . . . ?"

"Was deliberately intended to provoke an asthma attack that would cause Jennifer to use the inhaler? It's an interesting idea, but why make it so complicated? It's too much like a bad episode of *Murder, She Wrote.* Real killings aren't like that."

"Hey! I liked Jessica Fletcher."

"I know, and if you ever wonder how much I love you, think back on all those Sunday nights when I sat watching with you, resisting the urge to tell you all the different ways it went wrong."

Ash's eyes bulged out. "Honey, who the heck do you think you're kidding? Half the time I couldn't hear the dialogue over your running commentary on the show's faults."

"I may have made an occasional critical observation," I said sheepishly.

"And conducted the occasional crime

reconstruction using the kids and sometimes the dog to illustrate how something couldn't happen the way Jessica said it did."

"I don't remember that." My cheeks began to grow warm.

With a gleeful grin, Ash whipped the wireless phone from the satchel. "How about I call Heather and Chris right now to see if *they* remember?"

"All right, I'll admit it: I was a colossal pain in the butt. I'm sorry. Can we get back to discussing the actual murder?"

"If the present topic is embarrassing, of course, darling."

"The bottom line is that there's no point in speculating until we do two things: We've got to learn as much as we can about everyone involved, including Jennifer, and then figure out how the suspect entered their room twice without being noticed."

"Todd was Jennifer and Tony's partner. He might've needed access to the room, so couldn't he have been issued a key?"

"Considering how jealous Tony is, that's about as likely as The Beatles getting back together. Still, I'll have to check that out. Speaking of The Beatles, do you know what John Lennon would say right now if he were alive?"

"No, what?"

"Let me out of this coffin!" I half-shouted while frantically shoving my hands upward against an invisible and closed casket lid.

A trio of women, each carrying teddy bears, paused in front of our table to peer at me in consternation. Then, muttering amongst themselves, they continued down the aisle. Ash gave me an I-can't-believe-you-said-that-in-front-of-normal-people look and I made a quick mental note to myself to reserve my dead Beatle jokes for venues other than teddy bear shows.

At last she said, "So, tell me, since we don't have any access to the police computer system, how are you going to do the background checks?"

"I'll start by going up to our room and using the laptop to Google everyone involved. It's a long shot, but maybe I'll find something useful. After that, I'll do some discreet witness canvassing back down here in the hall and hope the cops don't notice."

Ash squeezed my hand and stood up. "Well, I'll leave you to brainstorm, because I'm going to find the woman that Mulvaney chased off. She liked Brenda Brownie, and more importantly, we don't need her wandering the exhibition hall telling everyone that we were arrested. Then, when I get back, you can start investigating."

Once Ash was gone, I reached into the satchel, pulled out a steno pad and began making some notes. It was a little difficult to concentrate because the exhibit hall was growing crowded and very noisy. I looked up periodically from my notebook to check out the passing crowds, and saw Sergeant Delcambre approaching our table. I snapped the steno pad shut and slid it into the satchel. The very last thing I wanted to advertise was the fact I was conducting my own investigation.

Delcambre heaved a sigh that was a mixture of frustration and exhaustion. "Hey, before we go back to headquarters, I want to apologize to you for my boss's behavior."

"It wasn't your fault, but thanks. It must be difficult working with someone who's perpetually going off half-cocked."

"It's . . . challenging."

"Yeah, I'll bet. If you don't mind me asking, just what is her major malfunction?"

"You ever see the old movie, *Sunset Boulevard*?" Delcambre jutted his chin out and did a fairly credible job of mimicking Gloria Swanson's imperious tone, "I'm ready for my close-up, Mr. DeMille."

"So, she's Norma Desmond, huh?"

"And sometimes I envy Bill Holden at the bottom of the swimming pool." He glanced down the aisle and lowered his voice. "From the outset, she was always a marginal detective, but not long after she was promoted to investigations she worked a couple of slam-dunk, smoking-gun homicides. For instance, one of them was the murder of a pawn shop clerk where the crook left his freaking ID on the counter."

"Call Sherlock Holmes and the Baker Street Irregulars."

"Exactly. But the media made a huge deal out of it because she was one of the first female homicide investigators on the department. They created a monster."

"You have my sympathies. So, what's up with Tony?"

"Mulvaney arrested him. He's being transported to police headquarters for questioning."

"You think he did it?"

"The murder weapon was in his room, so there's probable cause to make the arrest."

Noticing the oblique answer, I said, "Yeah, I don't think he did it either."

"Let's just say, I have questions."

"Such as why he took the inhaler back up to his room and then gave you consent to search."

"Yeah."

"You know, Mulvaney was so focused on

browbeating us that she missed the chance to pick up some pretty important information. You interested?"

Delcambre pulled his notepad and pen from his jacket pocket. "Of course."

"I saw Jennifer use that inhaler on Friday morning, shortly after I stopped Tony from going *Raging Bull* on her. She had it in her purse."

"When did that happen?"

"Call it ten-twenty."

"So, if it's the same inhaler, we're talking a twenty-two-hour window for the suspect to burg the room and alter the inhaler."

"That's how I see it."

"Anything else?"

"Did anyone tell you about the disturbance at breakfast this morning?"

"What? You think the woman . . ." Delcambre began to flip through the pages of the notepad.

"Donna Jordan."

"Yeah, Jordan. You think she has something to do with it?"

"I'm not accusing her, but there's definitely bad blood between them."

"Over what?"

"Donna accused Jennifer of stealing her teddy bear designs."

"And she'd kill her over *that?*"

"They were apparently the same designs the Swifts just sold to Wintle Toys for three hundred and fifty grand — not that you need a six-figure cash amount as a motive for murder. I worked a homicide once over the theft of an Our Lady of Guadalupe medal that was worth two dollars and eighty cents retail. People often kill for stupid reasons."

"Good point."

"And add this to the mix: there's also the possibility that Todd Litten, the guy who wrote the books for her teddy bears, was suffering from a serious case of unrequited puppy love for Jennifer."

"We heard about what Tony said."

"It's worth following up on. In fact, it'd be premature to eliminate him as a suspect."

"I know, but if he was in love with Jennifer, what would his motive be?"

"How about something as simple as 'if I can't have her noboby else can either'? I've worked a few of those."

"Me, too. But the problem is that Mulvaney is absolutely convinced Tony did it and she's using Litten as our main witness."

"How so?"

"He can testify to Tony's ongoing physical abuse of Jennifer and how frightened she said she was of him." He glanced toward the exhibition hall door. "And I've got to take off, because she's waiting outside in the car. But . . ."

"If I come up with anything, I'll call you. Got a card?"

"Thanks, man." Delcambre dug a business card from his badge case and handed it to me. Then he gave me a wry, knowing grin. "Oh, and should I be concerned as to what might lead you to think that you'd come up with evidence pertaining to an official murder investigation?"

"Do you really want the answer to that question?"

"Nah."

"I didn't think so."

Nine

Once Delcambre left, I resumed work on my notes and was jotting down a rough chronology of events when I heard someone clear their throat to announce their presence. I looked up and realized that if Ash returned in the next few moments, there was an excellent possibility that I might witness a second murder this morning. The lady teddy bear judge who'd made the suggestive "big one" remark was standing in front of our table, fondling one of our bears. It was apparent she wanted to chat and I knew it was no coincidence that she'd arrived while my wife was gone.

Furthermore, the judge had dressed up for her visit. She was wearing a tight raspberry-colored pullover shirt with a low neckline that showed off more than a little décolletage, snuggly-fitting slacks, and a lip-glossed smile I think was intended to be coy. There was a pale circular indentation at the base of the ring finger on her left hand, which told me she'd probably removed her wedding band only a few moments earlier. Another thing I noticed was that she was eyeballing me in the same longing manner that Kitchener has when staring at a pizza crust and, for the life of me, I couldn't understand why. My hair is the same color as the brushed aluminum on a DeLorean, I'm lame, and I thank a merciful God for the invention of "relaxed fit" jeans. So, what was the attraction?

"Hi, remember me?" she asked.

"Of course, you were here yesterday with the judging team looking at our teddy bears. Thank you for the nomination."

"You're welcome. I didn't get the chance to introduce myself yesterday. I'm Lisa Parr and I have to tell you that you were amazing this morning at breakfast."

"It was just standard CPR and I couldn't have done it without my wife. She'll —"

"But you were the one in charge."

"— be back in a minute so you can also thank her."

"Call me old-fashioned, but I adore a man who takes command."

"Yeah, me, too."

Lisa gave me a quick puzzled look. After a moment, she said, "Did you hear the news?"

"No. What?"

She leaned over to speak confidentially and provide me with a panoramic view of her cleavage. "Someone told me they heard a policewoman say Jennifer is dead."

I pretended to look shocked. "Really? That's too bad."

"And that isn't all. She also said that some detectives just took Tony Swift out to a police car and he was wearing handcuffs. What do you suppose that means?"

"I really wouldn't know."

"Do you think he might have killed her?"

"That's kind of hard to believe. From everything I could see, they were the perfect couple." I lied with the easy grace of a congressman, hoping Lisa might reveal some useful gossip about the Swifts.

"You don't know them, do you?"

"No, my wife and I are still pretty new to the teddy bear show circuit, especially on the East Coast."

"He's a pig and for all her snooty attitude, Jennifer always made me feel as if I should check my purse to make sure my wallet was still there when I finished talking to her."

"So, could there have been some truth to the accusations Donna made this morning?"

She looked thoughtful. "There might be. A far as faces are concerned, their bear designs are pretty similar. But how do you prove who had an idea first and if someone stole it from you? It happens. I've had designs ripped off, but you've just got to trust that you're a better artisan than the thief and move on."

"You grin and bear it."

Lisa laughed a little too heartily at the feeble pun, straightened up, and turned to perch herself on the edge of the table so that I could survey her derriere, which was less than two feet away. She smiled when she saw that I was studiously keeping my eyes on her face. "Let's talk about something else. I heard you're a retired homicide detective from the San Francisco police."

"That's true."

"That's *so* exciting. I'll bet it was dangerous."

I thought: *If my wife shows up in the next couple of seconds, not half as dangerous as what you're doing right now, because you're dicing with death.* Instead I said, "Mostly it was a lot of paperwork."

"I think you're being modest. You know, I write articles for the teddy bear magazines and I'd like to do one about you."

"I can't think why."

"Because there aren't many male teddy bear artisans with your background. I wonder if we could get together sometime before Sunday night so that I could interview you."

"With my wife, of course."

She gave me a little pout. "Actually, I was hoping we could meet privately, so that I could get a more . . . intimate and *in-depth* profile of you."

My cheeks flushed and I realized that she'd just crossed over the line from relatively innocent flirty banter into what sounded suspiciously to my finely honed investigative ear like an invitation to dance the horizontal naked mamba with her. I also knew I had to acknowledge and politely decline the invitation, because if I chose to ignore it, Lisa would view my passive response as a tacit signal to proceed with plans for the in-depth meeting.

I said: "You know, you're a very attractive woman and I'm flattered and frankly perplexed by your interest. But I have to tell you that I'm very much in love my wife and it wouldn't be right for me to be alone with you under any circumstances."

"That's so sweet. I can't tell you how refreshing it is to meet a man with principles." She stood up, gave her tresses a shampoo commercial flip, and smiled warmly. "I have to go now, but we'll talk more later. Bye."

I'll tell you, I was feeling pretty good about how I'd handled the situation, which only goes to show you that as far as the subject of women and how they think is concerned, I haven't seen the ball since kickoff. That point was firmly driven home when Ash returned to the table a few minutes later and I casually told her of the encounter, while striving to keep the self-satisfaction from my voice.

When I finished, she asked incredulously, "And you actually think she understands that you're off-limits?"

"Umm . . . yeah."

"Wrong. Honey, all you did was encourage her."

"Okay, I'm officially confused. How did I do that?"

"Because you've made the prospect of seducing you more challenging. You're a much bigger prize now, because there's the extra thrill of knowing that she's trying to take you away from another woman."

"The fruit from the Forbidden Tree being the sweetest, huh?"

"And what could be more forbidden than a man who says he's in love with his wife?"

"But what's the attraction?"

"Brad, one of the nicest things about you

is that you don't realize how wonderful a husband you are. There are probably a couple of hundred women at this show that envy and despise me because I got one of the few good ones. She — you said her name was Lisa, right? — Lisa just happens to be a little less moral than most."

I looked down at the tabletop. "Well, if that's the case, it makes me wonder if the only reason she picked Dirty Beary was because she had ulterior motives. Maybe he really isn't good enough."

"Which is another excellent reason to break that chick's neck the next time I see her." She took my hand and continued in a more tender tone, "Honey, your bears are wonderful and I'm convinced that Beary would have been nominated regardless of who was on the judging team. So, don't let a bad and selfish person ruin everything."

"If you say so."

"I do. Now, forget about Lisa and tell me what your next move is on the investigation."

"To go upstairs and run some quick computer checks and then change clothes. We didn't bring a tie did we?"

"No, this was supposed to be a casual event. Why do you need a tie?"

"If I'm going to commit the felony crime

of impersonating a homicide detective, I'd better be dressed like one."

"And why do you need to impersonate a cop?"

"Because we need to know if there were any extra card keys issued to the Swifts' room and the hotel staff won't give that sort of information to an average citizen." I kissed Ash on the cheek and pushed myself to my feet. "Love you. I'll be back in awhile. Oh, and I'm assuming you found that woman. Is she coming back for Brenda Brownie?"

"She said she might, but I don't think so. Mulvaney really scared her off."

"You know, taking into account we've so far dealt with domestic disputes, drunken rants, murder, bullying cops, and predatory trollops, I vote that we pass on the Baltimore Har-Bear Expo next year."

"The motion passes unanimously. Please be careful, honey."

Tucking the steno pad under my arm, I headed for the exit, passing crowds of happy people and table after table loaded with sweet-looking teddy bears. This was my life now and I wondered for just a second why I was voluntarily going back into the revolting universe of murder investigation. I guess the bottom line is that although I'd been removed from the homicide bureau, the homicide bureau hadn't yet been removed from me.

Leaving the exhibition hall, I noticed the doors to the adjoining banquet room were closed and a plastic DO NOT DISTURB sign hung from one of the handles. I knew that meant there were Baltimore detectives and CSI techs inside, photographing the murder scene and searching for evidence. The last thing I needed was for any of the cops to spot me, so I continued on down the corridor.

I went through the lobby, avoiding the registration desk, and saw a sign pointing the way toward the gift shop, which was apparently down a side corridor. Passing the hotel's glass entrance doors, I saw the rain was coming down in gray sheets and caught a glimpse of a parking valet standing out in the storm, his old-fashioned fisherman foul weather gear billowing in the gale. I applauded the Maritime Inn's commitment to creating a wooden-ships-and-iron-men atmosphere, but that was just insane, especially since I knew the valet was probably making nothing more than minimum wage, tips, and whatever personal information he could boost from the cars to commit identity theft.

The hotel gift shop was about what I expected. The clerk was a young woman playing some sort of computer game on her cell phone who paid no attention to me as I entered the store. Inside, I found usuriously priced candy bars and bags of salty snacks, a small and well-thumbed assortment of glitz, financial, and computer magazines, cheap sunglasses, Maritime Inn commemorative teddy bears made from shoddy tangerine plush and looking as if they'd been stuffed with sawdust, a collection of royal blue Maritime Inn baseball caps that had obviously been on the shelf since the mid-1980s because the brims were decorated with that hokey military-style gold braid so popular back then, and since a high-class shopping expedition always works up a big thirst, twenty-ounce sodas at five bucks a pop in the small refrigerator. I also found the small collection of men's ties at the back of the shop hanging next to a display of T-shirts the color of baboon rumps, silk-screened with the message, "My Mom and Dad Went to Baltimore and All I Got Was This Stupid Shirt."

The selection of ties was limited — again, no big surprise. My choices were either second-team Warner Brothers cartoon characters such as the Pepe LePew and Sylvester the Cat, or hideously asymmetric geometric designs in neon tones reminiscent of Japanese anime that looked as if they'd been designed by a nine-year-old boy who couldn't draw and who'd consumed way too much sugar. In the end, I selected one of the ugly Pokemon ties and managed to attract the clerk's attention away from her game long enough to pay her $22.95 for the polyester assault on the eyes.

A few minutes later, I entered our room on the fifth floor. The bedclothes were still in disarray, which signified the maids hadn't gotten to our side of the hotel yet. It also meant that there wasn't anything but a package of decaf for the room's miniature coffee brewer, so there wasn't any point in starting a pot because hot water from the tap would be much quicker and be just about as tasty. Windblown rain spattered against the window, creating a gloomy, Monetlike, monochromatic view of the Baltimore Inner Harbor cityscape off to the west.

Turning on the laptop, I accessed the hotel's high-speed Internet connection and whimpered with joy. I love living out in the country and wouldn't dream of moving back to a city, but our house is so isolated that the only Internet service available is telephone dial-up that moves at a speed best measured by geological epochs — that is, when the connection isn't dropped. Anyway, before long I was typing Jennifer Swift's name into the search box on my Internet provider's homepage.

The reason why I started my inquiries with the dead woman is that I look at murder as being very similar to investigating a two-vehicle traffic accident. A crash doesn't just happen; it's the result of different vehicles on separate routes that somehow violently collide, which is also how most murders occur. I didn't know who the killer was, but by studying Jennifer's journey toward death I might develop some insights into the path she'd been following and how that might have played a role in causing someone to hate her enough to kill her.

There's a surprising amount of personal information available on the Web and I soon had her home address and telephone number in Basingstoke Township. Running another search, I found that the Basingstoke Township *Blade-Tribune* newspaper had a Web site with a wonderful archive section and I located a feature article from 2004 about her burgeoning success as a teddy bear artisan. Then the well went dry. All I could find after that was her Cheery Cherub

Bears Web site and a long list of e-tailers and stores selling her stuffed animals.

Next, I entered Tony's name into the search engine and had greater luck. The newspaper Web site contained a story about how Tony had pled guilty to felony domestic violence against Jennifer, who'd suffered a broken wrist during the attack. The piece included the requisite idiotic statement from his defense attorney that the big guy was undergoing "anger management" therapy. Just for fun, I considered looking up the liar-for-hire's telephone number and calling him to break the news that the therapy hadn't worked and Tony was in jail for murdering his wife, but it was Saturday, so I knew the law office was closed and the lawyer wouldn't have cared anyway.

I clicked on another newspaper story and read about Tony receiving some twenty-five-dollar gift certificate from the big-box retailer where he worked for being salesperson-of-the-month. Having briefly worked retail myself before joining the army, I suddenly understood why Tony wanted so badly for the Cheery Cherub Bears business to take off.

I entered Todd Litten's name next and came back with next to nothing. The *Blade-Tribune* Web site had a couple of small articles about car crashes and medical emergencies where he was mentioned in passing as one of the paramedics. Another news story said that he'd been a presenter at a fire department safety fair, back in September. The only other information was from the sports page, which reported he'd bowled a three-hundred game in 2005. A check of the person-locator Web site revealed that he lived in the town of East Stroudsburg.

Then I began running Donna Jordan. She also lived in Basingstoke Township, was cross-referenced with a few teddy bear e-tailers, and her name also appeared connected with James Polk High School, in nearby Lititz. I clicked on the high school Web site and clicked again on the faculty icon. Scrolling down the page, I found her name and my pulse began to pound as fast as Buddy Rich doing a drum solo on meth. Donna Jordan taught chemistry, which meant that she would know the lethal effects of superglue on human lungs.

Donna clearly had a motive and the technical know-how to commit the crime and I felt bad for so cavalierly dismissing Ash's theory that the confrontation at breakfast was deliberately intended to provoke an asthma attack. Suddenly, it made perfect sense. The important thing now was to prove Donna had the opportunity to sabotage the inhaler and that meant going down to the lobby and trying to find out how many card keys had been issued for the Swifts' room, to whom they were given, and when those cards were handed out.

Shutting the computer off, I quickly — well, as quickly as I'm able with this bum leg — changed clothes. I put on my dress slacks, a twill shirt, knotted the retina-searing Pokemon tie around my neck, and slipped my sports coat on. Studying myself in the mirror, I hoped I could still generate some of my old homicide dick persona. I switched my wallet containing my gold SFPD "retired" inspector badge from my trousers to the left inside pocket of my jacket, where I'd customarily carried it during my career as a cop and felt a little more comfortable.

However, I had a far more challenging task in recapturing some of my arrogant swagger long enough to fool the hotel staff and that was my need to abandon my cane while I was at the front desk. I had to appear as if I were fully ambulatory, otherwise the clerks might suspect I was a fraud. Theoretically, I can walk short distances without my cane, just as, theoretically, Carrot Top is a comedian. I knew it would be impossible for me to make it from the room to the elevator and then to the registration desk without my cane, so I decided to use it until the last moment and then find someplace to hide it temporarily.

Another potential problem was if the same desk clerk who'd checked us in yesterday morning was working today. Then again, what were the odds that he'd recognize me? It was a huge hotel, hundreds of new guests had registered the previous day, and it was unlikely he'd remember me . . . especially when he'd been paying such close attention to Ash.

I rode the elevator back down to the first floor and decided that I'd attract far more attention to myself if I wandered around trying to find the perfect place to hide my cane, so I leaned against an end table beside some chairs that were just around the corner from the registration desk. Then, taking a deep breath and steeling myself for the effort, I began walking as normally as I could. The first few steps didn't hurt, but after that the pain started in my shin and began working its way upwards to my hip. By the time I reached the desk, I was gritting my teeth.

There were two female clerks behind the counter and I guess, what with my angry grimace and white complexion, I must have looked a little intimidating. When the older woman saw me, she gave her younger counterpart a he's-all-yours look, snatched up a phone, and pretended she was handling a call.

The younger woman sighed and said, "Yes, sir, can I help you?"

Reaching into my jacket, I pulled the badge case and flipped it open and shut quickly, hoping she didn't notice that I'd just shown her a seven-pointed gold star as opposed to the silver shield worn by the Baltimore detectives. "I'm Detective Callahan from Homicide. Lieutenant Mulvaney told me to come down here and get some information."

"Yes, sir. Are you all right, sir?"

"Sure. Why?"

"You look like you're in a lot of pain."

"Acid-reflux. I shouldn't eat doughnuts, but I do and I pay for it afterwards," I said as if confiding a slightly shameful secret.

The woman nodded and I noticed the tiniest hint of a sneer. One of the most popular American myths — a belief that almost amounts to occupational bigotry — is that cops eat nothing but doughnuts and

I'd proven my identity as a peace officer by mentioning my addiction to gut bombs. She said, "How can I help you, Detective?"

"I want some information about the Swifts' room." I panicked for a second, realizing I didn't know the room number. There was no other recourse but to brazen it through. "Lieutenant Mulvaney wants to know how many card keys were issued for room . . ."

I began to flip through the pages of my steno pad and the woman said, "Room seven-forty-six."

"Right. Seven-forty-six."

The woman bent over the keyboard and typed some information into the keyboard. Studying the monitor screen, she said, "A total of . . . three."

"Why three? There were only the two of them in the room."

"It says that two cards were issued when they checked in yesterday —"

"Which was about ten-thirty."

"Yes, sir, and then a third key was issued to Mrs. Swift last night at about seven-forty-five. The notation says that she lost her key and needed a replacement."

"Is the employee that issued her the replacement key here now?"

"No, sir. He's on the night shift, so he

won't be in until four p.m."

"His name?"

"Terrell Slessor."

"Fine, I'll be back at four to interview him. Your name, please?"

"Bethany Gibbons."

I wrote the name down in my notebook and then pointed to the TV camera on the wall behind the registration desk. "Would that incident have been captured on your security camera?"

"I suppose so. The camera is on all the time."

I thought: *Great, there'll be incontrovertible evidence of me impersonating a peace officer. I wonder if they serve Chesapeake Bay crab cakes in the Maryland State Penitentiary?* Instead, I said: "Contact your security manager and put that tape into safekeeping. We'll want it later."

"Yes, sir."

"And thanks for your cooperation, Bethany. I'll be getting back up to the room now."

Turning slowly so that I didn't trip, my leg throbbing so badly I wondered if I could even move it, I stomped back toward the corridor leading to the elevators. The moment I was around the corner, I grabbed my cane and collapsed into one of the chairs. But the pain was worth it because I'd just obtained another piece of important information.

I was certain Jennifer Swift couldn't have requested a duplicate card key at 7:45 p.m., because she was present at the reception until at least 8 p.m., when we left. Therefore, another woman had pretended to be Jennifer and bluffed the desk clerk into giving her a spare key. Add those circumstances to the fact that Donna Jordan *had* left the reception before 7:45 p.m., after telling us about how much she hated the Swifts, and I began to see the outline of a brilliant plan: murder the woman that betrayed you and frame your victim's repugnant spouse for the killing. Donna could have easily slipped back into the banquet room during the confusion while we were doing CPR, grabbed the inhaler, and planted it in the Swifts' room. Furthermore, her behavior after the murder was consistent with someone tortured by guilt.

Maybe I should have called Sergeant Delcambre then, but — sore leg notwithstanding — I was enjoying myself too much. So, I decided I'd talk to Donna myself.

Ten

After changing out of my homicide detective costume and tossing the ugly tie into the wastebasket, I went over to study the fire escape map on the inside of the room door. I couldn't run the risk of being recognized as I passed the registration desk on my way back to the exhibit hall, which meant finding another way. I was confident there had to be a stairwell on the opposite side of the hotel and if there wasn't, when I was finished investigating this murder I'd be calling the Baltimore Fire Marshal to report a major building code violation. Luckily, there was another stairway, and I hobbled down the length of the building and started downstairs, one step at a time.

The first floor stairwell opened onto the corridor near the exhibit hall and as I headed inside I saw some further evidence that Jennifer's death was no longer a secret. A woman television reporter and her camera operator had just come through the main doors and they were shaking rainwater from themselves and their equipment like a pair of soggy golden retrievers fresh from a pond. I suspected they were merely the vanguard of a local media invasion and I wondered how they'd learned of the murder so quickly. Call me suspicious, but I figured Mulvaney had made a discreet phone call to the newsroom — after all, you can't be the star if there are no cameras.

Going into the exhibit hall, I brought Ash up-to-date on what I'd learned.

"You really think it was Donna?" She didn't sound convinced.

"I'm just saying that the pieces and time line seem to match up. Furthermore, she fits the profile, because women, being smarter and more cunning, have always been far more prone to use poison than men."

"Always?"

"At least as far back as fifty-four A.D."

"Should I remember that date?"

"Not unless you're a student of the history of murder. That was the year Agrippina murdered her husband, the Roman emperor Claudius. She fed him poisoned mushrooms and if you ask me, it served him right for marrying his niece."

"Eww." Ash looked nauseated.

"Yep. Talk about a close family — you needed a crowbar to separate them."

"Can we please change the subject to something just a little less disgusting?"

"Such as premeditated murder. So, you were about to tell me why you don't think Donna's good for the murder."

"It's because of the way she behaved last night when we talked to her at the reception."

"Go on."

"If we follow your theory that she's the killer, Donna was only minutes away from tricking the hotel clerk into giving her a key to the Swifts' room so that she could fill the inhaler with superglue. So, why would she do anything to draw attention to herself?"

"By behaving like a drunken banshee. That's a good point. Of course, there's always the chance she was trying to generate some liquid courage to go through with her plan and over imbibed."

"Maybe, but even so, would she have acted that way in front of *us?* She had to know that you're a retired cop."

"I see what you mean." I grimaced as an ugly thought struck me. "Jesus, if you're right, I might have been able to prevent the murder."

"What are you talking about?"

We suddenly had to hit the "pause" button on the conversation because standing in front of our table was one of the rarest things you see at a teddy bear show: A wife with her middle-aged husband in tow who wasn't checking his watch every four seconds and sighing, rolling his eyes, or shaking his head in scornful amusement at all the people in ecstasy over stuffed animals. In fact, he looked like he was having a pretty good time. We chatted with them and he insisted on buying Suzy Cinnamon Streusel because his wife had fallen in love with the bear. They were holding hands as they walked away and their obvious love for each other restored a little of my faith in the human race.

Once the couple was out of earshot, Ash said, "Okay, what were you going to say about feeling a little responsible for the murder?"

"Here's a hell of a what if: What if that scene last night was a huge cry for help? Maybe you're right and she knew I was a former homicide detective and she hoped I'd say something to make her see that murdering Jennifer wasn't the answer. At least you tried to comfort her. All I did was stand there, caring guy that I am, and hope she was going to dish out some embarrassing and entertaining dirt about the Swifts."

Ash peered at my event name tag. "Sorry, the name says Bradley Lyon, not God. Honey, there's no way either of us could have known what she was intending . . . if she actually killed Jennifer."

"But before we eliminate her as a suspect, there's something else to consider: When I went to check out her booth, Donna was just coming back from somewhere. She was a total basket case and acted as if she was certain that Jennifer was dead."

"Why didn't you say anything?"

"That lunacy with Mulvaney made me forget."

"And she knew Jennifer was dead?"

"It could've been a lucky guess or maybe even wishful thinking, but she was in full Lady-Macbeth-after-the-murder mode."

"So, what are we going to do now?"

"I'm going to go talk to her."

"You mean, *we're* going to go talk to her. I don't want to miss any of this."

"I don't see how you can go."

"Why?"

"Aside from the fact that there's something a little disturbing about your fascination with murder, there's the tiny issue of someone having to stay here at the table."

"We'll only be gone for a few minutes."

"And what if somebody wants to buy a bear or, worse, decides to steal our stuff?" I gestured toward our array of stuffed animals. "One of us has to watch the store."

"Nobody's going to steal our bears."

"Sweetheart, I hate to remind you of this, but there's already been a murder here today, so I wouldn't be too quick to rule out grand theft as the next unique feature of this show."

"But if I put up a note saying that we'd be back in a few minutes and asked one of our neighbors to watch our table while we're gone . . ." She grabbed a sheet of paper and a red marking pen from the satchel.

"I'm not going to win this debate, am I?"

"No."

"Okay, we'll go together. And thank you for resisting the urge to point out that I've *never* won a debate with you."

Ash dimpled. "You're welcome."

She quickly finished the note, asked the nice lady at the adjoining booth to watch our table for a few minutes, and covered our bears with an old bed sheet. A minute later, we were standing in front of the spot where, just over an hour earlier, Donna's Ivanhoe teddy bear display had stood. Now it was as empty as a professional baseball player's solemn promise to a congressional committee that he'd never used anabolic steroids.

"She's gone," said Ash.

"Yep and this is what we used to call 'suspicious' in the homicide investigation trade."

"Oh, my God. Maybe she *did* kill Jennifer."

"Could be, but if you're on the run from a murder rap, you don't come back to disassemble your booth and carefully pack up your teddy bears. You just make tracks."

"That's true."

"Hey, are you guys looking for Donna?" Dolores called from the adjoining booth.

"Yeah, we needed to talk to her for a second," I said, trying to sound casual.

"You just missed her. She said she wasn't feeling well and was heading back home."

"How long ago was that?"

"Just a minute or two ago. Like I said, you just missed her."

"Thanks." I turned to Ash and quietly continued, "Head for the parking structure and I'll catch up with you as fast as I can."

"What do you want me to do if I find her?"

"Try to stall her. Tell her that we know what really happened and that we'll call the cops if she runs."

Ash took two quick strides toward the exit, then stopped and pivoted. "Now that you mention it, *shouldn't* we be calling Lieutenant Mulvaney?"

"Not yet. We don't have anything even close to probable cause to arrest Donna. If we called now, the only thing Mulvaney would do is send some cops over to arrest us for interfering with her investigation."

"If you say so. I'll see you in a couple of minutes."

"I'll hurry and please be careful." I reached out to squeeze her hand.

"That's my line. Don't worry, I'll be fine."

Ash headed for the door, but as she neared the end of the aisle, Lisa rounded the corner from the opposite direction and the two women almost walked headlong into each other. Talk about a showdown-at-the-O.K.-Corral moment. Ash paused for just a second to give the other woman a glare cold enough to cause frostbite and continued toward the exhibition hall exit. Lisa watched her go, wearing a realistic look of puzzled innocence. Then she turned and saw me hobbling along in apparent pursuit of my wife. I realized that it must have looked as if Ash and I had just had an argument and it made me angry when I saw the nascent glee in Lisa's eyes.

"Gee, is everything all right between you and your wife?" she asked solicitously as she moved directly into my path and stopped.

"We're fine. I don't have time to talk with you right now."

"Then later, I hope. I'm a very good listener."

"I don't need a good listener; I'm happily married to one already," I said, pushing past her.

She touched my wrist. "Of course you are. Bye."

Even if they had no intention of actually straying, most men would take pleasure in Lisa's amorous overtures since being considered sexually desirable by an attractive woman inflates the male ego to the size of a Macy's Thanksgiving Day Parade balloon. However, I wasn't enjoying it and not just because I utterly love my wife. The nasty delight I'd seen in Lisa's eyes told me that Ash had been right about one thing. Lisa wasn't interested in me because I was a candidate to become her second — or maybe third — husband. She couldn't care less about me personally. I was merely the pawn in her most current game of subverting other women's husbands merely to see if it could be done. That knowledge made me want to stop in a restroom and wash where she'd touched me, but there wasn't any time.

Out in the corridor, two TV news cameras were videotaping a cop in a baggy blue jumpsuit, kneeling on the floor and putting a fresh trace evidence filter container into a forensic vacuum cleaner. I limped around the group and was almost clear when I heard the subdued buzz of conversation. One of the cameras swiveled in my direction and I cursed under my breath. During my years as a homicide inspector, I'd met many television reporters and the overwhelming majority were decent enough people. But they serve in an industry that exploits tragedy for ratings points, which, in my opinion, makes prostitution seem a squeaky clean profession in comparison. Suddenly a microphone was thrust under my nose as the camera operator shifted to a position in front of me.

"Sir, would you mind speaking with us for a moment?" The reporter was a twenty-something kid wearing a black blazer with the station's logo embroidered on the left breast and dandruff on the shoulders.

"I have nothing to say." I kept walking and the camera operator began backpeddling to keep me on camera.

"But we understand that you gave the victim CPR. Did you know she's dead?"

"No comment." I kept walking and now had to contend with another camera in my way.

"How do you feel about that?"

"Excuse me, but unless you want your afternoon news teaser to be 'Reporters Trip Cripple — Stay Tuned for the Full Story *and* Details about the Personal Injury Lawsuit,' please get out of my way before I lose my balance and fall."

The journalists scurried to make room and I passed through the lobby, not caring whether or not the registration clerks recognized me.

As I pushed open the heavy metal door leading to the parking structure, I heard a car door slam and Donna shout, "Leave me the hell alone!"

Donna's vehicle was a boxy older model Plymouth Town and Country minivan with silver paint so oxidized that it looked as if the van had eczema. It was parked near the door with the engine running. A nearby empty luggage trolley told me that Donna had just finished loading her bears and was ready to leave.

Ash raised her voice to be heard over the

engine. "Donna, please listen. If you run —"

"Get away from my van!"

Then Ash did something that absolutely chilled my blood: She reached inside the minivan to get the keys. One of the most important things a young street cop learns — if he or she wants to become an old street cop — is to never, never, *never* lean into a vehicle with someone behind the steering wheel and grab the keys. That's because the driver can take off and if you get stuck, you'll experience the automotive equivalent of shooting rocky whitewater rapids without a raft as you're dragged along the pavement. I obtained this knowledge the hard way back in 1982 when I tried to prevent a drunk driver from leaving a traffic stop. Half a block later I hit the asphalt, my uniform trousers in shreds and both knees bloodied. However, I'd been lucky. Cops have fallen beneath the wheels of vehicles and died under identical circumstances and it was that knowledge that made the scene unfolding before me so terrifying.

I yelled, "Ash, get away from the van! Let her go!"

But it was too late. Donna popped the van into drive and, as I feared, when the vehicle started to roll quickly forward, Ash began to trot alongside the driver's window. Although I couldn't see inside the van, from the angle of her shoulders I was pretty sure Ash's arm was caught in the steering wheel.

Ash screamed in pain and alarm, "Donna, please stop!"

Realizing I only had a second or two to stop the van, I grabbed the luggage trolley and shoved it hard into the path of the minivan, hoping Donna would slow down or stop long enough for Ash to free herself. However, Donna apparently wasn't paying attention to the roadway in front of her because the van was still accelerating when it hit the metal cart, which fell over on its side. The trolley began to crumple and collapse beneath the van's undercarriage as Donna stomped on the brakes and Ash was sent sprawling onto the cement pavement. At the same time, the minivan swerved away from Ash and ran headlong into a large concrete support pillar. There was a loud metallic crash that echoed throughout the parking structure and the van's engine died with a sputter.

I hobbled as fast as I could to Ash, who'd rolled over and was sitting up. Kneeling down, I asked, "Are you all right?"

"I think I'm okay."

"Jesus, you about scared me to death." I

touched her cheek and noticed my fingers were trembling.

"And now you know how I felt for twenty-five years," Ash said softly and then took my hand and kissed it.

"You're really okay?"

"I may end up with a bruise on my bottom."

"I'll give it a kiss later tonight. In the meantime, please stay here while I go over to say howdy to Donna."

"Don't be mean to her. She's very upset."

"Mean? Me?" However, as I approached the wrecked vehicle, my rage was suddenly rekindled. I threw the door open and brandished my cane. "Get out of the van right now, you freaking maniac!"

I don't think the words registered because Donna was crying uncontrollably as she tried to disentangle herself from the airbag, which had deployed during the crash. Then she hunched over and grabbed the steering wheel as if it were the last lifesaver on the *Titanic* and the ship's band had just finished playing "Nearer My God, To Thee." At last she opened her eyes and sobbed, "Please don't hurt me."

Realizing that Donna was petrified, I lowered the cane and said in a somewhat calmer tone, "I won't. But for God's sake, lady, you nearly killed my wife."

"I was scared. I was just trying to go home and her arm got caught. I didn't mean to hurt her."

"Uh-huh. Just like you didn't mean to hurt Jennifer Swift?"

"I didn't kill Jen," she said between ragged breaths.

"But you were in her room last night."

"No, I wasn't."

"You lie as badly as you drive. I know you tricked the desk clerk into giving you a duplicate card key."

"All right, I was in her room, but I didn't kill her."

"Who did?"

"Tony, I think."

Either my homicide interrogation skills were deteriorating or she was a world-class liar, but it sounded as if she were telling the truth.

A man and woman came through the doors into the parking lot and paused to look at the crash. I heard Ash tell them that there'd been a minor accident, but that no one was hurt. The couple didn't seem particularly concerned and went to their car. However, with the hotel packed with more cops than a police convention, I knew it was only a matter of time until someone told them about the traffic accident.

I said, "Look, we need to talk, but not here. I want you to come to our room and tell me the entire story."

"Why should I?" She was becoming a little more pugnacious as she recovered her composure.

"Because even if you didn't kill Jennifer, you're custom-made to take the fall for it. You've got motive, means, and opportunity and the only thing standing between you and a charge of first-degree murder is my good will. Now, let's go."

ELEVEN

When no cops or security guards arrived to check on the wreck, I decided we should tidy up the scene before leaving. If we left the damaged van in its present position, half blocking the roadway, someone would soon let the Maritime Inn management know . . . if it hadn't happened already. The staff would tell the detectives working at the hotel and, after that, it would only be a matter of time before news of the crash and the vehicle registration information was passed along to Lieutenant Mulvaney, who'd undoubtedly recognize Donna's name from the witness statements. However much Mulvaney was convinced Tony was the killer, she'd want to know why the woman who'd announced her hatred of Jennifer to a roomful of people, five minutes before the murder, had tried to flee the teddy bear show.

Ash started the minivan, and although the

engine was making a loud thumping noise like the kind a clothes washer makes when all the wet bath towels end up on one side of the tub, she managed to coax the damaged vehicle into a parking spot. Meanwhile, I dragged the broken pieces of the luggage trolley out of the traffic lane and tucked the wreckage between the cement wall and the front of the van. When we finished, I found myself pondering a legal question: had Ash and I just committed two fresh counts of interfering with Mulvaney's investigation or, if it turned out that Donna actually was the killer, was our offense the more serious felony crime of harboring and aiding a fugitive? But I decided the problem wasn't worth any further brainpower because we already had so many potential charges pending against us that the punishment for any new ones would hinge on us living past a hundred.

With Ash and I flanking Donna, we went back into the hotel and stopped near the elevators.

I said, "I'll take Donna up to our room and I think it would be a good idea if you went back to the exhibit hall."

"Why?"

"Because the longer both of us are gone, the more likely it is that someone's going to notice and word will get back to the Baltimore cops. Mulvaney may be gone, but she hasn't forgotten about us."

"I suppose you're right."

"It's been known to happen occasionally."

Ash's eyes got hard. "And if I get some spare time maybe I can look up your new friend, Lisa. What is wrong with that woman? She just stood there smirking at me as if she'd already seduced you."

"I know and I'm sorry."

"What did the little trash-truck say once I left?"

"Uh . . . just that she was a good listener."

"Really? I wonder how well she'd listen with a pair of fourteen-inch teddy bears rammed into both her ears?"

Donna hadn't spoken since apologizing to Ash out in the parking lot, but she emerged from her silent funk to shyly ask, "I don't mean to pry, but are you talking about Lisa Quesenberry?"

"No, Lisa Parr. She's a judge for the teddy bear competition," I said.

"And one of the things she apparently wants to judge is my husband's performance — and not as a teddy bear artist." Ash glowered.

"Same Lisa, new last name. I suppose she's gotten remarried since the last time I attended a show." Donna glanced at Ash. "If you want, you can go back to my van and get a couple of the knight bears. They have miniature wooden swords, so they'd be a little more painful when you shove them into her ears."

"That's very thoughtful, thank you," said Ash.

I pressed the elevator button and then leaned over to kiss Ash on the cheek. "I'll be back in a little while, so please hold off on any mohair mayhem until I can be there to watch."

"I'll be good, so long as she keeps her distance."

Two uniformed cops in wet yellow rain jackets appeared from the around the corner and the conversation died faster than the notion that having Roseanne Barr sing the national anthem at a baseball game had been a good idea. One of the officers was carrying a cardboard box packed with four mermaid-decorated cups of overpriced coffee while the other was lugging a large metal case that likely contained some sort of forensic equipment that was needed in the Swifts' room. At last, the elevator doors opened and Donna and I stepped inside while Ash headed toward the exhibit hall.

The cops followed us into the elevator and

I asked, "Floor?"

"Seven. Thanks."

I pressed the buttons for the fifth and seventh floor. The doors slid shut, and we rode in silence, all four of us watching our reflections in the polished metal door. I was nervous. Being a novice criminal is stressful. I couldn't tell for sure how Donna was handling the tension, but I looked down and noticed that she was gripping her brown leather purse so tightly that her fingers were white, so it was a good guess she was frightened, too. The short ride up seemed to take forever but the doors finally opened and Donna and I got out on the fifth floor.

A minute later, we were in our room and I hung the DO NOT DISTURB sign on the outside door handle. The maid had cleaned the room and made the bed while I was gone. Better yet, there were two fresh foil packages of real coffee next to the brewer. I made a mental note to leave the maid a nice tip when we checked out.

Donna said, "Can I use the bathroom before we start?"

"Of course."

A minute or so later, she emerged from the bathroom and put her purse on the dresser. Walking over to the window, she turned her back on me to look out at the stormy panorama.

"Coffee?" I asked.

"No, thanks."

"You mind if I have some?"

Donna's voice was surly again. "It's your room. Can I ask a couple of questions?"

"Sure."

"Is it true that you're a retired police officer?"

"That's right. I worked as a homicide detective in San Francisco."

"But you're hiding me from the police. Why?"

"Because I'm conducting my own private investigation of Jennifer's murder."

"Is that legal?"

"Nope."

"Then why are you doing it?"

"Ego, mostly, and a desire to get even with the Baltimore homicide detective working the case. I react badly when my wife and I are falsely accused of murder."

"I heard that Tony was arrested for her murder."

"Yup."

"But you don't think he did it?"

"I strongly doubt it — not because he isn't a brutal scumbag. It's just that he doesn't impress me as being bright enough to have pulled off such a sophisticated murder."

She turned around to face me and folded her arms across her chest. "And so you think I might have killed Jen?"

"I think it's possible, but I'm not as convinced as I was an hour ago."

"How reassuring. So, what do you want from me?"

"Just some truthful answers."

Donna jutted her chin out. "Why should I talk to you? Couldn't I just call that detective and tell her my story?"

"Sure." I jerked my head in the direction of the phone on the nightstand. "But a word to the wise if you decide to talk to Lieutenant Mulvaney — pack a toothbrush."

"Why?"

"Because it won't make any difference what you tell her. Once they match your fingerprints to the latents they're almost certain to have recovered from the Swifts' room, you'll be a permanent guest at the Razor-Wire Courtyard by Marriott."

"So I'm stuck with you as my protector? Wow, I feel so much better."

I was beginning to find the acidic sarcasm annoying. "If you don't like the situation, there's the door. And just so that we thoroughly understand each other, I'm not your protector. I'm just trying to find out who killed Jennifer and if I decide you did it, I won't think twice about giving you the patented Judas Iscariot kiss and handing you over to the cops."

"You're a rat bastard. You know that?"

"Here's a news flash: It isn't a beautiful day in the neighborhood and I'm not Mr. Rogers. Nice guys not only always finish last, they never solve murders." I tore the foil package open and inserted the paper cartridge containing the coffee into the brewer. "So, if you're done venting on me because the world is so cruel, sit down."

I took the carafe into the bathroom and filled it with water. When I returned, Donna was seated on one of the wooden chairs next to the worktable. Her fingers were interlaced in her lap and her left foot was tapping out a quiet nervous tattoo on the floor. I poured the water into the coffeemaker and the brewer had already begun to hiss by the time I'd taken a seat in the other chair. Grabbing several pages of Maritime Inn stationery from the drawer, I wrote the date and time at the top of a sheet.

"Are you going to walk or talk?" I asked.

"I'll answer your questions and I'm sorry for snapping at you. It's just . . ."

It's just that your mood changes are as volatile as gasoline prices right before a holiday weekend, was what I wanted to say.

Instead, I said, "Forget it. People get upset and say things they don't necessarily mean when they're angry and frightened."

"And I am frightened. Thank you for your understanding."

"You're welcome. So, how long had you known Jennifer?"

"Since middle school." There was a long pause. "God, it's so weird to refer to her in the past tense."

"How old were you when you met her?"

"I was going into eighth grade. Her family moved to our town from somewhere near Wilkes-Barre."

"You became friends?"

"Not right away, but a few months later."

"Tell me about her. Can you remember why you considered her your best friend?"

Donna's eyes seemed to glaze over. For just a second there was a slight bittersweet smile, and I knew she was remembering the good times with Jennifer. At last, she said, "Everybody thought she was this dull wallflower, but she could be so wickedly funny and she was very smart. She should have gone to college . . ."

"But?"

"But she ended up marrying Tony. I could never figure that out."

"Why?"

"You've seen Tony. He wasn't fat back then, but other than that he was completely the same. A loud-mouthed, know-it-all loser."

"And violent?"

Donna gave a snort of disgust. "They hadn't been married much more than a month when she came running over to my house after he'd kicked her in the thigh. God, you should have seen that bruise."

"Yet from everything I've been able to piece together, Jennifer loved him. Any ideas why?"

"None that made any sense to me. Once, she told me that it was always very nice after one of Tony's 'episodes' — that's what she called the beatings, by the way — because he was very attentive and sweet."

"And he bought her gifts and took her on special vacations."

"How did you know that?"

"It's a normal cycle of domestic abuse."

"That's sick."

"And far more common than you can guess." The coffee brewer began to sputter and gurgle. I went over and poured myself a cup. "You sure you don't want any?"

"No, thank you."

Returning to the table, I said, "I realize you two had been on the outs for some time, but is it possible she could have been having a relationship with another man?"

"An affair? I don't think so."

"Why not? There's some evidence that another man is in love with her."

"Then he's just another victim of one of her con games. We didn't talk about it a lot, but Jen wasn't a big fan of sex. It was too sweaty and personal for her. In fact, one of the things she appreciated about Tony was his patriotism."

"Huh?"

"He was a Minute Man." Donna's face twisted into a wry grin.

I gave a humorless chuckle. "You mentioned her having a 'wicked' sense of humor. I guess that's an example?"

"She could be cruel."

Ordinarily, I'd have spent a great deal more time eliciting background information about Jennifer, but I decided to move forward more quickly and aggressively with my questioning. There were a couple of reasons for this. I realized the clock was ticking and that it wouldn't be long before the cops began looking for Donna. Also, I knew it was only a matter of time before her mood switched back to Joan Crawford–mode and there was no assurance that she'd continue the interview after that happened.

I gently asked, "Cruel enough to make someone want to kill her?"

"Yes."

"You, for instance?"

She blinked at me in confusion as if she hadn't quite heard me correctly. "No. I told you that once already."

"Call me a nasty old cynic, but people have been known to lie when they're looking at life in prison."

"I'm not lying. I didn't kill her."

"But you hated her."

"That's not the same thing as wanting her dead."

"Say for the sake of argument that's true. If you didn't want her dead, what did you want?"

Donna seemed to be holding her breath. At last she said quietly, "An acknowledgement from her that she'd betrayed me."

"But you knew that wasn't going to happen, didn't you?"

"Yes." She looked down at the tabletop.

"Do you know how Donna was killed?"

"The only thing I heard was that she couldn't breathe."

"She was poisoned. Somebody removed the medication from her asthma inhaler and replaced it with superglue."

"Oh my God." Donna looked up and her

eyes shone with a sick horror. “A big enough dose of cyanoacrylate fumes would shut her lungs down almost immediately.”

“Uh-huh. Not many people are aware of that, much less the chemical name for superglue. But it’s exactly the sort of information I’d expect a high school chemistry teacher to know.” I put the pen down and sat back in my chair.

“How did you find out that I teach chemistry?”

I nodded in the direction of my laptop on the table. “I Googled you. Your name came up on the high school Web site.”

“And so you immediately decided that I killed her?”

“Put yourself in my place. What would you think?”

She locked eyes with me. “I didn’t sabotage the inhaler or kill Jennifer.”

The interrogation of a homicide suspect involves as much tactical listening as it does asking questions. A skilled interviewer pays close attention to phrasing, use of tenses, metaphors, body language, and five or six other indicators to determine if the suspect is providing an honest answer or false information. Crooks almost always try to qualify their answers because, deep down inside, they recognize they aren’t smart enough to remember their lies and they want some wiggle room when they're eventually forced to explain disparities in their stories. Think of a former president quibbling over the precise meaning of the word "is" and you have an idea of the sort of word games that criminals can play. Yet, Donna had answered directly and hadn't sworn to it on her mother's grave, which is a guaranteed signal that a suspect is being frugal with the truth. I was forced to conclude that she'd answered honestly.

"I believe you, but you've still got a major problem."

"Being in her room last night."

"*Breaking* into her room," I corrected, "after falsely identifying yourself as Jennifer to the hotel clerk and then later making statements to a hundred or so witnesses that could be construed as threats. You're Tony's get-out-of-jail-free card."

"Do you think he actually killed her?"

"Unlikely." I took a sip of coffee. "Like I said earlier, he's a thug. Blunt force trauma is his style. He's not smart enough to use poison."

"And I am," Donna said bleakly.

"Yep."

"Well, what about Todd Litten? Couldn't he be a suspect?"

"I'll admit he probably has the brains to have done it, but what was his motive?"

"I don't know." She sounded frustrated.

"Neither do I and your problem is that the police have already crowned him as their star witness."

Donna's gaze dropped to the tabletop. "Now what do I do?"

"Tell me why you went into her room."

Twelve

Donna put her elbow on the wooden arm of the chair and rested her chin in her palm. She studied me in silence for a few moments and then finally said, "Tell me something. Did *you* really design and make that bear? The one that was nominated for the award?"

"Of course," I answered a little stiffly.

"Your wife didn't help?"

"Not unless you count the couple of hundred hours she spent teaching me how to avoid sewing my fingers together as helping."

"I wouldn't blame you if she helped. She's good."

"It's my work."

"The clothes, too?"

"I got the shoes from a doll supply shop. Other than that, it's all my own work, including the gun and sunglasses."

"That's hard to believe."

"So is the idea that sane people actually paid seven-fifty to see *Gigli.* We live in a strange universe."

For the moment, we'd switched roles and she was the interrogator. Back when I was a young and inexperienced detective, I'd have bristled at this change in circumstances and sought to immediately reassert myself as being in control. But now that I was older and a little wiser, I understood that we were at that pivotal point in an interview when fundamental trust was being established. Donna's decision as to whether she was going tell me the rest of her story hinged on how I answered her questions.

"How long have you been making teddy bears?" she asked.

"Just since last October."

"Why did you begin making them?"

"Two reasons, I guess. The most important one is that I get to spend time with Ashleigh. My job kept us apart way too much."

"And the other reason?"

"I like them and having them around makes me a better man. Twenty-five years of cop work in a city like San Francisco tends to give you a pessimistic view of the human race. Yet, artisan teddy bears are proof that people aren't all bad." I paused to take a sip of coffee, slightly taken aback by a sudden realization. "Which, I suppose, is the real motive for why I'm investigating Jennifer's murder."

"I don't understand."

"A murder at a teddy bear show is as bad as a murder in a church. Worse, as far as I'm concerned. Most of the wars in history were caused by religions, but no one's ever started a crusade, massacred a town of heretics, or declared a jihad over a teddy bear."

Donna slowly sagged back into the chair. "Are you a parent?"

"We have two children. My daughter is a police officer. My son is a vintner."

"I had a son . . . Benjamin. He was the sweetest little boy. We used to play a kissing game every night before he went to bed."

"What happened to him?"

"Eleven days after his third birthday he was diagnosed with severe muscular dystrophy."

"I can't even begin to imagine how terrible that must have been."

"No, you can't, but thank you for not saying you're 'sorry.' It's a word people use when you've made them uncomfortable and they want you to change the subject."

"Were you still married when this happened?"

"Could I have something to drink?"

"There's some coffee left. Or would you like some water?"

"You don't have anything else? I'm not picky." Donna tried to sound blasé, but there was an undercurrent of shame in her voice.

I realized that she wanted something alcoholic and, as a matter of fact, there was an unopened 750-milliliter bottle of Frangelico in my suitcase. Ash and I don't drink much, but we occasionally enjoy small glasses of the sweet hazelnut liqueur as a nightcap. I'd brought the bottle along because the only thing more obscenely overpriced than a hotel bar drink is a CEO's golden parachute retirement package. Back when I was a homicide inspector, I wouldn't have even considered giving her an alcoholic beverage, since any statement given afterwards would probably be suppressed in an evidentiary hearing. Judges tend to frown on the practice of liquoring up witnesses, much less potential murder suspects, before an interview. However, this wasn't an official police investigation and it was clear that I was going to have to prime the pump before Donna continued her tale.

"I may have something here." I limped

over to the closet, opened the suitcase, and held up the monk-shaped brown bottle. "Will this do?"

"Yes, thank you."

"You want it in some coffee or straight?"

"Straight, please. You must think I'm pretty pathetic."

"People do the best they can do." I grabbed a clean water glass from the bathroom and returned to the table. Unscrewing the bottle top, I poured about three finger's worth of the fragrant amber liquor and slid the glass across the table to her.

Liqueurs such as Frangelico are made to be sipped, but Donna knocked back half the Benedictine joy-juice in two swallows. Giving me a weak grin, she said, "Better. You know what they say?"

"No."

"I'd rather have a bottle in front of me than a frontal lobotomy, but . . ."

"You'd opt for the lobotomy, if it made you forget."

She nodded and her eyes grew moist. Ordinarily, I have a very low tolerance for boozy self-pity, but it was pretty clear that her son had died, so she had a better reason for wallowing in it than most folks. I sat down and kept silent, waiting for her to resume speaking.

Donna wiped at her eyes with the back of her hand and then drank the rest of the liquor. "Here's an *Oliver Twist* moment: May I have some more, sir?"

I poured two fingers worth this time and said nothing.

She stared down into the glass. "My husband's name was Gus — Augustus. He wanted us to wait to have children."

"Which can mean increased health risks to both mother and infant."

"I don't like you and you shorted me on my drink, but you're very smart."

"Thank you."

"Finally, he gave in and I got pregnant. I was thirty-nine. There were serious complications with the delivery and it turned out that this was going to be the one and only time I could give birth." She took a small sip of the liquor. "You know, this tastes like candy."

"Glad you like it. How'd Gus deal with the arrival of a new baby?"

"At first, he was a really good dad, but a few years later, when we found out just how sick Benjamin was . . ."

"Why do I have the feeling that you're about to tell me that Gus pulled a D. B. Cooper?" I asked, referring to the legendary skyjacker robber.

"Huh?"

"Did he bail out and disappear?"

"He told me he couldn't deal with the situation. That he had a life to live. That . . ."

"He was a selfish, dishonorable bastard?"

"No, but I appreciate you saying that." Fresh tears welled up in her eyes. "Gus blamed me for Ben's illness. He said that if I hadn't insisted on having a child at my age, this never would have happened."

"And so he skied." I shook my head in disgust.

"He left. The last I heard, he was living someplace in Nevada. If it hadn't been for Jen, I don't know what I would have done."

"I assume you were teaching then. How did you manage to keep your job?"

"I needed to stay home with Ben, so I took a sabbatical."

"Which meant no income and — oh God — no health insurance."

"No, I was able to keep the health insurance through the school district. My parents are fairly well-off and they kept up the monthly premiums, but they couldn't completely support me." Donna swallowed a little more of the Frangelico. "I needed money and something I could do from the home, so that's what made me start making teddy bears. I'd always wanted to make them and it turned out I was talented."

I stood up and carried my empty coffee cup over to the brewer. Pouring what remained in the carafe into my cup, I asked, "What did you do? Sell them at regional bear shows?"

"There, and at craft shows, and to a bear shop in Lititz, and even on eBay. I began to develop a collector customer-base and it looked as if I was on my way to a new career."

"How did Jen help?"

"At the time, she lived just down the block. She came over every morning to visit after Tony went to work. She'd play with Ben and talk to me while I worked on the bears. Eventually, I ended up teaching her how to make the bears."

"Was she any good?"

"Not at first, but she improved. Sometimes Jen would stay all day and then Tony would beat her because his supper wasn't ready." Donna smiled ruefully.

"Yeah, as if he should have been concerned over missing a meal." I sat back down at the table. "What happened to change your relationship with her?"

"Ben had the best medical treatment, but he kept getting sicker and more weak. By the time he was four, he mostly stayed in bed. But he never complained. He was such a sweet boy." She held out the empty glass for a refill. When I'd poured some more Frangelico, she continued, "He loved teddy bears and so I began making some especially for him — some that I never intended to sell, because it would have been like selling part of Ben."

"The Cheery Cherub Bears?"

"My cheery cherub's bears. I hung them up with fishing line from his ceiling, so it looked like they were flying around his room. Then I made fabric clouds and began attaching them to the walls with the bears sitting on them."

"Sounds beautiful."

"Ben loved them. In the end there were probably fifty bears and, and . . ." Donna's lower lip began to tremble and tears were running down her cheeks. "And I told him that that was what heaven looked like, so he shouldn't be afraid of going there."

Suddenly, she was wracked with sobs and slowly bent forward to bury her head in her shaking hands. I wanted to touch her arm, but somehow knew that she wouldn't tolerate even the slightest sign of intimacy from me, and with good reason. I wasn't her friend. I was the cold-hearted son of a bitch making her relive the most terrible and anguished episodes of her life. It was one of those moments as a cop when you know that you're doing the right thing by digging for the truth, but you still hate yourself. So, all I could do was sit there and watch silently as she wailed and wept. When the crying finally guttered to a halt I held out a Kleenex box. Donna grabbed a wad of tissue and mopped at her eyes and nose.

"When did Benjamin die?" I asked.

"Two and a half years ago," she whispered.

"You were devastated."

"Yes. There were times when I thought about just stepping out in front of a train or something . . ."

"And killing yourself?"

"But I didn't. I toughed it out." Her nostrils flared and I heard a subtle yet unmistakable tinge of pride in her voice. "After the funeral, I went back to my teaching job and tried to get on with my life. But I couldn't continue making the teddy bears, because they reminded me too much of Ben."

"How soon was it after Ben died that you learned Jennifer had stolen your idea and designs and was making the Cheery Cherub Bears?"

Donna blew her nose and frowned. "Four weeks to the day after the funeral."

"What happened?"

"We need to back up a little bit for you to understand why I hated her so much. The day after the funeral, Jen came over to help me pack up everything in Ben's bedroom. I had to clean it out completely, otherwise it would have ripped my heart out every time I went in there."

"I'd have done the same thing."

"We took all the cherub bears down and put them into three big cardboard boxes. I asked Jen to take them over to Lancaster General Hospital and donate them, thinking that maybe some other sick child would like a teddy bear. Jen said she'd take care of it."

"And then?"

"After that I saw less and less of Jen. I figured she was just tired of listening to me cry. Hell, *I* was tired of listening to me cry."

"But?"

"But a few weeks later I understood the real reason why. I was over near York taking care of some errands."

"What is that, about thirty miles from Basingstoke Township?"

"Maybe a little farther."

Donna took a swallow of the liqueur. "It was a Saturday and the last thing I wanted was to go back to that empty house. There was a craft fair and I decided to go in."

Spontaneously, I knew where the story was heading and, although as a cop you smugly imagine that you've seen the very worst the human race is capable of, people can still surprise you with their capacity for sheer vileness. I said, "Oh, no. Please don't tell me she was there, selling the bears you'd asked her to donate to the hospital."

"She and Tony had a booth and, yes, she was selling Ben's angel bears along with some others that she'd made, as if it were all her own work. I guess they figured that York was far enough away that I wouldn't find out what they were doing."

"Christ Almighty, talk about stealing the pennies from a dead man's eyes. What did you do?"

"At first I just stood there in shock, because I couldn't believe what I was seeing. She was supposed to have been my best friend."

"Did they see you?"

"Yes, eventually."

"How did they react?"

"Tony looked away. I could tell he was embarrassed."

"And with good freaking reason. What about Jennifer?"

"She just jutted her jaw out and stared

right at me as if daring me to say anything. That look was just like being slugged in the stomach. She'd traded our friendship for a little money and you could tell that it didn't bother her at all."

"And then what happened?"

"Nothing. It was the final betrayal. First Gus, then God killing my little boy, and then Jen. I couldn't deal with it, so I just skulked out of there with my tail between my legs."

"And your grave-robbing 'friend' went on to turn the bears you'd made to comfort your dying son into a cheesy but lucrative enterprise. How long was it before you made another bear?"

"Almost two years."

"What made you start up again?"

"It was either that or drink myself to death and I missed my friends from the teddy bear community."

"Yeah, for the most part they're good people. When you signed up for this show, did you know that Jennifer would be attending?"

"Of course. You saw the pre-event brochure with their smug pictures plastered on the front."

"Were you planning some sort of showdown?"

"No, I was going to ignore them."

"But something happened to change your mind."

"It was their booth."

"Huh?"

"That vulgar booth with the flashing lights and music. My son died surrounded by angel bears and that filthy pair of monsters had them on display like they were cheap prizes at a third-rate carnival. First it made me sick. Then it made me mad."

"So, you weren't upset over them signing the big contract with Wintle and the cartoon series?"

"This wasn't about money," Donna snapped.

"I understand."

"It wasn't enough that Jen stole those bears, she'd turned them into something tawdry and vile and in doing so deliberately dishonored the memory of my son. She might as well have set that goddamned booth up on Benjamin's grave."

My brain couldn't quite follow the logic, but my heart did and I nodded in full agreement. "So, what did you do?"

"Last night at the reception, I started drinking and the drunker I got, the more I wanted to remind Jennifer of just what an evil thing she'd done."

"Where did you go after you finished talking to Ash and me?"

"Out to the lobby. You were right. I pretended to be Jennifer to get a key card to their room. The clerk didn't think twice about issuing a new one."

"And what did you do then?"

"I went up there and — I'll admit it — for a few seconds I considered either destroying or stealing the angel bears they had stored in their room." Donna glanced away for a second, clearly embarrassed at the admission. "But, I didn't do it."

"Actually, I'm not as worried about the fact that you considered committing vandalism and theft so much as whether or not you put superglue into Jennifer's inhaler."

"How many times do I have to tell you? I didn't kill her."

"Any idea of who did?"

"Probably someone else she stabbed in the back and if I knew the name I certainly wouldn't tell you or the police. And let me ask *you* a question." She pointed a finger at me. "Would it be so wrong for Tony to go to jail for Jen's murder? Both of them were very bad people."

"They may have been, but that doesn't mean it's okay to commit a brutal murder and imprison a man for life for a crime he didn't commit. That's dangerous thinking because what happens if somebody decides that *you're* evil and deserve to die?"

"I suppose." She didn't sound convinced, however.

"So, what did you do in their room?"

"I took one of the angel bears from a box and propped it up on the bed next to the pillows. Then I got a picture of my son that I used to carry in my wallet . . ." Donna took a deep ragged breath. "And I put it so that the bear was holding the picture. Then I left."

"That's it?"

"That's all I did. I wanted to remind her of what a ghoul she was."

"Yet you didn't get the response you were hoping for from Jennifer."

"I — how did you know?"

"Your B-52 strike that I regret interrupting at breakfast. Something obviously happened to make you even angrier than the night before."

"Late last night, Jen called my room and told me that she wasn't going to tolerate any further harassment and that if I so much as blinked at her wrong, she was going to have me arrested for stalking and trespassing."

"Not exactly the penitent response you

were hoping for."

"No, and then she told me I was crazy. She said that the cherub bears were her idea and that I was just jealous of her success. How could she have lied like that?"

I chuckled humorlessly. "Sorry, I don't mean to laugh. But this woman was so sleazy that she stole your dead son's teddy bears, which were supposed to be donated to a hospital, and you're actually surprised that she lied to you?"

"When you put it that way, I guess it does sound ridiculous."

"But at the time you were angry."

"Furious."

"Enough to go back to their room this morning while they were at breakfast?"

"No. Besides, I couldn't. Right after I got off the phone with Jen, I began worrying that she was going to call the police or hotel security."

"So you got rid of the card. Where?"

"I threw on some clothes and went down the hall to the elevator. There was a trash can there." Donna emptied the glass again. "Can I have some more?"

"Just a little. I want to save some for my wife." Once I finished pouring, I sat back and rubbed my eyes, suddenly weary. "What do you suppose happened to the picture of

Benjamin?"

"I'm assuming she threw it away."

There was a pair of gentle taps on the door. Donna gave me a nervous look.

"It's okay. It's probably Ash."

I limped over to the door and received an ugly surprise. No sooner did I press down on the handle far enough to disengage the latch, than the door slammed into me with enormous force. I fell backwards, bounced off the dresser, and crashed to the floor, landing hard on my hip. Meanwhile, a platoon of heavily-armed cops came piling through the doorway in a never-ending stream, like clowns from a car, all of them shouting, "Police! Get your hands up!" Behind me, Donna screamed.

Although I often find fault with the mystery novels that Ash loves, the supposedly more realistic thrillers can be just as fake. For example, the male protagonists in thrillers are usually endowed with an uncanny ability to immediately identify the manufacturer, country of origin, model, and caliber of the firearm being pointed at them. Even more amazingly, they sometimes can even venture a guess as to the sort of ammunition inside the gun, which should qualify as some sort of extra-sensory perception. Real life is a little different, however. Having had guns aimed at me several times during my career as a cop, I can assure you that your thoughts aren't: *Gosh, that's an American-made, Smith & Wesson brand, Model 4040PD, .40 caliber, semiautomatic pistol with a black matte finish — and probably loaded with hollow-point bullets — being pointed directly at my melon.* Rather, your brain simply registers it's a gun as you try not to wet your pants.

So, although I didn't recognize the guns, I did know one of the persons holding them as they charged into the room. It was Lieutenant Sarah Mulvaney and, insofar as her frozen facial muscles allowed, she was smiling. With her gun pointed directly between my eyes, she said, "Hey, wiseass, move and you're dead."

It was a bad bit of dialogue from a Grade B cop movie, but I decided not to say anything. Nor did I move.

Since my prone body completely blocked the pathway into the room, two of the uniformed cops ran across the top of the bed to get to Donna, who was whimpering with fear. They quickly handcuffed her and then dragged her back over the bed. Just before they got to the door, it occurred to Donna that I was the most recent in a long line of people to betray her, so she let loose with such a volley of inventively obscene insults that all the cops paused momentarily to listen in admiration. And I'll allow it was a magnum opus performance as she abused my parentage, sexual practices, gender orientation, eating habits, weight, physical equipment or lack thereof, and how I loved my mother. Her voice continued to echo from down the hallway until she was ushered into an elevator. Meanwhile, Mulvaney continued to keep her pistol — by now I'd been looking at it long enough to tell it was a semiauto — pointed at me.

"Am I allowed to ask what this is all about?"

"Yeah, it's *about* twenty-five years, if they don't give you the lethal injection." Mulvaney slowly raised the pistol and nodded at a trio of waiting cops. "Get him up and in handcuffs."

They yanked me to my feet and a second later I was wearing a set of stainless-steel bracelets — and not the kind that's the hot look in jewelry in Italy this year. I looked around for Sergeant Delcambre, but couldn't see him, so I assumed he was still at the police station.

Leaning against the dresser, I said, "I didn't kill anybody."

"We've got information that says otherwise."

"Information from who?"

"An anonymous informant who called the front desk at the police station to tell us we could find evidence linking you to Jennifer Swift's murder in this room."

"Why am I not surprised that you're one of those dishonest cops who likes to run the 'anonymous informant' hoax?"

"We actually received a call," Mulvaney said hotly.

"Right, as if I don't know how this game is played. I refused to give you permission to search my room and, what do you know? Some 'anonymous person' — that you'll never have to put on the witness stand, because he doesn't exist — was kind enough to telephone you and provide you with precisely the information you wanted. It's a freaking miracle."

"Believe what you want." She turned to a uniformed officer. "Search him."

One of the cops patted me down for weapons and pulled my wallet out. He flipped it open to show my SFPD badge to Mulvaney. She took it and stuffed it into her jacket pocket.

"There'd better be sixty-eight bucks in that wallet when you hand it back to me."

"For a killer, you're a funny guy." Turning to the doorway, she yelled, "The evidence techs can come in now."

"I'd like to see your search warrant," I said, wishing this didn't feel so much like the final scene of *The Treasure of Sierra Madre.*

"I don't need a warrant. This is a search incident to a lawful arrest."

"I'm under arrest?"

"That's right. For the murder of Jennifer Swift."

"You're making a huge mistake."

"Why don't you just shut up until we get back to headquarters?"

I watched as two investigators in dark blue jumpsuits came into the room. One had a digital camera while the other carried a metal suitcase that undoubtedly contained evidence collection equipment. Both immediately went into the bathroom. There were several bursts of white light as the camera strobe flashed. Then one of the techs emerged from the bathroom dangling a clear plastic bag with some items inside, but she was too far away for me to make out what they were.

"It's here in the trash can, all right," she said.

"What's here?" I demanded.

Mulvaney snatched the bag from the tech and shoved it under my nose. "This. The proof you killed Jennifer Swift: a pair of latex gloves and two empty superglue tubes. You're dead meat, Lyon."

THIRTEEN

I'll tell you, I felt pretty stupid. We're talking world class-stupid: racing to beat a fast train at a railroad crossing-stupid; joking about having a bomb in your carry-on luggage to Transportation Safety Administration guards at an airport-stupid; the kind of breathtakingly transcendental stupidity that caused the NFL to contract with an outfit like MTV to produce the Super Bowl halftime show and then be shocked when there was a "wardrobe malfunction."

It was all suddenly and painfully clear. Donna *was* the killer and the gloves and superglue tubes used to turn the inhaler into a murder weapon had been hidden inside her purse right up until the moment she'd dumped them into my wastebasket. It'd happened when she claimed she needed to use the bathroom. For all I knew, maybe Mulvaney had told the truth about the anonymous caller. Perhaps Donna had a cell phone in the purse, too, and had quietly duked in the call to the Baltimore cops while supposedly powdering her nose. And then she stalled me with a teary dog-and-pony show until they arrived.

However, an awful lot still didn't make any sense. For instance, why hadn't she planted all the evidence in the ventilation duct in the Swifts' room when she framed Tony? Why hang onto it? Another thing I couldn't figure out was why the cops had arrested her. But I guessed I'd have a good long time to figure that out. The bottom line was that I felt like a first-class idiot and with good reason: I was.

Yet the thing that bothered me the most was the knowledge that my arrogance was going to cause Ash pain and upset. My only option now was to focus on keeping her from being sucked into the whirlpool, which meant portraying my wife as being completely unaware of my unofficial investigation.

Mulvaney dangled the evidence baggie a couple of inches from my eyes. "This was stupid."

"You're a mind-reader."

She tossed the baggie to the evidence tech and then jerked her head in the direction of the Frangelico bottle and glass on the table.

"And this is a cozy little scene. Does your wife know that you're up here entertaining another woman?"

"No, and that other woman is —"

"Donna Jordan. I know all about that disturbance she caused this morning at breakfast. We've been looking for her."

"Good, because she's the killer."

Mulvaney's eyes glittered with merriment. "Nice try, but I know exactly who murdered Jennifer Swift. My only question is whether your wife helped with the killing."

"She knows nothing about this."

"Well, maybe I'll arrest her, too, just to cover my bases."

"Leave her out of this and I'll provide you with a complete statement." I hoped that Mulvaney wasn't paying close attention to the careful way I'd phrased the proposal, because I hadn't offered to confess, although that's the way I'd intended it to sound.

"You'll tell me everything?"

"Everything." Which, again, was technically the truth. "If Donna's not a suspect, why did you arrest her?"

"Hit-and-run and accessory after the fact to murder. I figure the threat of criminal charges will improve her memory and make her a better witness when it comes time to get a statement from her."

"So, if she doesn't remember things your way, she goes to jail."

"Basically."

"And after perjuring herself to implicate me, the real killer goes free. Do you have any idea of just how dishonest you are?"

She shoved me in the direction of the door. "You can tell me all about my ethical shortcomings over at district headquarters. Then, when you're done, you can tell me why you killed that woman."

As I left the hotel room, the crime scene techs began to take more photos before searching for evidence. There were a couple of cops out in the hall and they fell in behind Mulvaney and me as I shuffled down the corridor. My bad leg makes walking challenging enough, but with my hands secured behind my back, I felt as if I were about to lose my balance at any moment. We arrived at the elevator and rode it down to the ground floor, where my day immediately went from bad to worse.

The door slid open and the bright spotlights from no less than four TV video cameras blinded us. Somebody had obviously alerted the media that Mulvaney was about to escort a homicide suspect through the lobby and you didn't need to be the

Amazing Kreskin to know who'd tipped off the tragedy merchants. Microphones were shoved in our faces and I heard several voices simultaneously ask if Mulvaney or I had something to say. I glanced at Mulvaney and saw that she was wearing the patented police I'm-far-too-professional-to-grin-but-we-caught-the-bastard expression.

It hit me all wrong and so, just to prove that my colossal misjudgment of Donna wasn't a fluke, I did something else extremely stupid by saying, "Yes, I'd like to make a statement."

The cops began to push me toward the door, but the reporters kept pace. Someone shouted, "Did you kill her?"

I leaned close to a microphone. "No, I'm innocent. I've been arrested for a murder I didn't commit, but I don't blame Lieutenant Mulvaney on account of her medical condition."

Mulvaney paused to shoot me a surprised and questioning look.

"What medical condition?" The question came from the reporter with the dandruff.

"This poor woman has had so much BOTOX injected into her face, that it's leaked into her brain and paralyzed it."

There was a moment of silence and then several of the reporters began to chuckle.

Mulvaney gave me a venomous stare and jerked me toward the doors. As we passed through the revolving glass doors, I heard the officer behind me trying to smother her laughter, while the shoulders of the cop in front of me were quivering. However, I wasn't feeling particularly jolly, because I realized that I might have just talked Ash into jail. Outside beyond the portico, the wind-driven rain was pelting down. It was cold, but not half so much as Mulvaney's expression.

She growled, "Innocent, huh? I thought we had a deal."

"We still do, but you had that coming."

"What are you talking about?"

"I agreed to cooperate and then you parade me through the lobby for the media like I was some sort of big-game trophy? That was just wrong."

Her gaze flicked downward. "I had no idea that was going to happen."

"Yeah, and I'm the Sultan of Brunei. But don't be upset. Think how good you're going to look at the press conference when you modestly tell all about how you got the wise-cracking killer to give a full statement."

"You'd better, otherwise I'll be back for your wife. Are we clear on that?"

"Crystal." I sighed and watched the steam

from my breath vanish in the wind. “You know, it would have been nice to have my coat.”

“You’ll be warm enough in jail, especially after I let the other prisoners know that you’re a retired cop.” Mulvaney pulled open the door to a patrol car. “And don’t bother watching your head as you get in.”

The atmosphere inside the cruiser smelled faintly of urine, vomit, unwashed flesh, and cigarette smoke — the olfactory components of the “glamour” of police work. If you’ve never been in the backseat of a patrol car, it’s cramped and I had to sit a little sideways in order to stretch my bad leg out. Once I was seated, one of the uniformed cops leaned in to put the seat belt on me.

Outside, Mulvaney told the other officer that she’d meet us at the station and I watched as she stalked through the rain to an unmarked police car. A moment later, we were headed northward up Broadway. One of the survival habits you quickly pick up as a cop is to pay close and constant attention to your location, because you must know where you are at all times, just in case you have to call for the cavalry. So, I automatically watched the passing street signs and when the police cruiser made a right turn, I noted that it was Eastern Avenue.

As we slowly made our way through stop-and-go traffic, I wondered how Ash was taking the news of my arrest. Undoubtedly the reporters had my name by now and that would lead them to my wife in the hope of securing an emotional sound bite to spice up an already juicy story — not that they'd get anything for their efforts but an icy and disdainful stare. Ash is a veteran of media ambush tactics. On the day I was shot, the reporters arrived at our house long before someone from the PD could deliver the news. They stood on our front porch, aimed cameras through the living room window and shouted questions about how she felt. Ash's response was that she "felt" like getting the garden hose and dousing everyone until they left our property, which she did. When things go to hell in a handbasket, she's the steadiest and strongest person I've ever known, which was why I was worried that she'd immediately come to the police station to demand my release.

Next, I reflected on what I was going to do when we arrived at the police station. Under ordinary circumstances, I'd say nothing and get a damn good lawyer, but that wasn't an option. I had to talk; otherwise Mulvaney would arrest Ash for murder. My best hope was to confess to my unofficial investigation, share my information, and hope that I could convince Mulvaney — or more likely, Delcambre — that Donna was the killer.

We continued eastward, driving past a large park and a little while later passing under Interstate 895. About six or seven blocks after that, we turned into the parking lot at the rear of the Baltimore City Police Department's Southeastern District Headquarters. We parked near the rear entrance and I was ushered slowly toward the building through the pouring rain. I was pretty soaked by the time we got inside.

The investigations division office looked like almost every other detective bureau I've ever worked in or visited. There were four rows of gray modular desks, each with a computer, and all separated by cubicle walls, creating an overall effect reminiscent of furnished cattle stalls. It being a Saturday, it looked as if there was only a skeleton crew of detectives on duty.

I was led to an interview room where the male officer removed my handcuffs. It was a relief to have the hooks off and I rubbed my wrists where the metal had created indentations in my skin. He motioned for me to sit in a hard plastic chair that stood on one side of an old metal table.

Obeying the silent instructions, I said, "Can someone get me some paper towels or something? I'm soaked."

The officer nodded, left the room, and shut the door behind him. Meanwhile, the female officer leaned against the wall with her arms folded, watching me. Looking up, I saw a glass and metal camera housing on the ceiling and knew that my interview was going to be videotaped. It gave me an idea. A few seconds later, the other cop returned with a half-inch thick stack of brown paper towels. I thanked him and began to dry my face and hair.

A few minutes passed and then Mulvaney breezed into the room with a manila folder tucked under her arm. She told the uniformed officers, "You can go now."

Delcambre entered the room next and he wore an expression that was a combination of puzzlement, wariness, and slowly simmering anger. It was clear that he was still undecided as to whether I'd lied to him, but if he did conclude that I'd played him for a chump, I knew which one of the detectives would take the bad cop role when they hit me with the Mutt and Jeff routine.

Once the detectives were seated, Mulvaney opened the folder and said, "This is Baltimore City Police case number two-zero-six-six-eight-one-alpha, a homicide investigation. My name is Detective Lieutenant Sarah Mulvaney."

"And I'm Detective Sergeant Richard Delcambre."

Mulvaney glanced up from her paperwork at me. "Could you please identify yourself, sir?"

Now I was absolutely certain that we were being videotaped, otherwise she wouldn't have asked me to state my name. A videotaped interview is a wonderful investigative and prosecutorial tool, but it's also a double-edged sword: detectives who might be more worried about their conviction batting average than justice can't conveniently forget or ignore statements that would tend to show a defendant's innocence. Furthermore, the videotape must remain on continuously throughout the interview — detectives can't turn it off if they don't like the answers they're getting from a suspect.

"My name is Bradley Lyon and can I clarify something before we go any further?"

"What's that, Mr. Lyon?" said Mulvaney.

"Am I under arrest?"

"No, you came here voluntarily."

"In handcuffs . . . in the back of a police car . . . after being taken from my room at gunpoint? If that's voluntary, I'd sure hate to see your version of coercion."

Delcambre's jaw dropped and he turned to look at his boss in shock.

"That's not how it happened." Mulvaney tried to sound imperious, but the words sounded more like a whiny complaint.

I looked up at the camera on the ceiling. "Hi there, future defense attorney and jurors. Just for the record, I am under arrest for murder, I haven't yet been read my constitutional rights although I *have* been questioned, and the only reason I agreed to come to the police station was because Lieutenant Mulvaney threatened to arrest my wife if I didn't confess to a crime I didn't commit."

Mulvaney tossed her pen on the table. "We've got solid evidence on you!"

"You've got nothing." I locked eyes with her. "Donna Jordan put those gloves and superglue tubes in the trash can because she killed Jennifer, but you wouldn't listen when I tried to tell you that. And here's the freaking punch line: you won't even be able to use that evidence against her because it'll all be suppressed. You needed a search warrant to come into my room."

"We had exigent circumstances!"

"Really? Back at the hotel you told me that it was a search incident to a lawful arrest, which of course, we know it wasn't."

"I never said that."

"Yes, you did, but let's examine your 'exigent circumstances' theory. It's supposed to mean you had reliable information that someone's life was in imminent danger or that the evidence was about to be destroyed." I lifted my hand to my ear. "You hear that? That's the sound of a defense attorney sharpening his carving knife as he prepares to slice, dice, and turn that silly ass argument into julienne fries. There were no exigent circumstances and you've got no evidence."

"You promised to confess."

"Think back. I promised to make a *statement* and here it is: I did not murder Jennifer Swift. However, I have developed significant information since the last time we spoke that will help you prove that Donna Jordan is the killer. I'm willing to work with you and share that information, but I have a couple of conditions. If you don't agree to them, I'm going to invoke my right to remain silent and you can chat with my attorney."

Mulvaney snapped the manila folder shut. "You aren't in any position to dictate terms. This interview is finished."

Up until that moment, Delcambre had

remained silent. He said, "With all due respect, Lieutenant, will you shut up for a second? Mr. Lyon, what are your conditions?"

"They're real simple. First, no more threats to arrest my wife."

"Done."

"Second, I was dragged out of that hotel in handcuffs with every TV station and newspaper reporter in Baltimore watching. I want Ms. Javert there" — I nodded in the direction of Mulvaney — "to call a press conference and tell everyone that she made a terrible mistake and that I'm not under arrest for murder or anything else, for that matter."

Mulvaney blinked in bewilderment, but Delcambre, who'd obviously read *Les Miserables,* rubbed his mouth to conceal his grin. "Agreed."

"And I need someone to go back to the hotel and get my cane."

"I'll send someone over right away."

"Finally, I want to make a telephone call and let my wife know that I'm all right before an F-five tornado with blond hair and blue eyes levels this police station."

"I think we've got a deal," said Delcambre.

Mulvaney was chalk-faced with rage.

"There is no deal and I ought to relieve you of duty for insubordination, Sergeant."

"Reality check, Lieutenant: the idea of no longer working with you is a relief, not a threat. And yes, there *is* a deal and you're going to go along with it."

"Why?"

"You've screwed things up so badly, we don't have a choice," Delcambre said impatiently. "I want to catch the real murderer and, even though I don't really care what happens to you, I'm not thrilled with the idea of Mr. Lyon owning my house because your incompetence dragged us into a seven-figure, false-arrest lawsuit."

Mulvaney was about to deliver a spiteful response when she heard me softly humming, "There's No Place Like Home." Gritting her teeth, she said, "But what will the captain say?"

"That's your problem, boss."

Fourteen

Delcambre led me out of the interview room and pointed to a vacant work cubicle. "You can use that phone."

"Thanks." I sat down in a frayed office chair and pressed the numbers for our cell phone. Although the interview room door was shut, I heard the argument between the detectives resume and quickly grow in intensity. Mulvaney attempted to launch a Vince Lombardi–like speech about how teams succeed or fail together. However, she didn't get much past the second stanza before Delcambre shouted her down, saying that if the team's captain was an imbecile that showed up at the wrong stadium on game day, it didn't make a difference how the rest of the players performed.

Ash answered on the first ring and her voice was almost crackling with tension. "Hello?"

In a bright and cheerful tone, I said, "Hi,

honey. Hey, a funny thing happened on the way back down to the teddy bear show."

"Where are you? Are you all right? They told me you were under arrest for murder."

"By they, you mean that hyena pack of reporters? I'm sorry you had to find out that way. I'd have called, but I had a gun screwed in my ear."

"Are you all right?"

"I'm fine and the good news is that, at least for the moment, I'm not under arrest."

"Bradley Aaron Lyon, this is not funny. I've been calling every police department number in the phone book trying to find out where they took you and all I could get were those damn voice menu recordings. Then I started calling nine-one-one and they told me to get off the line because it wasn't an emergency. And I was so frightened, because . . ." She paused to take a deep breath.

"Because it's way too much like the day I got shot." I looked down at the desktop, feeling awful that my lame attempts to lighten the mood with humor had upset her so badly. "You're right, it was really wrong of me to treat this like a big joke. I'm very sorry."

"You should be." There was a short pause. "Are you *sure* you're all right?"

"Other than being ashamed of myself and a bit damp, I'm excellent."

"Where are you?"

"Sitting at a desk in the detective bureau at the Southeastern District headquarters. Where are you? It sounds quiet."

"I'm up in Karen's room. She gave me her key. It was a madhouse with all those reporters wanting to know why you'd been arrested."

"I can imagine. You didn't spray anybody with a hose, did you?"

"No, but I might have accidentally splashed some of my sparkling water on this horrible woman reporter who kept asking me what it was like to be married to the 'Teddy Bear Terminator.' "

"Accidentally, huh?"

"Half the bottle."

"That's my girl."

"And did you have to make that comment about Mulvaney and the BOTOX?"

"I was misquoted."

"Right. So, why were you arrested for murder? I thought the police had already charged Tony."

"They had, but Donna changed all that by planting a couple of superglue tubes and some latex gloves in our bathroom wastebasket. Then she called Lieutenant Mulvaney to tell her where the incriminating evidence was."

Ash inhaled sharply. "You were right about her being the killer."

"Yeah, but if even half of what Donna told me about Jennifer is true, I'm not going to lose any sleep if the trial ends up with a not-guilty-by-reason-of-insanity verdict."

"Why?"

"Because Donna began making the angel bears for her little boy, who eventually died of muscular dystrophy. Then her 'best friend' Jennifer stole the prototype bears from the dead kid's room and began selling them. Later, when Jen ran out of hot angel bears, she began making pirated bears and claimed the design was her original idea."

"Oh my God, that's, that's . . . vile. It's . . ." It doesn't happen often, but my wife was at a loss for words.

"Yeah, the idea is so gruesome it's kind of hard to get your brain around it, isn't it? And I didn't even get to the part about how the bears that Jen ripped off were supposed to be donated to the children's ward at a local hospital."

"How could she have done those things and lived with herself?"

"I suspect that may have been exactly the question that Donna asked herself when she walked into the exhibit hall yesterday morning and saw the Tomb Raider and Tony hawking the bears. I'm certain it just unhinged her."

"It all fits together. But . . ."

I heard the uncertainty in Ash's voice and understood why. "But some things still don't make any sense. I know."

"I mean, if the police found the inhaler in the ventilation duct in the Swifts' room, why would Donna want to frame *you* as the killer?"

"Maybe she was afraid that I'd find the evidence in her purse when I took her to our room to talk."

"But why not plant it all in the vent? If you'd committed a murder, would you carry the evidence around in your purse for hours afterwards?"

"Depends on the purse. Do you see me with a Louis Vuitton or am I more a Dooney and Burke sort of guy?"

"Brad honey, focus."

"I'd have ditched the evidence ASAP," I said, remembering how Donna had talked about throwing the key card away after the warning call from Jennifer.

"Exactly."

"Which sounds very logical, but doesn't take into account the fact that Donna is a functional alcoholic. Remember our little chat with her last night?"

"Of course."

"And you think maybe that scene this morning was powered by booze?"

"I hadn't thought about that. Did you smell anything on her breath?"

"No, but that's why God created vodka. And a little later, she nearly dragged you to death with her van. Can anyone say DUI? Then she drank nearly half the bottle of Frangelico during our interview. It's possible that she was so drunk that she forgot to plant all the evidence in the Swifts' room."

"I see what you mean."

The verbal dispute in the interview room was growing louder by the second and then the door swung open with such force that it slammed against the wall.

"I am not going on TV and committing career suicide! We're in this together!" Mulvaney yelled over her shoulder as she stormed past the cubicle.

"*We?* Do you have a mouse in your pocket? *We* did not arrest the wrong man! *You* did! And if you think I'm gonna fall on my sword for you, you've been smoking crack!" Delcambre shouted back.

"Hang on for a second, sweetheart." I put

my hand over the phone's mouthpiece. "Hey, can you kids keep it down? Dad's on the phone."

Delcambre paused to look over the cubicle wall and give me a frosty look that clearly told me I was pushing my luck.

Uncovering the phone, I said, "I'll call you back in just a bit, honey. We've got a little crisis here and Mr. Empathy is needed."

"I don't think I've ever met him," Ash said sweetly.

"I happen to know that you sleep with him."

"Nope, still doesn't ring a bell. Why were you elected peacemaker?"

"Because I caused the argument."

"Gosh, what were the odds of *that?* When can you come back here?"

"Very soon, I hope. First, we have to figure this thing out, because if Donna didn't try to frame me . . ."

"Then we're back to Tony being the main suspect."

"Except he couldn't have planted the evidence in our room, because he's been in custody."

There was a thump and then a crash from the far corner of the room that sounded suspiciously like someone kicking a chair over. Then the argument flared up again.

"Look, I've really got to go. They're starting to break things. I love you, sweetheart, and one other thing: we aren't coming back to this teddy bear show next year."

"I love you, too. Is there really any point in me telling you to be careful?" Ash tried to sound light-spirited, but there was an undertone of wistfulness.

"I like hearing it . . . and I do listen. It's just that things seem to happen to me."

"I've noticed."

"And I hope you've also noticed how much I love you. Now, go back downstairs to the teddy bear show."

"But the reporters —"

"Are going to be leaving there very shortly to come here for a press conference. Promise me that you'll try to relax and enjoy yourself with all the bears."

"And you'll be here as quickly as possible?"

"Just as soon as I can get a talking Pomeranian to come here to take over the case."

Hanging up, I hobbled along the aisle between the desks to a cramped office where Mulvaney and Delcambre were working themselves into a fairly credible imitation of the Battle of Guadalcanal. A black plastic nameplate on the door said it was Mulvaney's workplace and the first thing I noticed was the small and lovely Tiffany-style leaded-glass lamp on the desk. The lamp shade was a rich mosaic of pastel-colored wildflower bouquets and looked as out of place on the stark and utilitarian desk as a DVD player in a hearse.

Next, I looked at the wall to my immediate right, where about a dozen framed color photographs were hanging. All the images featured Mulvaney posing or shaking hands with a bunch of other anonymous people. If my life depended upon it, I couldn't have identified any of the other folks and that included the guy wearing the Baltimore Orioles baseball team uniform. My guess was that the other people were minor politicians, obscure entertainers, and local TV newscasters — the archetypal big fish in the small ponds. Suddenly, I felt a small spark of pity for the lieutenant, because the pictures told me that she was so insecure and felt so inconsequential that she'd plastered her wall with photos of her brief encounters with a bunch of nonentities, in order to be "somebody." It also explained why she so desperately craved the spotlight.

Somebody once wrote that "To know all is to forgive all." I think that's mostly nonsense; however, now that I had some notion of what made Mulvaney behave the way she did, I couldn't find it in my heart to continue to ridicule her. It was like making fun of a cripple — and being a fellow cripple, I know how that feels. At the same time, I don't want to give you the idea that I was ready to sit around a campfire with her, eating s'mores and singing "Kumbuya." She'd behaved recklessly by arresting me and committed the unforgivable sin of threatening my wife. I didn't like Mulvaney and never would, but as long as she believed I was intent on destroying her career — and therefore, her life — we wouldn't get anywhere.

I guess I'd been gathering wool, because I realized that the argument had stopped and Mulvaney and Delcambre were watching me. I said, "I know things are a mess, but what do you do when life hands you lemons?"

"The only thing I hate more than lemonade is advice from get-well cards," Mulvaney said sourly.

"I'm not talking about making lemonade. You permanently stop the flow of lemons by getting a backhoe and digging the tree up by the roots."

"What are you getting at?"

"Look, we got off to a bad start, but that doesn't mean it has to continue that way.

There are three of us. We're all good homicide detectives. Let's get some lunch in here and sit down and solve this murder."

"But the press conference . . ."

"Call it, but they can wait in the lobby until you're ready to talk to them. In fact, it might work to our advantage if the real killer thinks I'm still under arrest."

"The real killer? You told us it was Donna," said Delcambre.

"Yeah, and up until I talked with my wife, I thought so, too. Hey, is there anyplace to get decent Chinese takeout here? I love living in the Shenandoah Valley, but it isn't exactly famous for its Szechuan cuisine."

"Chin's has pretty good food," Mulvaney offered in a cautiously friendly voice. "It's just down the street."

"And if this is a real detective bureau, I'll bet you have their menu and one from every takeout and delivery restaurant in a five-mile radius."

"They're tacked to a bulletin board in the squad room."

"Then let's eat and get to work."

Mulvaney telephoned the BCPD's Public Information Officer to announce the impending news conference to the media outlets, while Delcambre went to get lunch. Thirty-five minutes later we were seated around Mulvaney's desk and the air was redolent with the aroma of spicy food. Mulvaney and Delcambre were eating with plastic forks while I used chopsticks for the first time since leaving San Francisco. The food was excellent and hot enough to be considered a violation of the Geneva Convention rules prohibiting chemical assault, which is exactly the way I love it. As we ate, I brought them up to speed on what Donna had told me. When I got to the part about Jennifer stealing the teddy bears and selling them at a craft fair, both detectives gaped at me in disbelief.

Delcambre dropped his fork into the cardboard box containing shrimp lo mein. "That's so sick, I just lost my appetite."

"Yeah, and isn't it funny that Tony didn't mention *that* part of the story? The only thing he told us was that Donna broke off her friendship with Jennifer because she was envious of how well they were doing with the angel bears," said Mulvaney.

"What else did he say?" I speared a chunk of Szechuan shredded beef and popped it in my mouth.

"Not much. He lawyered up right after we found the sabotaged inhaler in his room. But you don't think he's the killer, do you?"

"You talked with him. Unless the guy is

periodically channeling the spirit of Albert Einstein, does he impress you as being bright enough to have come up with such a sophisticated murder weapon?"

"No. What made you believe Donna might have done it?"

"Because she was in the Swifts' room last night during the cocktail reception." I wiped some perspiration from my scalp and snared another piece of blistering-hot meat. "God, this food is great."

"I'll take your word for it, because it's making my eyes water just being in the same room with that stuff. So, what made you change your mind about Donna?" said Mulvaney.

"Part of that's going to depend on what your evidence people found in the Swifts' room. Did it look like the maid had cleaned before you guys got there?"

"No."

"Then they should have found a color picture of Donna's little boy. More than likely, it was in the trash."

"The CSI team is still there. I'll call and see." Delcambre grabbed the phone and began pressing numbers.

I used the chopsticks to push some steamed rice into the fiery sauce and braced myself for another bite. "By the way, where is Donna?"

Mulvaney grimaced. "At the hospital. She started hyperventilating so badly that she got chest pains and someone decided she was having a heart attack. I've got no idea of when they're going to release her."

"The same hospital where they took Jennifer?"

"Yeah. It's ironic, now that you mention it."

"And for sheer weirdness, how about this: 'breathe,' which Jen couldn't do and Donna is having trouble doing, is an anagram for 'the bear.' "

Mulvaney looked over at me with arched eyebrows. "You're a very strange guy."

"It's been remarked."

After about a half-minute of conversation, Delcambre hung up. "There was a photo in the waste basket that'd been torn up into little pieces, but it looks as if it was a picture of a young boy."

"And that's why I don't think it was Donna. She told me she went into the room to drop off that picture to remind Jen that her success was the result of having betrayed a friend and committing the next best thing to grave robbery. The photo corroborates her story."

"Because if her actual purpose was to

sabotage Jennifer's inhaler, the last thing she'd do is leave a piece of evidence that would lead the cops directly to her," said Delcambre.

"Precisely."

"So if it wasn't Tony or Donna . . . or you" — Mulvaney paused to give me a faint sardonic grin — "we're back to square one."

"Which is your star witness, Todd Litten," I said.

Realizing her partner had told me about the police interview with Todd, Mulvaney shot Delcambre a hard look and then said, "Why him?"

"I'd love to pretend I'm being brilliant, but it's simply because we're running out of innocent people to suspect." I gave her a crooked smile. "But the question of Todd brings us to one of the lynchpins of this case: Access to the hotel rooms — first, the Swifts' room to sabotage the inhaler and plant the evidence and then, later, ours. Now, we know that there were a total of three card keys issued for room seven-forty-six."

The forkful of tangerine chicken stopped just short of Mulvaney's mouth. "We knew that. How did *you?*"

"As long as we're getting along so well, I suppose it's time to tell you that I kind of falsely identified myself as a Baltimore PD homicide detective to the hotel clerk. I had to find out if and when another card key was issued and that's what led me to Donna."

Delcambre chuckled. "*Now* it makes sense. The desk clerk copped a major attitude and told us that she'd already given the information to another detective. We were wondering who the hell Detective Callahan was."

"That'd be me."

"As in 'Dirty Harry' Callahan?"

"It seemed cute at the time."

Mulvaney slowly put the food in her mouth, carefully chewed it, and swallowed. Delcambre and I waited for the explosion, but it didn't come. She carefully dabbed her lips with a paper napkin and then said, "You were telling us about the card keys."

"There were three issued. Donna said she threw hers away last night, which means some lucky cops get to search the hotel dumpsters in the rain. In the meantime, can we account for the other two key cards?"

Mulvaney and Delcambre stared at each other and I could see that they were silently asking each other if they could remember whether they'd seen the key cards.

"Let me go back to the holding cell and get Tony's property envelope," said Delcambre, standing up and heading for the door.

"Jennifer's purse was still in the room. And I'll get a squad car to bring it over here from the hotel," said Mulvaney, grabbing for the phone.

"And I hate to be a pest, but can they bring my cane, too, please?"

"Who're you kidding, Lyon? I've known you less than half a day and I can tell that you love being a pest," Delcambre called as he left the office.

"You really shouldn't believe everything my wife says about me."

I gathered up the food containers and looked for a trash can.

Mulvaney said, "For God's sake, please take that stuff out of here. The fumes from your lunch are like being pepper-sprayed."

There was a break room just across the corridor. I dumped the rubbish there and went back to the office. Delcambre returned a couple of minutes later with a large and slightly bulging manila envelope. He dumped the contents onto the desktop. There were car keys, a cell phone, a handful of coins, emergency provisions in the way of a bag of peanut butter M&M's, and an overstuffed and shabby-looking gray nylon wallet.

Delcambre opened the billfold and removed the paper currency. "Just so there aren't any questions later on, I see a total of one, two . . . nine whole dollars."

"Yeah, he and Bill Gates were going to have dinner together later tonight," I said.

"And we have a driver's license and a credit card, and a credit card, and a credit card." Delcambre tossed each item onto the table as he spoke. "And a credit card, and a health insurance card, a gym ID card, another credit card, and I believe this is what we're looking for: a Maritime Inn card key."

Mulvaney took the card and put it into a separate evidence envelope. "There's the first one."

While we waited for the purse to be delivered, I went to the restroom. I was returning to the office when a young uniformed cop in a dripping wet yellow rain jacket slipped past me. He was carrying a rain-spattered brown grocery-sized evidence bag in one hand and my cane in the other.

I said, "Whoa there, son. Ginger Rogers and I are going dancing tonight, so I need my cane."

The officer handed me the cane and continued on to the office. By the time I got there, Jennifer's purse was on Mulvaney's desk and my stomach did the sort of nasty flip-flop that's like the sudden onset of seasickness. The brown shoulder bag was the one I'd seen Todd Litten reaching into yesterday morning as I'd passed the Cheery Cherub Bears booth. Jennifer's back was turned to him and her eyes had been closed, so she couldn't have known he was rifling her purse.

With a start, I remembered something Donna had told me and realized that her words were far more important than either of us could have guessed at the time. When I'd asked her if she knew who the murderer was, she'd replied something to the effect that it was probably someone else that Jennifer had stabbed in the back. There was only one other person present at the teddy bear show who might fit into that category and I began to wonder if Todd had come to view Jennifer's refusal to return his love as a stab in the back . . . or maybe, more appropriately, the heart. Then I realized that I'd completely overlooked a pivotal piece of information, but I kept silent until we confirmed that the key card wasn't in the purse.

Mulvaney carefully emptied the purse's contents out onto the desk. There was an assortment of cheap cosmetics, a tube of skin lotion, another cell phone, and a maroon-colored leather wallet. Mulvaney went through the wallet, but as I now expected, there wasn't a key card.

"Nothing," she said, tossing the wallet onto the table.

"And the CSI team says that it isn't in the room either."

"So, where did it go?"

"Actually, I have an idea about that, but I need to use your phone first."

FIFTEEN

Mulvaney stepped to the side and nodded for me to go behind her desk.

I sat down, grabbed the phone receiver, and pressed the number for long-distance directory assistance for the 717-area code, which covers south-central Pennsylvania. A computer-generated woman's voice answered, asked me what number I wanted, and I replied, "The Basingstoke Township Fire Department."

I listened as the artificial voice told me that in the event of an emergency I should hang up and dial 911 immediately, which is always helpful advice in the event your house is aflame. Then the computerized operator began reciting a series of telephone numbers and I jotted down the one for the non-emergency line. Disconnecting, I pressed the new number and a real woman answered this time, saying, "Basingstoke Township Police, Fire, and Rescue Dispatch. How can I help you?"

"Hi, I'm Detective Sergeant Richard Delcambre from the Baltimore City Police, down in Maryland. I'm conducting a murder investigation and I need some information from your agency," I said, glancing at Delcambre, who was rubbing his temple as if he had a headache.

"What sort of information, sir?" asked the dispatcher.

"You have an employee by the name of Todd Litten. He's an EMT and it's vitally important that I speak to his supervisor immediately."

"Has something happened to Todd?"

"No ma'am. He's absolutely fine. It's just that he tried to assist our murder victim before she died and we need to follow up on a little information before moving on with our inquiries," I said, figuring the simultaneously misleading and truthful reply would secure me more cooperation than stating point-blank that Litten was about to become a "person of interest" in a homicide investigation.

"Let me see. Litten . . ." said the dispatcher. I could hear the quiet clicks of a keyboard being tapped and knew she was consulting a schedule. "He works for Captain Gallagher and . . . and that shift is off today."

"I know you can't give me his home phone number, but will you please call Captain Gallagher and ask him to call me at the Baltimore City Police Department as soon as possible? It's very important." I waved to Delcambre, shoved a notepad in his direction and silently mouthed, "Write down the number and this extension."

"And can I have your name again, sir?" asked the dispatcher.

"It's Delcambre." I spelled the name. "I'm a detective sergeant at the Southeastern District Headquarters."

"And your number?"

I read it off from the notepad. "And will you please call me back to let me know if you couldn't contact Captain Gallagher? Again, I can't stress enough how important this is."

"Yes, sir."

Once I disconnected from the call, Delcambre said in an amused tone, "Before we talk about Litten, I've got to know: Do you suffer from multi-personality disorder?"

"No, I just asked the questions that you'd have asked fifteen minutes from now, if we had the time to waste. But if my using your name really bothers you, I'll be Lieutenant Mulvaney if and when Gallagher calls back."

"Do you actually think you could do her voice?"

"I'd probably sound more like Kathleen Turner after smoking a pack of Camel non-filters, but I'm willing to give it a try."

"Can we concentrate on the murder, please?" said Mulvaney. "You're talking about Todd Litten, the guy who wrote the books that the Swifts sold with the bears, right?"

"I didn't know you'd met him," I said.

"He was in the hospital waiting room when we got there and volunteered to tell us what happened, up until the point when you and your wife stepped in."

"Did he happen to mention where he was while Jennifer was dying?"

Delcambre said, "He told us that he was so upset and angry over people believing Tony's insinuations about him having a romantic relationship with Jennifer . . . and you shoving him aside, that he went upstairs to his room."

"To sulk?"

"Basically."

"Did any of the witnesses at breakfast say otherwise?"

"At the time, we thought Tony was good

for the murder, so we didn't ask about Todd."

"So he *could* have grabbed the inhaler during the commotion while we were doing CPR." I began tapping out the bass riff to the jazz-fusion classic, "Birdland," with my middle finger on the desktop, a nervous habit of mine when I'm excited.

"You still haven't explained why you think Litten's involved," Mulvaney said.

I pointed toward the purse. "For starters, I saw him reaching inside *that* thing yesterday afternoon — call it some time around one-thirty. I didn't think it was significant at the time."

"Where'd this happen?"

"Inside the Cheery Cherub Bears booth at the teddy bear show. Jennifer had her back turned to Todd and was trying to ignore him. My guess is, he lifted the card key then."

"I hope you have something more than that," said Delcambre.

"I do and it's the classic wild card. Todd was in love with Jennifer."

"How do you know that?"

"I chatted with him briefly last night at the cocktail reception and he thanked me for stopping Tony from clobbering Jen."

"You're referring to the incident in the

parking garage that morning?"

"Yeah. And while we were talking he had this sad-puppy-dog-I-love-Jody-Foster-so-much-that-I'll-shoot-the-president look and then he asked me why Jennifer stayed with Tony when he could give her a better life. From the way Todd was behaving, I thought they were having an affair."

"Were they?" asked Mulvaney.

"My wife doesn't think so, and I trust her judgment."

"But should we trust her judgment, considering she married you?" Delcambre deadpanned.

"One little mistake and she's tarred for life."

Mulvaney chopped at the air with her hand in frustration. "Can we please give the Marx Brothers routine a rest for just a couple of minutes? What are you trying to say, Lyon?"

"The one thing we know about Jennifer is that she didn't have any compunctions about using people. As far as she was concerned, they were nothing more than tools. So, what if she gently encouraged Todd to think there was a blossoming romance, when in fact, it was nothing more than a convenient scam?"

"But why?"

"I don't know. Maybe she wanted to make Tony jealous. Maybe Todd actually was her boy toy. Maybe the guy writes a hell of a children's book. Regardless of the reason, I think something happened to make Todd realize he'd been played for a fool. How did he react when you told him that Jennifer was dead?"

"About the way you'd expect someone would when you tell them that a friend just died." Delcambre rubbed his chin. "You know: The standard Oh-my-God-I-can't-believe-it."

"And having been to more than a few death scenes as an EMT, he'd have the shocked reaction down pat. However, we now know Todd considered Jennifer far more than just a friend." The phone trilled and I snatched up the receiver. "Homicide. Sergeant Delcambre speaking."

"Yes, this is Captain Darryl Gallagher. You asked me to call?" In the background, I could faintly hear voices from a TV. I listened more closely and recognized them as belonging to Joseph Cotten and Trevor Howard and realized I was missing *The Third Man* on Turner Classic Movies.

"Yes, sir, thank you for calling back so quickly."

"Before I answer any questions, is Todd in

trouble?"

"No, sir, not at all. In fact, he did his best to save a woman's life earlier this morning. You should be very proud of him."

"That's not surprising. He's one of our very best people. So, how can I help you?"

"I just have a couple questions. Your department sponsored a community safety fair back in September and Todd was one of the presenters, right?"

"Yes."

"Do you remember what topic he covered?"

"Of course. It was a class that he gave to a bunch of high school kids on the dangers of huffing inhalants. You know: spray-paint, toluene —"

"And superglue?"

"That would have been one of the chemicals. Sure." In the background I could now hear a zither playing.

"Did Todd have any special qualifications to teach that class?"

"Absolutely. He'd taken a course at the State Fire Academy over in Lewistown and was nearly an expert on the subject."

"I think that's all I need, so I'll let you get back to your day. Thanks for everything, Captain Gallagher. Oh, and I almost forgot, should we send Todd's letter of commendation to you or to the fire chief?"

"The fire chief, definitely."

"And can you do me one more little favor?" I injected a large dose of warmth into my voice. "Please don't call Todd and let him know that we're doing this. He was really embarrassed and said he was just doing his duty when we told him what a great job he'd done. We'd like this to be a nice surprise."

Delcambre put his hand to his mouth and puffed his cheeks out, pretending he was on the verge of being violently ill, while Mulvaney shook her head in reluctant admiration. However, I wasn't feeling particularly clever.

"I sure won't," said Gallagher.

"And again, thanks for your cooperation." I hung up the receiver, slouched back into the chair, and massaged the bridge of my nose. "Just so that we're all clear on this: I'm a freaking idiot. Earlier this morning, I Googled everybody involved in this mess. Among other things, that's how I learned Donna Jordan is a high school chemistry teacher and I wrongly assumed that her specialized knowledge made her the logical suspect. However, while I jumped on that piece of information, I completely missed the real clue."

"Which is?" Mulvaney asked.

"Litten is an Emergency Medical Technician, which means that along with all his other medical training he'd also be acquainted with —"

"How inhalants work, too." She finished the thought for me.

"Exactly. And then, a couple of minutes ago, I remembered an article on the Internet about Litten that I'd seen on the local newspaper's Web page. It said he gave a seminar at a community safety fair, but it didn't mention the topic and I was way too interested in being brilliant and rushing to wrongly accuse an innocent woman of murder to bother to check my facts," I said with a sigh.

"And?"

"And Litten took a specialized course on inhalants at the Pennsylvania State Fire Academy. He's apparently an expert on aerated poisons." I gave Mulvaney a chastened smile. "By the way, I sincerely apologize for acting so arrogantly. My performance in this investigation hasn't been any better than yours. In fact, it's been far worse, because I had more information to work with than you did, yet made the same errors. So, just say the word and I'll happily excuse myself from anything else having to do with this inquiry."

It got so silent in the room I could hear the electric clock on the wall quietly humming and the distant grumble of traffic from outside. I reached for my cane and prepared to leave.

As I pushed myself to my feet, Mulvaney said, "You may have been wrong and there's no arguing the fact that you're an utter know-it-all, but you've gotten us this far. What would you recommend we do now?"

I discovered that I'd been holding my breath. Relaxing, I replied, "A couple of things. First, did your front desk really receive an anonymous call? If so, was it a male or female voice?"

"Male," said Delcambre.

"And the call wasn't made to nine-one-one, where the phone number would have shown up on the caller ID screen and been recorded. What does that suggest?"

"That the informant didn't want us to know his identity —"

"And that he was someone acquainted with how an emergency dispatch center operates," Mulvaney cut in.

I nodded. "And a fire department paramedic like Todd would have that knowledge. Sorry for suggesting you made the story up about the anonymous reporting party."

"I can't wait to get my hands on that little weasel," said Mulvaney.

"And charge him with what? We've got nothing on him, LT," I said.

"So, what's the plan?" asked Delcambre.

"We have to talk to Tony. We need an inside look at how Jennifer viewed her relationship with Todd and what was going on behind the scenes before the show."

"But, I told you. He invoked his rights, so we can't talk to him," said Mulvaney.

"Of course we can talk to him. Miranda doesn't mean we can't continue to ask him questions. It just means we can't use his answers against him. Once he understands we're giving him the opportunity to shove the blame onto Todd, believe me, Tony will talk."

"I see what you're saying, but don't we have to release him?"

"Not immediately. The inhaler you found in his room is enough to hold him for now."

"But Todd —"

"Is probably the killer. But all we've got at the moment is an interesting theory and some suspicious circs. There isn't a shred of proof to implicate Todd. However, you have solid physical evidence that, at least at face value, shows that Tony is the murderer. Correct?"

"That's true."

"And it's merely our mean-spirited cop opinions that he lacks the G-2 to pull off such a complicated crime," I said, using the old U.S. army term for military intelligence.

"So, we're under no lawful obligation to release him yet," Delcambre said.

"Give the man a cigar. We hang onto Tony for now because we need a twist on him. When I'm done, you can show him the door."

"But I'm not comfortable with you interviewing him," said Mulvaney.

"I'm not comfortable with it either. The guy hates my guts and if I don't remember to move my hands frequently, there's the chance he'll eat one. But, it has to be me, because we're running out of time and I'm the only one who knows the questions that have to be asked."

"Even if that's true, you don't have any authority to interrogate him."

"Who says?"

"Our department rules and regulations —"

"Which aren't the same thing as statutory and case law and, like all regulations, are probably too rigid when a situation goes fluid like this." I glanced at my watch. "Look, for the past hour or so, I've been acting as your de facto agent and you can't un-ring that bell. It's going to come out at trial, regardless of who's charged with murder. So, type up something formalizing my role in the investigation. I'll sign it and that will keep everything legal."

We heard footfalls and a moment later, a desk sergeant stuck his head through the doorway. "Lieutenant Mulvaney? We've got a bunch of TV crews and newspaper people starting to set up camp in the lobby, saying there's going to be a big press conference. It's the first I've heard of it."

"Sorry, Carl. I've been jammed here. I'll come out in a second to update you."

"Thanks. I'll be in the watch commander's office."

Once the desk sergeant was gone, Mulvaney said, "You're right, we're running out of time, so I don't have any choice. You can do the interview, but I'm going to be in there with you, while Delcambre monitors the video from the AV room."

"Absolutely. I want to upset Tony's equilibrium, and you being there will do just that."

"Why?"

"Because you scare him. Unlike his wife, you're a woman that would not only fight back, you'd kick his butt. However, I want your promise not to interrupt because I'm liable to say some things that aren't quite orthodox."

"Imagine my surprise at hearing that," Mulvaney said with a sigh.

I opened the envelope containing Tony's property, peered inside, and took out the wrinkled bag of peanut butter M&M's.

Delcambre looked nauseous. "Please don't tell me you're going to eat those."

"No." I tossed the candy into the air and caught it. "If you're going fishing, you need bait."

Sixteen

While Delcambre went back to the holding cell to get Tony and Mulvaney briefed the watch commander on what was happening, I used the phone to make a quick call to Ash. When she answered, I was relieved to hear the buzz of many voices in the background. It meant that she was back down at the teddy bear show.

"You're still at the police station, aren't you?" she asked.

"There's a déjà vu moment. How many years have you been asking that question, my love?"

"Twenty-six. I thought it was going to stop once you retired from SFPD and became a teddy bear artist."

"It would have, if I hadn't been promoted to Chief of Fur-ensics."

Ash groaned.

"I take it the reporters are gone?" I asked.

"They took off out of here about a half-hour ago."

"And does everyone there believe I killed Jennifer?"

"Nobody knows what to think . . . except for your *special* friend, Lisa. She came by our table a little while ago to offer her support."

"Oh, no."

"Oh, yes." Ash began to mimic Lisa's syrupy voice and I winced. "Gee, Mrs. Lyon, I'm surprised that you aren't at the police station trying to help your husband. When you see Brad, please tell him that *I* don't believe he killed anybody."

"I'm stunned the cops weren't called back out there to investigate another murder."

"No, because that's exactly the response she wanted. So, even though I wanted to break her bones in alphabetical order, I stayed cool."

"Really?"

"Yes, I did, and I'm proud of myself." Ash sounded tranquil. "I just smiled and told her that I was certain the foremost thing on *your* mind at the moment was some tramp's opinion of you."

"That must have left a mark."

"Nope, she just gave me a nasty little smile and strolled off. So, when are you coming back here?"

"Soon."

"Brad honey, that word has no meaning when you use it."

"I know, but we're on the verge of breaking this case and I need to ask you a question: have you seen any sign of Todd?"

"He's down at the Cheery Cherub Bears booth. Why?"

"I don't have time to explain all the details, but it's looking more and more as if he's the real killer. When did he show up?"

"About a half-hour ago. It looked like he made some sort of little memorial speech and now there's a crowd of people around the booth —"

"And the bears are flying off the shelves faster than plywood panels just before a hurricane, right?"

"How did you know?"

"With Jennifer dead, it's the last bunch of angel bears she actually made. They've become instant collector's items."

"God, I hadn't looked at it that way," Ash said, the distaste palpable in her voice.

"That's because you're like most bear collectors. You buy them because you love them, not for their investment value."

"So, why did Todd kill her?"

"I don't know yet, but more than likely it has something to do with Jennifer's proclivity for shivving people who made the mistake of thinking they were her friend."

"Which also means he planted the evidence in our room. Why?"

"One unsolvable problem at a time, my love."

"What do you want me to do? Should I keep an eye on Todd?" she asked eagerly.

"No. Stay the hell away from him," I said, sounding far gruffer than I intended. At the risk of sounding like some overdramatic young teenager in the throes of puppy love, I couldn't envision life without her.

There was perhaps a moment's worth of silence. Finally, Ash said, "I promise not to go near him, darling."

"Thank you, and I'm sorry for snapping at you. But it's the 'nice guys' like Todd who have the potential to be extremely dangerous — Cody Jarrett-top-of-the-world-Ma dangerous," I said, alluding to James Cagney's masterpiece performance as a mad-dog killer in the old film, *White Heat*. "They figure they're trapped and already going down for murder, so there's no point in worrying about the final body count."

"I'll stay away from him. But do you want me to call you if he leaves?"

"Yeah, but I don't think that's going to happen."

"Why?"

"Because he's intelligent enough to realize that he'll attract suspicion if he suddenly bails. And, don't ask me why, I also have a feeling he won't leave until after the award ceremony this evening."

Ash was perplexed. "What does the award ceremony have to do with anything?"

"With Tony in jail and Jennifer in the morgue, Todd's the only member of the Cheery Cherub Bears team available to accept Jen's posthumous trophy for best bear in the costumed, five-to-fourteen inch category . . . and you know that's exactly what the judges are going to do."

"He'd stay for a trophy? That's crazy."

"Maybe, but he was in love with Jennifer and if he had to keep that a secret from everybody while she was alive . . ."

"He can pretend they're together now? Even if he hadn't killed her, that's just sick."

"Yeah, but it'll play well to people who, unlike us, don't routinely expect the worst from other folks." From out in the detective bureau, I could hear the muffled sound of Tony's protests as he was led into the interview room. I said, "Look honey, I've got to go now. I love you and I'll be there soon."

"There's that word again. Love you, too."

A sudden thought struck me. "Wait, wait . . . don't hang up. Are you still there?"

"I'm still here. What's wrong?"

"Nothing is wrong. I just want you to check your leather satchel and see if you still have your card key to our room."

"I'm going to have to put the phone down to look. Hold on a second." I heard Ash unzip the black bag and in the background I could hear the happy sounds of the teddy bear show that I was missing. She came back on the line. "Yes, it's right here."

"And I've got mine. Thanks, sweetheart and I'll explain later."

Hanging up, I made another quick telephone call. I walked out into the office area a minute or two later and met Delcambre, who'd just locked the interview room door. On the other side of the door, I could hear Tony complaining, but couldn't quite make out the words.

Noticing my quizzical glance at the door, Delcambre said, "There apparently wasn't enough for lunch. He's still hungry."

"Remind me to notify Amnesty International. Hey, a couple of things occurred to me when I was talking to my wife on the phone."

"What's that?"

"For starters, while we're in talking with

Wally Walrus, you need to contact your people at the hotel. Have them round up the fifth-floor cleaning crew for interviews, because I've got a pretty good idea of how Todd planted the evidence in our room."

"So, tell me."

"Detective Callahan strikes again. I just called the hotel and learned that there were only two card keys issued for our room . . . both of which are accounted for."

Delcambre tapped his forehead as if frustrated he'd missed an obvious clue. "And there was no forced entry, so the only way he could have gone in was while the maids were cleaning the rooms."

"Probably with a teddy bear in his hands, posing as me. I never saw the maids, so they wouldn't know me from Todd."

"And in fairness, they might have thought he was your son . . . or grandson."

"You're a cruel man, Richard. I guess that's why I like you. But back to the question of room access: the scenario also fits the time frame, because the maids cleaned our room between the time I was doing the computer searches and when I interviewed Donna."

"So, we're also going to need a photo lineup. I'll call the Pennsylvania State Police and ask them to send us a digital DMV photo of Litten ASAP."

"And here's something else you might want to jump on quickly: those latex gloves that were recovered from my room? I'll bet Todd doesn't know that it's possible to recover latent fingerprints from the inside of gloves."

"With the superglue fuming process." His eyes widened with surprise. "Oh man . . ."

"Uh-huh, the method of murder might also be the exact same process by which you identify the killer."

"And if we do recover latents, we can compare them immediately, because his prints will be on file in Pennsylvania."

"Because he's a public safety worker."

"Right. I'll also get the State Police to fax me a copy of his print card."

Mulvaney came into the detective bureau with a sheet of paper in her hand. She nodded in the direction of the interview room door. "Is he in there?"

"Yeah," said Delcambre.

"Before we get started, I need you to sign this." Mulvaney handed me the sheet.

"My secret agent credential. I might need it in Karachi."

"You might need it at the nuthouse. Or maybe I belong there," Mulvaney said with an anxious sigh, "because this is so far outside our policies and procedures, that I can't believe I'm doing it."

I said, "I know you're worried, but this is going to work out all right. It's always easier to explain why you crowded a department regulation if you've got the killer in custody. Trust me, I've been there."

I read the document. It was a boilerplate form on Baltimore City Police Department letterhead that essentially said I was temporarily acting as an agent of the police and that this didn't entitle me to break any state or federal laws. At the end, there was a statement saying I henceforth and forever surrendered any rights to sue the City of Baltimore or its employees if I were to be injured or killed during my time of service. The last bit was the standard "hold harmless" waiver that always gives a personal injury attorney a fit of the giggles, because it isn't worth the ink with which it was printed.

I signed the form, dated it, and handed it back to Mulvaney, who tossed it on a nearby desk.

I held my cane out for Delcambre to take. "It's probably best if you hang onto this. Just in case he cops to something criminal, we don't want some defense attorney later claiming that the only reason he confessed was because I threatened to cudgel him."

"Good idea, and here." She pulled my wallet from her jacket pocket and tossed it to me. "I forgot I had it."

I caught it and shoved it into my jacket pocket. "Thanks, Lieutenant."

Tony was seated at the table, his face buried in his hands. It was warm in the room and he'd taken off his heavy jacket, revealing the periwinkle I WUV CHEERY CHERUB BEARS T-shirt. When he looked up, he wore a heartbroken expression and it seemed as if his eyes were red from prolonged crying. However, I'd been a cop long enough to know that you can achieve the same effect by vigorously rubbing your eye sockets. His gaze flicked from the lieutenant to me and I noticed Tony's jaw tighten. My presence made him angry, which suited my purposes just fine, because if he wasn't in control of his emotions, someone else was going to be . . . namely me.

Tony snapped, "What the hell is he doing in here?"

"Mr. Lyon is helping us with our inquiries," Mulvaney said as we both sat down.

"I told you, I've got nothing to say. I want my attorney."

"Then don't say anything, you pinhead. Just listen for a few minutes," I said, knowing that the surest way to get someone like Tony to talk was to tell him to be quiet. "We think that Todd framed you for Jennifer's murder, but with your stellar background as a wife-beater and the way the evidence is stacked against you right now, you're in the same shape as a cork from an open bottle of wine."

"Huh?"

"Screwed."

"Todd? That little punk killed Jen?"

"That little punk's middle name should be Burlington-Northern, because he not only murdered your wife, he's railroaded you."

"I'll kill him!" Tony bellowed, as he jumped up from the chair.

Although Tony was a consummate actor, I realized that the explosion of unreasoning rage wasn't a performance. He was behaving in precisely the same manner I would if Ash had been murdered and I'd just learned the identity of the killer. Furthermore, I shouldn't have been surprised by the violence of his response, because, in their own twisted ways, abusers do love their spouses.

Tony began hammering at the door, shouting, "Let me out of here! I'll hunt him down and rip his goddamned heart out with my bare hands!"

I sat back in the chair and crossed my fingers on my chest. "Dude, you're missing the big picture. You're going to be in prison for a long time, so you aren't going to do *anything* to him."

"I'll —"

"You'll shut up and listen to me. Unless you like the idea of spending twenty-three hours a day in a tiny cell with the banjo player from *Deliverance,* while Todd assumes squatter's rights over the Cheery Cherub Bears, you'll give us the background information we need."

Tony turned on me with balled fists. "You think this is funny?"

It took every ounce of fortitude I possessed to maintain my relaxed posture. "No, it's just a sordid and very avoidable tragedy that began a couple of years ago when Jennifer stole a bunch of teddy bears from a dead kid's bedroom. Was that her idea or yours?"

The big man suddenly sagged a little, and his eyes wouldn't meet mine. "You know . . ."

"Yeah, I talked with Donna earlier today and she told me the whole heartwarming story. But what I don't understand is why you didn't accuse her of murder when the cops arrested you."

"For what, yelling at us at the breakfast? Hell, I figured we had that coming."

"Are you trying to say that you didn't know that Donna went into your room during the cocktail reception last night?"

"What?" The look of shock appeared genuine. "Then, couldn't she have killed Jen?"

"No, she just went in there to drop off a picture of her son to remind you grave robbers of what you'd done."

"I never saw a picture."

"Tell me what happened when you went back to your room last night."

"I unlocked the door. Jen went in first and I put the pizzas on the table."

I glanced at Mulvaney, who nodded. "There were two pizza boxes in the trash."

"And after you went into the room, what did Jennifer do?" I asked Tony, who'd lowered himself into the chair.

"I don't know. She was sitting on the bed, messing with a bear. I wasn't paying much attention because I was hungry and I'm not supposed to go near the bears with anything greasy."

"And she didn't mention finding a picture of Benjamin Jordan in your room?"

"No." There was a pause and then Tony continued in a softer and shame-filled voice,

"But then again, Jen wouldn't have."

"Why?"

"Because it was my idea that she take the angel bears and I kind of used to lose my temper when she talked about what a crappy thing we'd done."

"Is that a sanitized way of saying you went Mike Tyson on her if she made the mistake of saying something you didn't like?"

"I have anger-control issues."

"That sounds like a big 'yes.' Why did you make her take the bears?"

"We needed the money. I wasn't making enough at that lousy job and there was no other way."

"Enough money for what? Were you in danger of losing your house?"

"No."

"And you obviously have plenty of groceries, so what was the financial situation that made you decide there was no other way?"

"Is it such a big crime that I wanted a Harley?"

Tony's voice was growing increasingly whiny and I snapped, "Please forgive me for sounding a little judgmental, but if you don't make enough money to buy a motorcycle, you get a second job, or become a gigolo, or even sell one of your kidneys at an online auction. You don't solve the income problem by stealing teddy bears that were supposed to be donated to the freaking children's ward of a hospital!"

Todd winced. "You don't understand."

"And thank God I don't, because if I thought there was even the remotest possibility I could, I'd put my head in an oven and blow out the pilot light. Was it also your idea that Jennifer go into business making the pirated versions of the Cheery Cherub Bears?"

"Yes, sir."

"And then Todd came into the picture." I pulled the bag of M&M's from my pocket and tossed it onto the table in front of Tony as a peace offering. "I heard you didn't get enough lunch. You want some dessert?"

"Thank you."

"My pleasure. Now tell me about Todd."

SEVENTEEN

Tiny bonfires were ignited in Tony's eyes. "Everybody thinks that Todd is the greatest thing since canned beer. A paramedic, writes kiddy books, loves teddy bears . . . oh, he's Lance Armstrong, all-American boy, but he's a slimy son of a bitch."

Considering that only a few seconds earlier, Tony had rationalized his forcing Jennifer into a new profession in grave robbery as an unavoidable economic necessity, I was eager, and I'll admit it, a little creeped out at the prospect of learning what *he* thought constituted slimy behavior. I nodded for him to continue, deciding not to point out that he'd confused the Tour de France winner with a fictional character from an old radio show.

"That scene at breakfast . . . I wasn't being paranoid about him trying to put the move on my wife. He was always hovering around Jen, trying to show her how much better he was than me." Tony tore the M&M's bag open and poured several of the candies into his mouth.

"Yeah, it was obvious he was attracted to her. Did she feel the same way about him?" I asked.

"No . . . at least that's what she told me."

But the doubt in Tony's voice led me to deduce that Jennifer's denials of being attracted to Todd hadn't been very convincing — whether or not she actually was, it would have been an exquisitely cruel and satisfying mind game to play on the man who abused her.

"So, if you loathe him and Jen said she didn't have any feelings for Todd, how did he become such a big part of Cheery Cherub Bears?"

"The only way he got involved with our bears was because he forced his way in."

I was taken aback by the sheer effrontery of Tony's last statement and wanted to say: *Your bears?* However, I didn't want to interrupt his story by goading him. So, I bit my tongue and said, "How did he do that?"

"He blackmailed us. Me."

"When did this happen?"

"It started about fourteen months ago." Tony dumped another bunch of candy into his mouth and began crunching away.

"Was that when you met him?"

"Yeah. One night, Jen and I were having an argument and she started having trouble breathing." Tony raised his hand to ostensibly rub his nose, but he was actually covering his mouth, a Body Language 101 clue that he wasn't telling the entire truth.

"Asthma?"

"No. I uh . . ."

Suddenly, I understood why he was hesitant to continue. "Did you choke her?"

"She was calling me names and I reached out and accidentally grabbed her here." Todd motioned vaguely toward the front of his neck.

"Like this?" I asked incredulously, positioning my right hand in the same shape I would if I were holding a large glass tumbler.

The grip was what's known among cops as a C-Clamp. Applied perfectly, the fingers briefly pinch off the flow of the blood to the brain, rendering the victim unconscious in seconds. However, it's a physical restraint hold outlawed by almost every law enforcement agency in the United States. That's because you can easily miss the carotid artery, crush the windpipe, and kill someone with such a grip. I glanced at Mulvaney, who'd dropped her hand out of Tony's view and had unconsciously begun to open and close her hand into a fist.

Tony nodded sheepishly and muttered, "Kind of."

"So . . . you, 'kind of' actually strangled her and it really wouldn't be accurate to say that she was having *trouble* breathing when in fact, there wasn't any . . ." I stared at Tony, trying to will him to finish the sentence.

"Okay, she couldn't breathe! I didn't mean it."

"I know. It was that old anger-control problem. So, she's lying there gagging on the floor. What did you do?"

"I was scared, so I called nine-one-one."

"Good man. What happened then?"

"I remember thinking we were lucky, because the EMTs were already out on a call and were only a few blocks away. They got there in just a couple of seconds."

"And Todd was one of the EMTs?"

"Yeah, him and some real young guy who I could tell was a rookie."

"And then?"

"He had this oxygen tank and put this plastic tube partway down her throat and a second later she was breathing again."

"Hallelujah. Good as new and ready for some more roughhouse fun, right?"

Tony pouted. "It was an accident."

"Unlike all the other times. How did you explain how she got injured?"

"This happened in the kitchen and I told them that Jen had slipped and hit her throat against the edge of the counter."

"Slipped? On what, a banana peel? Why did you think anyone would believe a comic strip idea like that?"

"Because before the paramedics got there, I, uh . . . kind of poured some olive oil on the floor and . . . um . . ."

Realizing where the tale was going, I held my hands up in supplication. "Stop! Please don't tell me that you made slip marks through the oil with her shoes."

"They were slippers," Tony whispered.

"Yeah, I'll say they were. Let me get this straight: you took her slippers off, ran them through the olive oil, and put them back on her feet while she was lying there choking to death?"

I was laughing now as a defensive mechanism, because the interview had just descended into a new and lower level of horror in a Comstock Lode of squalidness. Beside me, Mulvaney was rubbing her forehead while glaring at Tony.

"I was on probation! They were going to send me to prison if I was arrested again,"

Tony wailed.

I managed to stifle my chuckling, wiped my eyes, and said, "Which is exactly where you belong, you scumbag and you want to know the hell of it?"

"What?"

"After everything you've done, you'll be a free man when you leave the police station. God, I wish I'd brought my cane in here." The spasm of gallows humor was instantly gone. "So, when did the police arrive?"

"How did you know about that?"

"It wasn't difficult to guess. One of the things that us mean ole cops do is make little notes of the houses where guys are victims of anger-control problems that cause them to hurt their wives." I glanced at Mulvaney, who nodded in tight-lipped agreement. I continued, "In fact, if Basingstoke Township has computer-aided dispatch, I'd wager they've got your number and home address red-flagged in the system for an automatic police response, because you've already been arrested for domestic violence."

"Oh."

"So, answer the question."

"The police got there maybe five minutes after Todd got Jen to start breathing again." Tony scowled, reliving an unpleasant memory. "He'd gotten her into a kitchen chair and he was kneeling there next to her, holding her hand and telling her that she was going to be all right and she was looking at him like he was so wonderful."

"How completely irrational of her. Did you think Todd believed the story about the olive oil?"

"No. He didn't say anything, but he gave me this who're-you-kidding look." Tony poured the remainder of the M&M's into his mouth, crumpled the wrapper in his fist, and tossed it onto the table.

"You think he knew you were on probation?"

"Probably."

I nodded in agreement. Life in Remmelkemp Mill had taught me that there was no such thing as a secret in a small town. "Then you must have been shaking in your space-boots when the cops arrived."

"I was scared."

"Yet, you're here instead of working in a prison chow-line. I'm dying to know why."

"There were two policemen and I told them the story of how Jen slipped on the oil . . . and they were standing there looking at me, just like you guys are looking at me . . . like you want to hit me." Incredibly, there was a tiny bit of self-righteousness in

Tony's voice.

"Sorry. Sometimes, Lieutenant Mulvaney and I have anger-control issues, too. Go on."

"Then one of the cops asked Jennifer what happened and she told them that she'd slipped."

I wasn't surprised. Remember what I said a little earlier about how, in his own bizarre way, Tony genuinely loved Jennifer? Well, the same thing was likely true of Jennifer. Despite the violence, like so many other battered spouses, she loved Tony and was willing to lie to protect him. I'm not going to pretend to understand all the psychological dynamics, but I've talked to far more domestic violence victims than I'd care to remember and I've learned something: many won't tell the truth to the police about how they were injured because they retain this pathetic hope that if they actively aid in the cover up of an assault, they'll somehow prove to their attacker that they're "good enough" and this will stop the violence. This vicious cycle can go on for decades until the victim finally wises up . . . or is injured so badly they're in no position to tell any further lies to the police because they're dead.

Emerging from my brief reverie, I said, "I'll bet the cops didn't believe Jen either."

"No. I think they knew she was covering for me. Then one of them tells Todd that he's not in the mood to listen to any more BS from me and wants to know how Jen really got hurt."

"Imagine a public servant saying that sort of thing about you. I hope you got his badge number and made a complaint."

Tony folded his arms across his chest. "Look, do you want to hear my story or make fun of me?"

"Both, actually, but I'll really try to keep my smart mouth shut."

Mulvaney shot me a look of sarcastic amazement that said: *Yeah, as if* that's *going to happen.*

There was a long pause, and I could see that Tony was weighing the pleasures of telling me where I could stick the interview against his need to clear his name in a capital murder case. Finally, he said, "So, the cop asks how she really got hurt. Todd looks at Jen and she's looking at him, like silently begging him not to tell what really happened. Finally, Todd tells the cops that he really thinks Jen slipped on the oil and that her injuries aren't suspicious."

"You think the cops believed him?"

"They were surprised and kept asking him if he was sure, but he stuck with his story."

"I'll bet you were shocked . . . and relieved."

"You could've knocked me over with a feather. At first, I thought I was wrong. Maybe he *had* bought the story."

"But?"

"But, once the police left, Todd sent his partner out to the paramedic truck. Then he starts talking to Jennifer about her teddy bears and how he's admired her since he saw the article about her in the newspaper. Then he asks to see the teddy bears."

"Did that annoy you?"

"A little, but I figure I gotta be nice to the guy because he saved Jen's life."

"Was it possible that you were also concerned that if you made him angry, he might change his mind about how she got hurt and tell the police what he thought really happened?"

"That's partway true. I mean, the guy didn't say anything right away, but I got this vibe from him like he thought he was in control." Tony's gaze went upward as he recalled the event. "Anyway, Jen shows him the bears and he's so interested that I begin to figure maybe he's weird or something, because normal guys don't get so loopy over teddy bears."

"Present company excepted," I said dryly,

while peering at the I WUV CHEERY CHERUB BEARS on his chest.

Tony realized where I was looking. "Hey, all I do is sell bears. I'm not like those losers that collect them."

"Hmm. At last count, my wife and I own over five hundred teddy bears and we'll probably go home with at least one more, because I've got my eye on one of Penny French's bears." I turned to Mulvaney. "Do I look like a loser to you? Be honest."

Mulvaney cleared her throat. "I think I'd rather be a loser than a procurer."

Tony flinched.

Looking back at him, I said, "But we digress. Todd is in your house making a fool of himself over the teddy bears, and . . . ?"

Tony took a deep breath. "Then he starts talking about how he's always dreamed of writing and illustrating kids' books and that he'd come up with a perfect idea a few months ago for Cheery Cherub Bears books, but that he was too shy to come and talk to her. All the while, he's looking at Jen like she's a big bowl of ice cream. Hey, you don't need to spell it out for me: I can tell he's sniffing around my wife."

"What an interesting way of putting it," I said. "How did Jennifer react to this attention?"

"In the beginning, she was nice to him."

"Do you think she was nice to him because she thought he was attractive or because she had to be?" I resisted adding: *Or because she knew the idea of her flirting with another man would drive you freaking nuts.*

"Because she had to," Tony snapped.

"Yeah, that's what I think, too. So, what happened then?"

"Todd keeps talking about the kids' books and how great they'd be with the bears. I'm starting to lose my temper, so I ask if he doesn't have someplace else to go. He turns to me and says that he'd really like to work with us on the bears, because it'll be good for his mental health." Tony's voice was growing more and more acidic. "Then he gives me this crap-eating smile and says, it'll help him to forget the bad things he sees as a paramedic."

"I guess *that* didn't need to be spelled out for you either," I said, noticing that Mulvaney's eyes were closed and she was shaking her head in disbelief.

"No. That was crystal clear. He was in . . . working with the bears and with my wife. Otherwise, he'd snitch on me and I'd go to prison."

"That was a pretty rotten thing for him to do."

"Tell me about it."

"And he could blackmail you until your probation expires. When does that happen?"

"I was released from it two months ago."

"So, Todd became part of the Cheery Cherub Bears team. What did Jennifer think of the situation?"

"She didn't like it."

"I assumed that, but did you tell her to be nice to Todd?"

"What do you mean by 'nice?' " Todd's tone grew hostile.

"You know, nice. Pleasant to be around."

"You'd better watch your mouth."

"Cool your jets, Tony. I'm not suggesting you pimped your wife to stay out of prison."

"You'd better not be."

"Count on it, because I know you'd have killed Jennifer before letting her sleep with another man."

"That's right!" Tony's mouth sagged open and his pupils were visibly constricting from fear. "I didn't mean that."

"Of course, you did. Jen knew it, too," I said gently. "That's why she'd never have had an affair with Todd. But you did ask her to be friendly with him, right? Just to keep things peaceful?"

"Yeah, but that's all it was. She thought the guy was a geek."

"So, if the motive wasn't romance, how about money? Tell me what happened with Todd and his books."

"There's nothing much to tell. Some people thought the books were cute, but we didn't really sell that many more bears." Tony put his hands behind his head, another telltale sign that he was lying to us. Think of what many animals do when they're trying to bluff an opponent. Cats arch their back and dogs puff their chests out and their tails curl upward. In short, they make themselves appear bigger and more menacing, which was what Tony was doing at this very moment.

"Okay, so they weren't successful, but who holds the copyrights?"

"Well . . ."

"Oh, my." Recalling the gathering of Wintle Toy execs at the cocktail reception and the sight of Todd receiving some very bad news, an ugly thought occurred to me. I continued, "Maybe I should have phrased that last question a little differently. Did Todd ever copyright his books?"

"I don't think so."

"And are they about to be copyrighted by Wintle Toys . . . say first thing Monday morning?"

"That's possible." Tony lowered his arms and began to fiddle with the balled-up candy wrapper.

"Is it also possible that you and Jen screwed Todd and that he won't get a penny out of this big merchandising contract you just signed with Wintle and that cartoon outfit?"

"Everything was done legally. We broke no laws."

"You learned that line from their corporate lawyer, didn't you? Please answer my question."

"The sneaky little bastard got exactly what he deserved. Whose fault is it if he didn't copyright his stuff?"

"Does Todd know yet?"

"No, it'll be a nice surprise . . . for us, I guess." Tony chuckled.

"And Jennifer went along with this?" Suddenly I understood what the couple had been arguing about on Friday morning.

"She was concerned about Todd suing us."

"She should have been more concerned about Todd killing you. Are the Wintle people staying at the Maritime Inn?"

"No, some other hotel. Why?"

It was all beginning to make sense, but I was lacking one vital piece of information.

"Who was there from Wintle? Was one of them a thin woman?"

"Yeah."

"And was she at the cocktail reception, wearing black pants and a black duster?"

"A what?"

"A long black coat."

"Yeah, that's Carolyn Fielding. She's the executive VP of licensing."

"I saw her breaking some sort of bad news to Todd on Friday night at the cocktail reception and he disappeared shortly thereafter, so I have to find out what she told him. What hotel are they staying at?"

"I don't know and it doesn't make any difference. They're flying back to El Paso this afternoon."

Mulvaney was already pushing past me and heading for the door, saying, "I'll call Baltimore-Washington International Airport. There can't be that many flights to El Paso and maybe they're delayed because of the rain."

"Leave me your notepad," I said to Mulvaney and she tossed it to me as she went out the door. I pulled a ballpoint pen from my shirt pocket. "What are the names of the other people from Wintle?"

"There was Mr. Wintle — his first name is Jeffrey — and Mr. Coburn, he's the corporate attorney, but I don't remember his first name. There was also one other guy that I think was the vice president of marketing, but I can't remember his name either."

I jotted the names down on the pad. "Kind of a sloppy way to do business. Would your lawyer know all the names?"

"What lawyer?"

"You didn't have a lawyer look over the contract before signing it?" I stared at Tony in naked disbelief.

"Lawyers cost money. Besides, I can read a contract."

"You know there's this old adage about doing things *pro per.*"

"Pro per?"

"It's Latin for not getting a real attorney and acting as your own legal counsel. The saying goes something like this: The person that acts as his own lawyer has a fool for a client."

"You know, I'm really tired of you talking down to me. Are we done here?" Tony barked.

"I just have one final question: What did Lucifer look like when you sold your soul to him?"

EIGHTEEN

By the time I left the interview room, Mulvaney was on the phone at a nearby work cubicle, saying, “No, it isn’t all right if you put me on hold. This is . . . hello?”

“And they put you on hold anyway, right?” I said.

“Yeah.”

“Here are a couple of the other names.” I slid the notepad in front of her. “And when you get them back on the line, don’t bother checking Southwest Airlines. They don’t have first-class seating and the Wintle group are definitely not the sort of folks to ride with the rabble in coach.”

“I’m not calling airport operations. I’m calling the Maryland State Police. The airport is under their jurisdiction.”

“And they can coordinate with TSA to run the names through the computer? Good idea.”

Delcambre came out of the audio-visual

control room looking irked. Handing me my cane, he nodded toward the interview room door. "I've been on the job for eighteen years and the one thing I've never gotten used to is the fact that nothing bad ever really happens to dung beetles like that."

"That's true, but I've found it helps a little to try and remember that dung beetles live their entire lives in a universe of crap and they're acutely aware of it. It never gets any better for them than that, which can't be pleasant."

"I guess," Delcambre said, not sounding convinced. He turned to Mulvaney. "I'm going to fill out the paperwork to release Swift. The faster we get him out of the station, the cleaner the air will be in here."

She nodded and held up her hand for silence. Speaking into the receiver, she said, "Yes, thanks for getting back to me today. I'm Lieutenant Sarah Mulvaney from the Baltimore City Police and I'm making an official request for information about passengers that are scheduled to fly to El Paso today. We're working a homicide here and this is an emergency. Yes, I know you have to confirm my identity. I'm going to give you the number for police dispatch, so you can call and ask them to transfer you to my extension. It's . . ."

Realizing that it was going to be at least a minute or two until Mulvaney could even request that the names be checked in the Transportation Security Administration database, I followed Delcambre over to his desk. He sat down, pushed the computer mouse back and forth until the machine emerged from "sleep" mode, and clicked on the word processing icon. A moment later, he was typing Tony's name and other personal information onto a form on the screen labeled, "Release of Prisoner Without Criminal Charges."

From the other side of the office partition, we heard the phone trill. Mulvaney answered it before the first ring was completed. "Southeastern District Robbery-Homicide, this is Lieutenant Mulvaney. . . . Okay, so now you know who I am. I need you to check your outbound passenger list. Last name is Fielding — common spelling — and first name is Carolyn, and I don't know the spelling, so it could be 'i-n-e' or with a 'y'. She's supposed to be flying to El Paso this afternoon. The next name is Wintle . . ."

Delcambre looked up from the computer. "I was thinking about that. A major toy company headquartered in El Paso? Isn't that kind of strange?"

"Not really," I replied. "The corporate offices are in El Paso, but I'll wager the factories are just across the border in Ciudad Juarez, where they don't have to pay that annoying American minimum wage or provide any benefits."

"Dung beetles."

"Yep. I'm going to go back and see what the lieutenant's learned."

Delcambre clicked on the "print" icon and his laser printer began to whine. "Yeah, I'll be with you in a second."

By the time I returned to the other cubicle, Mulvaney was bent over and writing on a note pad. "They're on what airline? Has the flight left yet? No? When? Okay, we're en route now, ETA driving time from downtown. Please listen carefully: I want you guys to contact all four people in that travel group. They are material witnesses in a homicide that occurred earlier this morning and I need to talk to them."

Delcambre walked past, headed toward the interview room. He asked me, "Success?"

"It seems they're still on the ground."

"Thank God for bad weather. I'll get Swift to sign this thing and get him out of here." Delcambre went into the interview room.

There were a few seconds of silence as

Mulvaney listened and rolled her eyes. Clearly losing her patience, she said, "Yes, I realize that they're just witnesses and you have no legal right to detain them. All I'm asking for is a little cooperation . . ."

"May I?" I held out my hand for the phone and Mulvaney slapped it into my palm. I said, "Hi, this is Inspector Callahan. This is what we want your officers to tell the Wintle travel group: we're coming out to ask them some potentially embarrassing questions about a murder and we can either do that in the first-class lounge in front of all the other Martini-sipping social elite or more privately in the State Police offices. We're easy. Got that?"

The woman on the other end of the line said, "Yes, sir."

"*Muy excellente.* When you hear back from your officers as to what the Wintle group has decided, call Baltimore City Police dispatch and have them relay us the information over the radio because we're about to make a code-three run to your location," I said, using the California police expression for driving with emergency lights and siren on.

"Yes, sir."

I was hanging up the phone as Delcambre opened the interview room door and motioned with his hand for Tony to come out. The detective said, "Let's go. As much as it disgusts me to say it, you're a free man. Follow me to the lobby."

"How do I get back to the hotel?"

"Walk. Call a cab. Swim through the sewers, for all I care," said Delcambre.

"Don't go back to the hotel," I cut in.

"Why not?" Tony demanded.

"Because, whatever your faults, I know you really did love your wife and you'll go back there to kill Todd."

"You can't tell me what to do or where I can or can't go! That little bastard killed my wife and I'm going to tear his head off and —"

I glanced at Mulvaney. "I'm not telling you what to do, but I'd lock him back up until we're done."

"For what?" Tony and Mulvaney asked simultaneously.

"How about deliberately providing false information to the police in a murder investigation? As I recall, he told you that I was the killer."

There was a flash of ruthless merriment in Mulvaney's eyes. "That's right, he did say that. Anthony Swift, you're under arrest for willfully interfering with an official investigation. Turn around so we can handcuff you."

"I'm not going back to that cell. You released me."

"For murder. This is a new and different charge," said Mulvaney.

"Oh, and please resist arrest, because I know the three of us would enjoy using only that physical force necessary to overcome your resistance," added Delcambre, making what I suspected was a quotation from the Baltimore Police regulations sound extraordinarily menacing.

Like all bullies, Tony was a yellow cur at heart. He apparently saw something in our faces that he didn't like, because he turned around and put his hands behind his back. Delcambre handcuffed him and started to lead him away.

"We don't have the time to fight traffic to get to the airport, so on your way back from the cells, grab a set of keys to a marked cruiser," Mulvaney told the departing detective.

"I'm driving," Delcambre called out as he led Tony around the corner.

Noticing Mulvaney's lips twitch ever so slightly, I asked, "Is that not a good thing?"

"Do you like amusement park thrill rides?"

"Not particularly."

"We won't actually go upside down, but it may feel like it. Let me go and grab my coat," said Mulvaney, heading for her office.

"Speaking of coats, you wouldn't let me bring mine when you arrested me. Do you have a spare jacket or something here?"

"Let's see." Mulvaney slowed her pace and began to visually inspect each work cubicle. Then she darted into one and came out with a blue coat. The jacket had Baltimore City Police patches on the shoulders and the word POLICE in bright yellow block letters on the back. She tossed it to me saying, "As long as you're impersonating a Baltimore cop, you might as well look like one."

A couple of minutes later, we crossed the parking lot to the police cruiser. The rain was no longer coming down in a blinding torrent, but it was still fairly heavy, which didn't bode well for a high-speed journey to the airport. I lowered myself into the backseat of the patrol car, while Delcambre got behind the wheel and Mulvaney belted herself into the front passenger seat. Delcambre fired the engine up with a roar and I was a little disturbed when I thought I heard him chuckle.

Racing through the parking lot, he turned the overhead emergency lights and siren on, and made a right turn onto Eastern Avenue. Then Delcambre accelerated in a fashion very similar to an F-14 Tomcat fighter jet being catapult-launched from the deck of an aircraft carrier. We went from zero to seventy in about seven seconds and I was slammed back into the seat by the insanely abrupt increase in speed. Then, without warning, he blew the red light and made a sluing right turn onto another street.

Several high-speed turns later, we were southbound on Interstate 895, otherwise known as the Harbor Tunnel Thruway. Now that we were off the city streets and on a freeway, Delcambre apparently decided he could really open it up and fly. However, there was a problem with that theory. Under optimum circumstances, other drivers are usually completely oblivious to the approach of an emergency vehicle, and our current conditions were awful. It was raining and all of the other motorists had their car windows up, so nobody could hear the siren and visibility was so poor that no one could see the flashing blue and red lights until the very last second. This tended to cause panicked reactions from the other drivers when they suddenly realized they had a cop car careening past them on the left . . . or right . . . or in the breakdown lane. I noticed that Delcambre wasn't partial to any particular path.

We ran into heavier traffic at the junction of the Tunnel Thruway and Interstate 95. Most sane people would have taken this as an unmistakable sign to slow down, but Delcambre simply increased the frequency of his zigzags. Not long afterwards, we descended into the Harbor Tunnel, where the roadway narrowed and Delcambre was actually forced to reduce his speed to *Star Trek* impulse power. However, he stomped hard on the gas pedal when we came out on the south side of the harbor, and when I idiotically looked over the detective's shoulder, I saw that we were doing a cool eighty miles an hour when we flew past the tollbooth plaza.

Not that I could hear anything in the backseat and over the siren, but I guessed there was a radio call for Mulvaney, because she snatched the microphone from its holder on the dash. There was a brief exchange of mimed conversation and then Mulvaney shouted back to me, "They've agreed to talk to us until three o'clock when their jet begins boarding, and they'll meet us at the state police offices at the airport!"

"It's two-twenty-five now, but please don't hurry on my account!" I yelled back.

We were about two miles from the interchange with the Baltimore-Washington Parkway when traffic began to clog and the roadway seemed filled with a solid brake-light wall of eighteen-wheelers. The rain was coming down hard again and so fast that the windshield wipers were almost useless. Delcambre swerved hard to the right, shot into the slow lane, and right there in front of us and nearly at a stop was a huge cement mixer truck. We were going maybe seventy miles an hour and I realized there was no room to stop and that we were about to die.

My brain was filled with a sudden and peculiar mélange of practical and esoteric questions, all occurring instantaneously. Was this going to hurt as much as I anticipated? How was Ash going to take the news that after all those dangerous years of cop work and with the joyful prospect of several decades ahead of us making teddy bears together, that I'd gone and gotten myself killed in a car accident? Why was this truck even out here, because what sort of fool pours cement in heavy rain? Was there a heaven? And more importantly, if there was and if, on account of some angelic paperwork mix-up I actually got in, would St. Peter be willing to explain to Ash, when she finally arrived, that she shouldn't be too cross with me? After all, except for the fact that I'd knowingly gotten into a car driven by an amateur auto stunt driver, and was aware in advance that we'd be traveling at breakneck speeds on a series of wet, slick, and crowded highways on one of the rainiest days of the year, I really *had* tried to be careful.

I shut my eyes, yet the expected collision didn't happen. Don't ask me why, since the only answer I can come up with is that Delcambre secretly possesses some sort of superhero powers that allow him to alter the flow of time or maybe the physical properties of the universe. It's the only thing that makes sense, because although there wasn't any room to maneuver, he somehow did. I heard a truck's horn blare, we veered hard to the right, and at the last second we swerved into the right-side emergency lane.

The other amazing thing about the episode was that Mulvaney didn't so much as grimace as we narrowly avoided being the guests of honor at a police funeral. I was impressed. And now that I knew her a little better, I was willing to give her the benefit of the doubt and attribute her stoic reaction to steady nerves and not face-paralyzing cosmetics.

Once we were clear of the tie-up and back on the highway, Delcambre looked over his shoulder at me. "Scared?"

"Not so you'd notice," I replied through clenched teeth.

"You need to do what I do."

"What's that?"

"Keep your eyes shut," he said with a giggle.

"You're killing me, Shecky. Hey, Lieutenant?"

"What?" Mulvaney said.

"I've got an embarrassing request to make."

"Do we need to stop at a restroom?"

"No, worse. Can you call ahead to the airport and have one of those golf cart things standing by for me? By the time I hobble to the State Police offices, it'll be five o'clock."

"I'll take care of it . . . and it's nothing to be ashamed of," said Mulvaney, reaching for the radio microphone.

"Thanks."

We made the transition onto Interstate 195 and in the distance I could see the tall parking structures that stand in front of Baltimore-Washington International Airport. Delcambre asked, "Are the State Police offices on the ground or upper level?"

"Upper," said Mulvaney.

Delcambre nodded and got into the lane marked for arriving flights. A moment later, we skidded to a stop in front of the terminal. There was a Maryland state trooper in a rain jacket, sheltering beneath an overhang and watching the flow of traffic. Noticing the arrival of the cruiser, she jogged over. Meanwhile, Delcambre opened the police car's back door and helped me out.

"I'm supposed to lead you guys to the office," said the trooper.

"Did you receive our request for the handicapped transportation?" asked Mulvaney, getting out of the patrol car.

The trooper pointed through the sliding glass doors. Inside the terminal, I saw a small white golf cart. It had a rotating yellow light mounted on its front bumper and a cheerful purple-haired lady who looked old enough to be my mother sitting behind the wheel. Knowing that the vehicle would also make a shrill beeping sound throughout its journey, I suddenly regretted having asked for the special transportation. However, there was nothing to do now but swallow my pride and accept the ride to the State Police offices.

We went into the terminal and as I clambered aboard the cart, the driver said, "Hi, hon."

"Pleased to meet you" — I squinted at her name tag — "Thelma."

"C'mon," said Mulvaney, as she, the trooper, and Delcambre began jogging through the concourse.

"Hey, can you do a tail job?" I did my best Humphrey Bogart, complete with facial tic.

Thelma grinned, obviously remembering the scene from *The Big Sleep* where Bogie asks the woman taxi driver to follow Joe Brody's car to the Randall Arms. "I'm your girl."

"Then follow them, but don't get too close."

The old woman gunned the cart and with yellow light flashing, we beeped our way through the terminal in pursuit.

NINETEEN

The State Police office was located down a corridor that led from the terminal's main concourse and by the time I arrived, Mulvaney and Delcambre had already gone inside. However, the trooper who'd met us at the curb was waiting for me, holding the door open. I came as close as I ever will these days to leaping from the cart, thanked Thelma for chauffeuring me through the airport, and hurried into the office. Inside there was a tiny lobby with the inevitable bulletproof-glass reception window and an armor-plated door that looked as if it could withstand an anti-tank missile strike. There was a buzzing sound as someone disengaged the electronic lock. The trooper pulled that door open and I followed her through an empty clerical office to a snug roll call room at the end of a short hallway.

It was like every other cop briefing room I've ever visited. At the front was a small table where the shift supervisor sat during roll call. A chalkboard was on the wall behind the desk and it bore the underlined message: ALL OVERTIME MUST BE APPROVED IN ADVANCE! Beneath it, some anonymous dissenting cop had scrawled: "Just as soon as I develop ESP and can predict when there'll be a last minute call, you fool." The tables and chairs where the troopers would sit were the usual ratty and mismatched assortment of hand-me-downs and throwaways that inevitably end up at police stations. There was a large blueprint-style map of the airport on one wall, a combination TV-VHS tape player on a table in the corner for watching training videos, and clipboards hanging from hooks loaded with wanted posters from the FBI that no one had ever looked at. The only thing missing were the state police officers; they were all out at work.

Instead, there were Mulvaney, Delcambre, and the foursome of plutocrats I'd seen at the teddy bear show cocktail reception the previous evening. It was warm in the room and everyone had taken off their coats. The Wintle execs were dressed in business casual for the flight home and none of them looked even remotely cheerful.

One of the men was making a big point of

studying his platinum wristwatch, which I had no doubt was a Rolex that had cost more than our Nissan Xterra. The man appeared to be in his early sixties with an aquiline nose that looked as if it had once been broken and imperfectly set. His glossy, perfectly styled hair was the same color as a polished silver dollar, his teeth were white and flawless, and his skin was that golden tone only attainable after many hours in a tanning salon. The only incongruous element was that his fingernails were bitten to the quick. From the way everyone was watching him, I assumed he was Jeffrey Wintle and Mulvaney confirmed this when she made the introductions.

The other three Wintle suits were the company's legal counsel, Steven Coburn, Peter Kinney, the vice president of manufacturing, and Carolyn Fielding, the VP of licensing. Coburn was short — maybe five-five — slight in build and those features, combined with oversized upper incisors, a receding hairline, and cold brown eyes, brought to mind the image of an attack Chihuahua. Kinney was a half-foot taller and older, with hair and a moustache that looked as if it had been dyed with Kiwi brand cordovan boot polish. Fielding was willowy, yet her face was fleshy and heart shaped. Her jaw was a little slack and the skin beneath her eyes was puffy and gray, which led me to believe that she was weary and had been so for some time.

"You aren't with the police." Wintle gave me an accusatory look and, although he lived in west Texas, his accent marked him as a transplant from somewhere in the urban Northeast.

"You know me?"

"I'm the owner of one of the biggest toy and stuffed animal companies in the country. It's my business to know you. Lyon's Tigers and Bears. Wife is Ashleigh, right? I like her work."

"So do I. Thank you and I'm impressed." It was no accident that he'd only commended Ash and ignored my work. I wasn't offended. In fact, my opinion of his expertise in teddy bears rose slightly and I was relieved that the guy wasn't going to give me a smoke-and-mirrors show.

"So, how come you're here with the police?"

"Back before I began to make mediocre teddy bears, I used to investigate murders for a living. I'm helping with this case."

"Then maybe you can start by telling me what the hell this has to do with us." He glanced at his watch. "Oh, and by the way, you've got seventeen minutes."

"It concerns you because Jennifer Swift was murdered this morning —"

"What?" Wintle gaped at me in disbelief.

I continued, "And the motive is more than likely connected with the licensing contract that she and Tony just signed with your company."

Kinney shook his head as if bewildered while Fielding turned to look at the map of the airport and then down at the floor.

Coburn put a cautionary hand on Wintle's shoulder. "Jeff, in light of the fact that this incident is probably going to generate a civil suit, I strongly recommend that you terminate this interview immediately."

"Mr. Wintle, neither you or your associates are considered suspects in this investigation," Mulvaney nervously cut in.

"We just want to know some details about the licensing contract," I added.

"Then I'd suggest you get a *subpoena dueces tecum* because we have nothing more to say. Good day." Coburn had precisely the sort of high-pitched raspy tone I'd expect from a talking Chihuahua that thought he was one cool and bad hombre. He nodded in the direction of the door. "Let's go, Jeff."

"Mr. Wintle, I realize we live in a world

full of ambulance-chasing lawyers." I shot a disdainful glance at Coburn. "And someone might file a lawsuit. But I'm asking you to do the right thing and help us."

"Jeff, let's *go.*" Coburn was slipping his jacket on.

"What if it was your wife or someone you loved lying there in the morgue and the killer was free?"

"Jeff."

Wintle shrugged and wouldn't meet my gaze. "Sorry. I'd like to help but . . . well, nothing personal, but this is strictly a business decision."

"Excuse me, Lieutenant?" Fielding asked diffidently. "Do you or the other detective have a blackjack or a sap?"

Mulvaney was baffled by the request. "No ma'am, those sorts of weapons are against department regulations. Why?"

Fielding gave me an imploring look. "Then could I borrow your cane for a minute, Mr. Lyon?"

"No, and, again, why?"

"Because I swear to God, if I hear one more person describe morally bankrupt behavior as 'just business' again, I'm going to hit them and I don't want to hurt my hand." Fielding erupted like one of those old Saturn V rockets that used to propel the

Apollo moon missions into orbit. "What are we, Wintle Toys or *Monsters Inc.*? Jeff, I've worked for you for over fifteen years and I've kept my mouth shut as you pulled off every sort of rotten legal stunt in the book. I even went along with you when you shifted our manufacturing out of the country to lower costs — and to avoid the child labor laws. But the era of me being a good 'team player' is officially done. We're talking about stonewalling over a murder that we might have helped cause and I won't go along with that."

The three men were stunned at her outburst and Kinney began to edge away from Fielding as though he'd suddenly discovered she had some sort of virulently contagious and fatal disease. Wintle's lips were compressed and I couldn't decide whether his cheeks were pink from shame or anger. Coburn was the first to recover his composure.

"I think it would be best if you calmed down, Carolyn." The lawyer sounded imperious, yet there was an underlying note of apprehension in his voice.

"And I think it would be best if you kept that sewer outlet you call a mouth shut, you revolting little shyster." Fielding's eyes were brilliant with anger. Turning to glare at

Wintle, she continued in a stiffly cadenced voice, "And you. For God's sake, Jennifer is dead and the only thing you're concerned about is damage control and the corporate profit margin. I had always hoped there was at least some limit to what you'd do for a buck, but I guess I was wrong. And here's the worst part —"

"Hey, you don't talk that way to me." Wintle raised a warning finger and pointed it at Fielding's nose.

"Yeah, how dare she suggest that you have some obligation to behave like a decent human being?" I sniped.

The CEO shot me a venomous look, but before he could retort, Fielding said, "You don't like what I have to say? Fine. So, fire me. No, better yet, I quit."

"Carolyn, you're overwrought." Coburn reached out to grab her right forearm, but she snapped it backwards and made as if to slap the lawyer.

"Don't touch me unless you want your little ass kicked, munchkin." Fielding turned to me. "I'll bet I can tell you exactly who you think killed Jennifer. It was Todd Litten, right?"

I nodded. "Yep."

"And you know why?"

"Tony told us part of the story. He basically said that he, Jennifer, and you guys all decided to screw Todd out of any share of the licensing contract. Whose idea was it originally?" I asked.

Fielding grimaced and swiped at some strands of hair that had fallen into her line of sight. "Jennifer's. She told us that Litten had forced his way into their original partnership and that he had nothing coming."

"Carol, let's go." This time Wintle reached to take Fielding's arm.

Delcambre swiftly moved between the CEO and Fielding, saying, "Ma'am, do you want any of these guys to touch you?"

"No."

"And you *do* want to tell us what happened, right?" Delcambre asked.

"Very much."

"Then we've got a new set of rules here, gentlemen." Delcambre put his hands on his hips and gave defiant stares to Wintle and then Coburn. "From now on, if anybody does anything to try and stop Ms. Fielding here from giving us a witness statement about this homicide, I'm going to arrest him for being an accessory after the fact to murder. Touch her and I'll add a count of battery. Do we understand each other?"

"You'd never get a conviction," said

Coburn.

"Maybe. You might beat the rap, but you won't beat the ride, counselor . . . the ride being in the backseat of a cop car to the police station in handcuffs. Right, Lieutenant?" asked Delcambre.

"There's nothing I'd like more." Mulvaney waved dismissively at Wintle, Coburn, and Kinney. "You three are free to go, if you want."

"We'll stay for now," Wintle grumbled.

"Fine, but no more interruptions. Brad, go on with your questioning."

"Thanks LT." I turned to Fielding. "When did Todd find out that the Swifts were in negotiations with Wintle?"

"Not until yesterday. Jennifer insisted that everything be kept a secret from Todd until after the contract was signed."

"How did he finally hear about the deal in progress?"

"He learned it from me." Although Fielding was speaking to me, her eyes were on Coburn and her lower jaw jutted out. "I went to the Maritime Inn yesterday morning, because I'm a fan of the books — which we were about to lawfully steal — and I wanted to meet the author." Fielding looked back at me. "It turned out that Todd had driven down from Pennsylvania the night before. He was sitting there in the exhibit hall, waiting like some dumb, loyal, patient dog in the empty spot where the Cheery Cherub Bears booth was going to be."

"And you liked him," I said.

"He was a refreshingly decent change from the people I work with."

"I'll bet you could tell he was in love with Jennifer."

"Of course." Her voice was bittersweet.

"And that upset you, didn't it?"

"Yes, it bothered me. The poor guy was about to not only be swindled out of his share of something he'd helped create, but also have his heart broken."

"So, what did you do?"

"What I thought was the right thing . . . at the time. I told him about the licensing agreement we were about to sign. But maybe if I hadn't said anything . . ."

"Jennifer would still be alive? I can understand why you feel that way, but don't. It's a waste of emotion and energy. Todd killed Jennifer, not you."

"I suppose." Fielding ran her fingers comblike through her hair.

"So, during this first meeting, how much did you tell Todd?"

"Initially, only that the contract was about to be signed and that he needed to talk to the Swifts."

"How'd he react?"

"Surprised over the contract, but mostly like an idiot in love. He told me that he trusted Jen implicitly and was certain she would never do anything to hurt him."

"Unless it was convenient."

"I hate to speak ill of the dead, but you knew her. Both she and Tony were sneaky crooks." Fielding glanced at the trio of Wintle execs. "And water always finds its own level."

"But Todd obviously came to a different conclusion later on. I saw you talking to him at the reception last night. What did he say?"

Fielding shook her head and said sadly, "He was distressed and didn't know what to think. He said that he'd asked about the licensing deal and that Jennifer had told him she'd simply 'forgotten' to mention the contract negotiations, but not to worry because she'd taken care of him."

"Which was the truth, although not the way she meant it to sound. What happened next?" I asked.

"I couldn't stand it. The contracts had been signed earlier that afternoon and somebody had to break the news to the poor sucker. I told him that the Swifts had completely leveraged him out of the deal.

He looked like he was going to faint and said that Tony must have forced Jennifer into signing."

"And you told him the truth."

"Yes, I did. I explained to him that I'd negotiated the contract and that Jennifer had made it very clear to me that she'd never wanted Todd involved with the bears in the first place and insisted on having him written out. He looked as if a ton of bricks had fallen on him."

"Did he say anything else?"

Fielding thought for a moment. "Just something I didn't quite understand. He mumbled that everything would be all right or good again — I can't be certain of the exact words — once he proved himself to Jen. Then he left and that was the last I saw of him."

"And he murdered Jennifer Swift about fourteen hours later."

"We never went back to the Maritime Inn, so we didn't know anything about that."

"This wasn't about money, was it?"

"No, he loved her very much and therefore did something extremely stupid."

"What's that?"

"Trusted another human being." Fielding rubbed the back of her neck and then grabbed her jacket from the table. "Is that all you need to know?"

"I think so. Thanks for your honesty."

"Before you go, can I please have your address and phone number?" said Mulvaney.

Fielding pulled a leather business card holder and pen from the inside pocket of her wheat-colored blazer. She wrote something on the back of the card and handed it to Mulvaney. "That's my personal cell number. I'll probably be moving, so call me next week and I'll give you all the information you need."

"Thank you."

"And now I'm going to get a ticket for a flight home on some other airline." Starting for the door, she paused to give Wintle a weary grin. "I'll be in on Monday to tender my formal letter of resignation and clean out my office."

"What are you smiling about? Is something funny?" he asked.

"No. It's just nice to have my conscience back."

Once Fielding was gone, Coburn said in a wooden voice, "We broke no laws. The books weren't copyrighted and, in any event, Mr. Litten had signed them over to Mrs. Swift. Everything we did was completely legal."

"Oh, I'm certain it was legal," I said with

a humorless laugh. "However, I can't help but notice that you didn't use 'ethical' to describe the deal."

Wintle made a contemptuous puffing sound and folded his arms across his chest. "Hey, who died and made you the judge of what's ethical or not? As far as I'm concerned, the deal was *ethical* as hell. The Swifts owned all rights to the bears and the books and I dealt with them. If Litten was too friggin' stupid to not look after his business interests, is that my fault?"

Although I hated to admit it, he had a point. I said, "No, I guess not, but it occurs to me that you have a major problem."

"Not from where I stand."

"Believe me, you do. You see, I'll bet there's something in that licensing contract that says Jennifer and Tony promised the bears were their original work."

"And?"

"Unfortunately for you, one of the things we've uncovered during this investigation is that the Cheery Cherub Bears concept and the designs were stolen from another artisan about two years ago. Which means the Swifts had no legal right to sell them to you."

"And you know this how?"

"Tony Swift told us."

Coburn snickered. "Yeah, as if he'll repeat that under oath in court."

"He won't have to." I gave the Wintle execs a wolfish smile. "Because we've got him on videotape confessing to the theft in detail. The contract you signed with the Swifts is null and void."

Twenty

Kinney shuffled his feet nervously while Wintle gave Coburn a swift calculating glance.

I said, "Uh-uh. I know what you're thinking: can you still ramrod the deal through, claiming you were acting in good faith, because you didn't know? The problem is, there were two upstanding and completely disinterested witnesses present when you were told the truth about who really designed those bears."

Mulvaney said, "And if we were subpoenaed, we'd have no choice but to testify to that under oath."

"And provide a copy of the interview videotape to the real designer's attorney," Delcambre added.

"Two witnesses? I count three. How about you?" Coburn asked.

"*I'm* not disinterested. In fact, I'd probably come across as so spiteful toward

Wintle Toys on the witness stand that a smart lawyer like you could easily paint my testimony as self-serving. You and I both know that all you'd have to do is imply that I wasn't outraged, but merely envious that you hadn't offered a licensing deal to my wife and me."

Wintle began, "Well, uh —"

"Which, by the way, wasn't a tacit suggestion that I was open to being bribed." I continued in an affable voice, "So, why put yourself and your company through that sort of aggravation and bad publicity? Besides, why would you want to do business with a wife-beater who forced Jennifer to steal the original Cheery Cherub Bears from a dead kid's bedroom days after his funeral?"

"Are you friggin' kidding me?" Wintle slapped his forehead.

"Nope. The original designer is a lady named Donna Jordan. You may remember her name from the teddy bear show. She was an exhibitor. Anyway, she made the bears for her young son, who was dying. Enter Donna's best friend, Jennifer."

"You're making this up."

"I tend to think the worst about people, but I'm relieved to know that even I couldn't dream up a story *this* ugly. And it gets better. Ready for the rest?"

Wintle shrugged helplessly.

"Tony gave Jennifer the choice of either stealing the bears or finding out what it felt like to be a slow runner at Pamplona during the running of the bulls. So, she decided to rip off a bunch of angel bears that were supposed to be donated to the children's ward of a local hospital. They sold some of the bears at craft shows and Jen used the others as prototypes for her pirated version."

"And you can prove all this?"

"If some enterprising attorney plays that videotape of Tony telling his tale to a jury, your claim to legal ownership will be as dead in the water as the *Exxon Valdez* and look twice as filthy. But don't just worry about the lawsuit."

Wintle understood what I was hinting at. "The media."

"Yep. It's precisely the sort of repulsive story that would grab and keep the public's attention," I said, making no effort to conceal my relish.

"And you're exactly the sort of SOB to tip them off."

"I consider that high praise coming from someone like you." I pulled out a chair and lowered myself into it, because my leg was really beginning to throb from standing so long.

Wintle turned to his attorney. “Steve, what do we do?”

“We call Swift right now and tell him the deal’s off, because he violated the terms of the contract. Then we follow up with a hard copy of the voided contract notification document via registered mail on Monday.” Coburn was already pulling the wireless phone from its leather case on his belt.

“You think he’ll sue us?”

“Probably. Better to deal with that scenario than his, though.” Coburn nodded in my direction as he clicked down the list of names in his digital phone book.

“He’s in jail, so you’re going to get his voice mail,” I said. “And I wouldn’t worry too much about him filing suit, because he can’t show he’s been damaged. Even the most predatory personal injury attorney will realize that since Tony and Jennifer never owned the rights to the bears, they had no legal standing to sell them.”

The attorney looked up from the phone’s tiny screen. “Go on.”

“It’d be like a burglar trying to sue a pawn shop because the honest merchant backed away from buying property when they learned it was stolen,” I explained. “The worst you'll have to deal with is a nuisance suit and that'll vanish faster than Vanilla Ice's career when you counter-sue, asking for the immense damages your company incurred as a direct result of Tony and Jen deliberately falsifying a legal document."

"Did you ever consider a career in law?" There was grudging respect in Coburn's voice.

"It was a childhood dream, but imagine how disappointed I was when I found out I couldn't be an attorney because I knew who my father was."

"Really? The way you act, nobody would think so." Coburn pressed a button on the phone and raised it to his ear.

As the attorney focused on the phone call, Wintle said to Kinney, "Production was going to begin when?"

Kinney's accent marked him as being originally from somewhere in the South and his voice was surprisingly rich and sonorous. "The thirteenth of next month. The only thing we were waiting on was the final go-ahead on the box artwork from Dumollard."

"Thanks for reminding me that the animation deal has just gone straight to hell, too. How much are we going to eat in unrecoverable losses?"

"That's hard to say," Kinney hedged. The

panicky look in his eyes told me it was a lot of money and he didn't want to be the one to break the bad news to his boss.

I said, "Before you scuttle the entire project, why don't you consider contacting Donna Jordan and offering her the licensing agreement?"

Wintle turned to me. "Do you think she'd deal with us?"

"I don't know. The only ax she had to grind was with the Swifts, so it can't hurt to ask."

"Interesting. Do you know how to get in contact with her?" Wintle was trying to appear nonchalant, but there was an unmistakable trace of eagerness in his voice.

"No, but I'll probably be seeing her sometime later tonight. However, our next stop is back to the Maritime Inn. Give me your business card. I'll explain to her what's happened and that you're interested, but I'm not promising anything. It will be completely up to Donna as to whether she calls you or not."

Wintle gave me the card and a shrewd look. "And what do you expect, a finder's fee?"

"No." I tucked the card into my wallet.

"A percentage of the action?"

"Nope."

"Not buying it, Lyon. Nobody does something for nothing. What's your payoff?"

"It allows me to retain my immature view of life."

"Huh?"

"It's childish, but even after twenty-five years as a cop, I still think that life should be fair," I explained. "So the payoff is seeing a hooligan like Tony screwed and Donna at least given the opportunity to decide whether or not she wants to sell the rights to her teddy bears. It's fun to pretend that things sometimes actually turn out the way they should."

Coburn disconnected after leaving a terse message on Tony's voice mail. "So, what's the plan?"

Wintle said, "Cancel our tickets. We're staying for now. There's a chance we can broker a new deal with the actual artist. Pete."

"Yes, sir." Kinney all but snapped to attention.

"Call Carolyn on her cell. Tell her I'm sorry for being such a jerk and that I refuse to accept her resignation. Then tell her I need her to be ready to negotiate a licensing contract with the artist that actually designed the angel bears."

"And that she'll be allowed to offer a fair

and beneficial agreement for both parties," I interjected. "Because, I'll bet if I read the fine print in the old contract and did the math, it'd reveal that the Swifts weren't going to get anything more than chump change. Right?"

Wintle gritted his teeth. "And tell her that, too, but not the last part."

"I understand, sir." Kinney fumbled with his phone and a few seconds later said, "It rolled right over to voice mail."

"Then go find her."

"The airport is pretty crowded, sir."

"She can't have gone far. Have her paged over the public address system. Go."

"Whoa!" said Delcambre, holding up his notepad. "Before anyone goes anywhere, I'm going to need your contact information for our report."

"And while you do that, I'm going to call my wife and let her know that I'm still alive," I said.

Pushing myself to my feet, I limped from the roll call room and sat down at an empty clerical cubicle that was decorated with Dilbert cartoons, a picture of a leering Johnny Depp from *The Pirates of the Caribbean,* and a hanging calendar featuring a weird color photo of a Skye Terrier with a computer-generated mushroom-shaped head and bulging eyes. I pressed the numbers for our wireless and braced myself.

"Honey, is that you?" Ash sounded both anxious and a little testy and with good reason. I'd promised to come back to the hotel and hadn't yet, I'd missed most of the teddy bear show, and had been incommunicado for over an hour.

"Yes, my love. I'm fine and I just wanted to call and update you."

"It's after four o'clock! Where *are* you?"

"I was abducted by aliens."

"Brad sweetheart, if they were smart enough to build a starship, they wouldn't have grabbed you. Where are you really?"

"Um . . . the State Police offices at the airport, but we'll be leaving soon."

"And you're at the airport because?"

"We had to talk to the Wintle management team before they flew back to El Paso. Tony told us that he and Jennifer finagled it so that they kept the rights to Todd's books while writing him out of the licensing contract. The suits confirmed that and told us a couple of other interesting things."

"What?"

"Todd didn't know anything about the pending agreement until early Friday morning, when a conscience-stricken VP tipped him off to the fact there was a contract in the works. She talked to Todd before the Swifts arrived at the teddy bear show."

"And obviously that's important, but I don't see why yet."

"You will once you have all the information. During that first meeting, the VP didn't tell Todd the Swifts were on the verge of swindling him . . . only that there was a licensing deal pending. Todd didn't learn the full story of how he'd been duped at Jen's urging until Friday evening when he briefly met the VP again. In fact, I noticed Todd talking to her and he disappeared a little later."

"To sabotage the inhaler."

"That's what I think, too. But, I'm also convinced he didn't come up with the idea spontaneously on Friday night. He'd been considering it for at least several hours, because I'm pretty certain I saw him stealing the card key to Jennifer's room from her purse on Friday afternoon."

"Which means he was already thinking about breaking into their room."

"Exactly, but I'm beginning to wonder if his motive was actually murder."

"How do you mean?"

I heaved a sigh of frustration. "I don't know yet. Something the VP said about

Todd is bothering me. By the way, where is he?"

"Still holding court at the Cheery Cherub Bears booth, I think. I've stayed away from him, just like you asked."

"Good. And how are our bears selling?"

"A fresh bunch of people came to the show after lunch, so we're getting a little more foot traffic at our table now. Before that . . ."

"I know. Almost everybody stayed away because the word got around that the cops thought I'd killed Jennifer. So, how many bears have we actually sold?"

"Just two, including Suzy Cinnamon Streusel from earlier this morning."

"Ouch. We aren't even going to cover our registration fee, much less the hotel bill for the weekend, are we?"

"Probably not . . . and thank you."

"For what?"

"For not reminding me that it was my idea for you to get involved in this investigation. This is all my fault and I'm sorry," Ash said gloomily.

"Ash honey, you didn't make me do anything and you've got nothing to apologize for. Would it make you feel any better if I told you that I'm having a blast?"

"A little, but that doesn't mean I'm happy

that someone had to die."

"Now, tell me: is the award ceremony still set for five?"

"Yes, but they've moved it to a different ballroom, because the CSI people are still processing the other room for evidence."

I looked at my watch. "And it's a little after four now. We'll be — hang on a sec, love."

Kinney emerged from the roll call room and half-jogged toward the exit. Hard on his heels were Wintle and Coburn, the trio apparently prepared to search the terminal on foot for Fielding. I hoped she'd hold out for a large pay raise along with her reinstatement. Next, the Baltimore detectives appeared.

Delcambre pointed toward the door and gave me a toothy smile. "Ready for another ride with the Road Warrior?"

I told Ash, "Sweetie, I've got to go now, but can you do me a little favor?"

"Of course. What?"

"I'm going to give Sergeant Delcambre the phone. He's bringing me back to the hotel and enjoys driving like a lunatic. Would you like to explain what you'll do to him if we get in an accident and that further delays me getting back to you and the teddy bear show?"

"I'd be happy to, darling. Please put him on the phone."

I handed the receiver to Delcambre. He didn't get much past saying a jolly hello before the grin began to slowly vanish. Ash didn't yell, so I don't know what she said, but before another ten seconds had passed, the detective was wearing an uneasy and alert expression that reminded me of how our dog Kitch looked when we lectured him on the evils of taking an empty pizza box from the trashcan.

Mulvaney noticed her partner's sudden transformation and said, "Can we put this on the speaker phone?"

Delcambre glowered at his boss and quickly covered the speaker button with his hand. Meanwhile, he was saying, "Yes, Mrs. Lyon . . . I understand, ma'am. . . . No, I wouldn't do that. . . . He was exaggerating a little, ma'am. . . . Just one, ma'am, and it wasn't my fault. . . . No really, someone else rear-ended my car. . . . You'd what, ma'am? . . . No, I don't think I'd like that. . . . I'll be very careful. . . . I promise you, Mrs. Lyon. . . . We'll be there soon — but not real soon. . . . Good-bye, ma'am."

As he gently lowered the receiver into its cradle, I asked, "So, are we ready to roll?"

"Your wife must really love you, because

she just told me that if you so much as got your hair mussed on the ride back to the hotel, she'd . . . just what is a whipstitch?" Delcambre sounded a little dazed.

"It's the way you hand sew fabric together very snuggly. A really good whipstitch — which I can't do, by the way — is so tiny it's almost invisible. Ash can do it, though," I replied.

Mulvaney did a double take. "How do you know that?"

"My wife taught me. And you know, as much as I'd love to be a homicide detective again, I really enjoy being a teddy bear artist and working with her." I turned to Delcambre. "Why did you ask about a whipstitch?"

There was a haunted look in Delcambre's eyes. "Well, apparently, she's going to whipstitch my . . . um, never mind. I'll drive very safely."

Twenty-One

Although my leg was aching, I passed on another electric cart ride, because it would have taken too long to have one dispatched to our location. Even so, it took ten minutes for me to hobble through the terminal and out to the patrol car. Outside, it wasn't raining now so much as misting, and off to the west, I saw a tiny patch of blue sky among the gray clouds. We got into the cruiser and after starting the motor, Delcambre surprised me by using a component of the steering system he'd thus far ignored: the turn indicator.

A minute or so later, we were clear of the terminal and traveling westbound along Interstate 195. Leaning forward to peer through the Plexiglas barrier and over Delcambre's right shoulder, I saw that he was locked on to the posted speed limit. Both his hands were on the steering wheel — at the two and ten o'clock positions — and he looked as if he belonged in an old drivers' education film. I looked to the rear and noticed there was an ever-growing mass of vehicles stacked up behind us because, of course, no one would pass the police car.

There was a burst of brief and undecipherable squawking from the police radio. Mulvaney grabbed the microphone to acknowledge the message. Then she pulled her wireless phone from her coat pocket and made a call. From the way she talked, it sounded as if she was receiving some mildly good news.

Once she disconnected from the call, Mulvaney turned around in her seat to face me. "That was district headquarters telling me that the media just left the station."

"Tired of waiting for the press conference?" I asked.

"That and there was a fatal car crash up on Loch Raven Boulevard."

"And people need *something* to watch over dinner. Any word on processing the gloves?"

"The techs just began fuming them. It'll be hours before we know whether there are even any latent prints, much less matching them with Todd's knowns."

"You can't wait that long to talk to him."

"I know."

"So, are you ready to give some thought as to how to work the contact with Todd?"

"Yeah. What do you think?"

"I'd just stroll up and say howdy. If you make it look like a formal interview, you're all but begging him to get a lawyer."

Mulvaney looked pensive. "Do we consider giving him Miranda?"

"Why read him his rights? You can't arrest him, so the contact will be consensual and non-custodial."

"And we don't have anything even close to P.C. to hook him." Delcambre signaled and gently guided the car into the lane that led to the Baltimore-Washington Parkway.

The P.C. that Delcambre was referring to was Probable Cause, the legal concept that allows cops to arrest people for felony offenses that didn't happen in their presence. It's the combination of objective information, evidence, and circumstances that would lead a normal person to conclude that a crime occurred and that the suspect committed it. Hunches, feelings, and unconfirmed suspicions can't be factored into the equation, which meant that Delcambre was absolutely right; there wasn't Probable Cause to arrest Todd.

In fact, we possessed next to nothing in the way of hard evidence. Until the crime lab completed its forensic work on the latex gloves and the Baltimore detectives had the opportunity to show the photo lineup with Todd's picture in it to the fifth-floor maids, all we had was an iffy motive and one observation on my part that might point to opportunity. What's more, the significance of what I'd witnessed was almost valueless, because I couldn't state for a fact that I'd seen Todd remove the card key from Jen's purse. I'd only seen him rifling the bag. However, there was nothing to prevent the detectives from talking to Todd.

As the police cruiser rolled sedately onto the northbound slow lane of the Baltimore-Washington Parkway, I said, "Can I make a few suggestions?"

"Absolutely," said Mulvaney.

"First, you guys have to talk to him without me being present. If Todd sees me with you, he'll realize that you've figured out that I was framed and assume you think he planted the stuff in my room."

"Which will mean he'll also know we suspect him."

"And you don't want to telegraph your moves."

"Makes sense. Where will you be?"

"With Ash at our booth or in our room.

And here's an officer safety tip: I'm done playing cops-and-robbers and she won't react well if you ask me to go anyplace else today. Come to think of it, if you ask me, I won't react well either."

"Yeah, right." Mulvaney made no effort to conceal her disbelief.

"It's true. This has been fun, but I'd forgotten just how sordid murder cases are. Also, ever since my retirement, my wife and I have been sort of joined at the hip and I miss her."

"Then we can handle things from here," said Mulvaney. "But we do . . . appreciate . . ."

"Don't start going Sally Fields at the Academy Awards on me, LT. It'll ruin my image of you."

"You really are a smart ass, you know that?"

"Uh-huh. Suggestion number two: I'm not telling you what to do —"

"No, you'd never do that."

"Hey, I prefer to think of myself as helpful. Anyway, don't hardball him. Treat him initially as if he's a witness who can clear up some troublesome points that have come up. Let him lie to you. Hell, encourage him to lie to you, because we all know how juries view that sort of behavior later on."

"As consciousness of guilt," said Delcambre.

"Exactly. Next, if and when you come to the point where the interview is transitioning into the accusatory phase, I wouldn't try to run a scam that you've linked him to the crime through physical evidence or a witness."

"Why not?" Mulvaney asked.

"Think about it. This guy is a paramedic. One of the main features of his job is going to violent crime scenes. He's seen how cops operate, so that means he'll know you're blowing smoke. Because if you had the evidence —"

"We'd just arrest him."

"Right, and another thing: don't talk down to him as if he were some sort of street hood or gangbanger. It'll insult him."

"And we wouldn't want to do that to a killer," said Delcambre. His gaze never swerved from the road ahead as he steered the car along the interchange ramp to the Harbor Tunnel Thruway.

"You really don't, Richard. I imagine this guy is just like the overwhelming majority of murder suspects we've handled during our careers. How many of them were actually Hannibal-the-Cannibal evil?"

Delcambre nodded slightly. "Just a few.

Mostly they're just stupid."

"And since there's no evidence that he's delusional or otherwise mentally incompetent, don't you think Todd is aware he's done something very stupid? He's about to lose everything. His career as a paramedic, his opportunity to write children's books, his freedom, maybe even his life, if he's smart enough to realize this could be filed as a capital murder."

"So, why rub his nose in it and endanger our chances for a confession? I see what you're saying."

"And he will confess if you're patient and remember something: people don't like to confess to murder, but they'll own up to making a mistake. So, let him depict the murder as a mistake."

"Sorry, but how can it have been a mistake if he broke into Jen's room to sabotage the inhaler and later planted murder evidence? That sure looks like premeditation to me," Mulvaney said.

"Maybe. But who cares whether it's the whole truth or not?"

"*I* do."

"You're missing the point. Which would you rather have, a confession from Todd that he poisoned Jen by mistake — a story you can later debunk faster than a James Frey memoir and portray as a nasty self-serving lie? Or, no statements from him and a theory of premeditation?" I said.

"When you put it that way, the confession."

"Then let it be a mistake." I saw that we were approaching the Harbor Tunnel entrance and glanced at my watch. "Can I make one final suggestion? It's four-forty now and you probably want to get to the hotel before five."

"Why?" Mulvaney asked.

"There's an award ceremony scheduled for five and you can be certain that Todd will be attending it, because there's a Cheery Cherub Bear up for a prize. You'll seriously hink him up if you pull him out of that event once it's started. So, you might ask your partner to drive just a *little* faster."

Delcambre's back stiffened. "I don't think so. Your wife distinctly said that she'd whipstitch me and she didn't sound like she was bluffing."

"But, if I assumed personal responsibility for the slightly higher speed then —"

"She said she was going to use an upholstery needle and her heaviest thread."

"That is a big needle," I said.

"So *this* needle isn't going any higher." Delcambre momentarily released his left index finger from the wheel to point at the speedometer.

"Then let's just hope that the award ceremony is like every other public function in the universe and starts the usual fifteen minutes late."

We passed through the tunnel, got off the Thruway at the O'Donnell Street exit, and headed westward through the city streets toward Fells Point. Along the way, Mulvaney radioed some officers at the hotel and instructed them to go to the lobby and await our arrival. My watch read 4:58 p.m. when Delcambre parked the patrol car in the fire lane in front of the Maritime Inn. I got out of the cruiser and took off the Baltimore Police jacket I'd been wearing.

Handing the coat to Mulvaney, I said, "Good luck and one final bit of advice from one egomaniac to another: you're a much better detective when you aren't completely stressed out over the need to be the star."

"Thanks. And by the way, I'd request a transfer to the parking enforcement division before I'd work with you as a partner . . . but you do know your stuff." Mulvaney gave me a quick handshake and then tossed the coat into the backseat of the cruiser.

Delcambre extended his hand. "Hey, you've got a spring broken in your head, but I like you."

"And vice versa. I'll tell my wife that we had a very safe and slow drive here."

"And to put that upholstery needle away."

"Yeah, that would be baste for everyone."

"Huh?"

"A bad sewing pun and you don't know how disturbed I am that I can make them. But then again, I'm a teddy bear artist now."

As we entered the hotel, I saw a small squad of uniformed cops standing in the lobby. Mulvaney waved them over into a loose huddle, while I headed for the corridor leading to the exhibit hall. Although I'd only been gone for a few hours, it seemed much longer, and I suddenly felt exhausted. It would be a pleasure to get back to Ash and relax. Plus there was the added relief of knowing that I wasn't going to be threatened with arrest again, at least for the rest of the day.

As I stumped along, I noticed that the CSI crew still had the ballroom sealed off, but a door was open on the opposite side of the hallway. I looked inside and saw the room was crowded with maybe a couple hundred folks. There was a small and elevated rectangular stage at the far end of the room and on it stood Lisa Parr with the other two members of the Har-Bear Expo judging team. It was obvious that the award ceremony had just started.

Assuming that Ash was there, I went inside and moved along the rear outskirts of the crowd, looking for her blond hair and the pink sweater I'd last seen her wearing. I also kept an eye out for Todd, but didn't see him. One or two people glanced at me as I moved past and I found myself scrunching my shoulders in anticipation of the hue and cry, but no one seemed surprised at my presence. Then again, Ash and I were still such newcomers to the teddy bear artist community that no one really knew me, so it's likely they didn't connect my face with the reports of my arrest for Jennifer's murder.

Meanwhile, up on the stage, Lisa announced Anne Cranshaw's bear as the winner in the "Undressed, Over Five Inches and Under Fourteen Inch" category. I recognized the artist's name because we had several of her mohair creations on our shelves at home. There was enthusiastic applause as Anne went up to receive her trophy.

As I stood there scanning the crowd, a buxom someone came up from behind, slipped her arms under mine, and hugged me tightly. I felt the brush of her hair against my neck, smelled the faint clean scent of her Pure Grace cologne, and knew it was Ash.

She gave me a kiss on the cheek and said, "Honey, I'm so glad to see you."

"Not as glad as I am to be here." I turned to face her. "Hey, I just came from that direction. Where were you?"

"Over in the exhibit hall. I came in behind you and I also saw the detectives out in the hallway. What's going to happen?"

"Once the event is finished, they're going to have a warm and fuzzy chat with Todd."

"So, that means you're all done?" Ash asked hopefully.

"They can talk to him. I sure as hell don't want to."

Up on the stage, Lisa had moved on to the next teddy bear award group: "Dressed or Accessorized, Over Five And Under Fourteen Inches," the category in which Jennifer's Cheery Cherub Bear was nominated. Ash realized this also and we both turned to watch Lisa as she read off the list of five nominees. There was a scattering of spontaneous applause as Jennifer's name was mentioned. Then Lisa opened a business envelope and pulled out an index card.

"The winner is . . ." Lisa's voice was larded with pathos and there was an understated yet dramatic sob. "Jennifer Swift's Cheery Cherub Bear."

The ovation was deafening and I felt badly for all the kind and decent people who'd been deceived into thinking that Jennifer deserved such applause. There was a ripple of movement to the right of us and closer to the stage and I saw that several people were encouraging and actually gently pushing a seemingly reluctant Todd toward the stage. He had a yellow Cheery Cherub Bear under his left arm and appeared a little chagrined at all the attention. At last, he shyly acquiesced and plodded through the crowd to accept the award.

Once he was on the stage, Lisa handed him the trophy, a nine-inch pewter figurine of the teddy bear in the Cap'n Crunch uniform on a marble base and gave him a chaste hug. Todd looked down at the prize in his right hand and then squeezed his eyes tightly shut. The applause continued and he held the trophy up while looking heavenward. Then Todd set the trophy on the podium and leaned toward the microphone.

When he began to speak, his voice was throaty with emotion. "I don't know why you're clapping for me, so please don't. Jennifer should be here for this, but . . . she's gone. But I want to share some thoughts about her, if you don't mind, because I loved her very much. She was the kind of person that people just naturally wanted to love. And the one thing I'll regret to my dying day was that I couldn't save her."

During the burst of clapping, Ash noticed that I'd suddenly become tense. She whispered, "What?"

"Do me a favor and go out and get Mulvaney and Delcambre. Tell them to come in and follow my lead." My eyes were locked on Todd like targeting lasers.

"What lead? What are you talking about, honey?"

"Promise me that you aren't going to be angry." I kept my voice low.

"Why?"

"Because I'm about to roll this guy," I said as I began to slowly move through the throng toward the stage.

"You're *what?*"

"Please, go get the detectives. Don't run, but hurry, honey."

"I will, but for God's sake be careful." Ash gave my hand a squeeze and began walking quickly toward the door.

"Most of you only knew Jennifer Swift as a superb teddy bear artist." Todd held the Cheery Cherub Bear up. "But she was much, much more than that. To those of us who were privileged to know her, Jen was warm and kind, thoughtful, caring —"

"And a two-faced, lying, manipulative thief who broke your heart," I announced in a loud voice as I pushed my way through the front of the crowd. "Which is exactly why she died."

TWENTY-TWO

I was fairly certain now that I understood what had happened and, more importantly, why.

Public safety professions such as firefighting, police work, and emergency medical service attract all sorts of people. Some are actually committed to serving the public. Others — like me — signed up primarily because the jobs are full of excitement and challenges. Unfortunately, there are also a few folks who embrace these vocations because they obtain an unhealthy emotional fulfillment in the role of a hero. They're "rescuers" and they secretly revel in the glory and adulation. In fact, they can become addicted to being admired as badly as a crystal freak is to meth. They've even been known to stage emergencies so that they can step in at the last moment and save the day.

And here's the really interesting part: If

you look up the listing for "loser" in an encyclopedia, you're liable to find a picture of a "rescuer." They devote themselves to saving other people because it allows them to minimize or even overlook their own huge personal problems. Often, they're lonely, vain, and immature, with tendencies toward monomaniacal relationships — which is just a fancy way of saying obsessive unrequited infatuation — and even stalking. As you'll have gathered by now, these behaviors were also a disturbingly accurate description of Todd's relationship with Jennifer.

The foregoing facts also confirmed my earlier advice to Mulvaney about how to approach the interview with Todd. The classic rescuer's self-image is of a modest and misunderstood knight-errant. If I could deftly shepherd our conversation along a path that allowed Todd to admit to an innocent error, while permitting him to preserve his aura of chivalry, there was an excellent chance he'd tell us what really happened to Jennifer. However, in order to do that, I'd have to give him someone to blame for being misled.

All these thoughts were racing through my brain as I mounted the stage with a grunt.

It was pandemonium for a few seconds. The air was full of stunned voices, gasps, and several calls for the police, which I suspected were for me to be arrested and not Todd. Meanwhile, Lisa and the other two teddy bear judges had edged away from us, but not too far. It was obvious they were apprehensive over the prospect of being at ground zero of a violent showdown, yet didn't want to be so removed that they'd miss the exciting details. Out of the corner of my eye, I thought I saw Ash come back into the room, with Mulvaney and Delcambre right behind her. I shifted a little to the right, hoping to block Todd's field of vision and prevent him from seeing that the detectives were present.

"What are you doing here?" Todd did his best to sound outraged, but it came out as just loud and petulant.

"You mean, why am I not in jail? That isn't important now." I paused to tuck my cane under my left arm and hoped that Todd didn't realize I'd done it so that I could use it as a bludgeon if things suddenly went to hell. "Let's talk about why Jennifer died."

"You killed her."

"Did I? Why?"

"Because . . . you were jealous of her success with the bears. The police have proof you did it."

"You and I both know that I didn't fill Jennifer's inhaler with superglue. And since that information about the evidence found in my room was never released to the media, how do you know that?" I asked gently.

"I, uh, heard some detectives talking."

"Then you may have also heard that a forensic expert can retrieve fingerprints from latex gloves. But, again, that's not important right now. Some mistakes have been made and we need to do the brave thing and own up to them like men."

Todd blanched slightly at my mentioning the gloves, but recovered quickly. "I don't know what mistakes you're talking about."

"I think you do and I'm saying 'we,' because I feel partly responsible for what happened. Do you recall last night at the cocktail reception when you asked me why Jennifer stayed with her abusing husband, Tony, when she could have a happy life with you?"

"That's not what I said."

"But it's what you meant. It's obvious you were very much in love with Jennifer."

"I loved her as a friend."

I gave him a bittersweet smile. "There's no shame in admitting it now, besides anyone with a set of eyes could see how much you loved her. Anyway, I wonder if I unintentionally misled you with my answer to your question."

Todd's eyes narrowed slightly. "How do you mean?"

"I told you that Jen probably stayed with Tony because she'd gotten used to the beatings and couldn't envision a better existence. Unfortunately, I also think I might have caused you to believe that she'd leave Tony, if she could just somehow see how good you were to her. Is that possible?"

Todd looked lost in thought. He barely nodded.

"God, I'm sorry. That'll teach me to psychoanalyze people I know nothing about, especially since it played a role in the decision you made."

"I didn't murder her."

I went on as if I hadn't heard him. "But in my defense, I'm not the only one that misled you and at least I didn't do it deliberately. But that wasn't the case with Jen, was it? And to make it worse, she forgot that she owed you her life."

"How do you know about that?"

"Tony told me about how he'd choked her and collapsed her windpipe and how you saved her." I paused as a buzz of unpleasant surprise from the audience swept the room. "It was an ugly story, except for your part. You did something that most of us only dream of doing: you were a genuine hero."

Todd swallowed hard. "I *did* save her life."

"And I wish you could have seen how envious Tony looked when he talked about the way Jennifer was gazing at you once she'd recovered consciousness."

"He was always jealous of me."

"With good reason. And because Tony was such a violent pig, you felt very protective toward Jennifer, didn't you?"

"Yes, because I knew — hell, everyone knew — that he abused her. She deserved a better life than that."

"Was that why you kind of inserted yourself into their lives? To keep Tony from hurting her again?"

"From killing her," Todd corrected me.

I nodded. "And the relationship also offered you the chance to help some other people, too, didn't it?"

"I don't understand."

"Your children's books. You wrote and illustrated them to teach kids how to behave like decent human beings. This was a way to get the books where they were needed most."

Todd's face brightened for a moment.

"That's true."

"And as you worked together, you fell in love with Jennifer."

There was a long pause. "Yes."

"But being an honorable man, you never said anything. Did you?"

"No. That . . . that would have been wrong of me."

"Do you think she knew how you felt?"

"I don't know."

"Actually, I think she did and what I'm going to say next is going to really hurt. Jen knew that you were head-over-heels in love with her and she couldn't have cared less. Believe it or not, she truly loved Tony."

"But, he . . ."

"Routinely brutalized her like some Nazi concentration camp guard? Yeah, he did, but she still loved him and don't ask me to explain why, because I can't," I said sadly. "And then on Friday morning, Carolyn Fielding broke the news to you that the woman you adored and whose life you'd saved was dumping you like last week's trash and stealing your books. You must have felt as if your heart was being cut out with a rusty chainsaw."

"Tony made her do it," Todd said in half-whisper.

"You and I both know that isn't true. Be

honest. I'll bet Jen had begun to start freezing you out about two months ago, hadn't she?"

"She was worried that Tony might realize how I felt about her."

"No, that's when Tony's probation was up. But being in love with her, you didn't want to face the truth that she'd strung you along to keep Tony out of prison."

"She told me that everything was going to be all right." Todd clutched the teddy bear against his chest.

"And yesterday morning you realized that was just the latest in a long string of lies. God, it must have hurt. But you loved her and you were willing to forgive her. Then, at some point, you came up with the idea that if you could only just make her understand how good you'd been to her, that she'd return your love."

Todd cast a panicked look in the direction of the door.

"Oh, don't do it, son. Don't run. All that will do is make a jury believe you did it deliberately and that isn't what happened, is it?"

"Please. I . . ."

"You wanted to be her hero again. You'd saved her life and maybe if you did it a second time, she'd come to her senses and realize that you were standing there offering her all the love in the world. Isn't that right?"

"Why couldn't she see?" There were tears running down Todd's cheeks.

"We'll never know why." I heaved a huge sigh. "But I do know one thing: an honorable man acknowledges when he's made a mistake."

"I didn't mean for it to happen."

"I know that. All you intended was for Jen to get sick, so that you could step in and handle the medical emergency, while Tony stood there looking helpless. Right?"

"Yes."

"So you stole Jen's card key, broke into their room and loaded her inhaler with superglue."

"I thought I only put a little in."

The crowd was beginning to become agitated and I hoped that didn't mean the detectives had decided it was time to move in, because I wasn't done yet. When I spoke again, my voice was tinged with disappointment. "You misjudged. But what's worse, in the end, you failed her by not being there."

"I was scared and you said that *you* could handle it," Todd sobbed accusingly as his shoulders slowly sagged forward.

"Nobody could have handled it. You put

enough superglue in there to kill a freaking rhino." I allowed my voice to become a little sterner. "But you could have prevented it. All you had to do to stop Jen from sucking death into her lungs was to say something. Why didn't you?"

"I just couldn't. My brain was frozen."

"No, it wasn't. You didn't say anything because you were ashamed of what you'd done and admitting that you'd tried to poison her would have meant giving up any chance to be her hero. Right?"

"Yes."

"Better she should die, I guess. But hey, I don't mean to sound judgmental. I've never been a hero, so I don't know what it's like." Now that I had an admission of guilt, I could drop the constricting Father-Brad-there's-no-such-thing-as-a-bad-boy persona and really burrow for the truth.

Todd cringed. "I panicked."

"But you apparently weren't so paralyzed with fear that it stopped you from grabbing the inhaler while we were doing CPR — thanks for the help by the way."

"I just couldn't watch what was happening to Jen."

"Especially since you'd done it to her. However, it did occur to you to trot up to Tony's room and plant the evidence there."

"That son of a bitch deserves to be in prison for the things he did to her! It wasn't my fault it turned out this way! It was his!"

"Maybe, but he never poisoned her. And why drag me into it by planting the evidence in my room?"

"I was so scared."

"Of me? What did I ever do to you?"

"Of being arrested. When I was at the hospital, I started wondering if I'd hidden the inhaler too well. Tony hadn't been arrested. What if the police didn't find it?" Todd was blubbering.

"And you knew that once they expanded their search for suspects, they'd eventually find out about the Wintle contract and how Jennifer and Tony screwed you out of the profits. That would lead the cops to take a closer look at you."

"Then I overheard the detectives talking to Tony. He told them about what happened in the parking lot and it seemed as if he'd convinced them that you'd killed Jennifer."

"So you went into my room while the maids were cleaning, dropped the evidence in the wastebasket, and then put in a call to the cops."

"I'm sorry."

I waved my hand in disgust. "Gee, that

makes everything all better. As long as you were trying to frame somebody, why didn't you plant all the stuff in Tony's room?"

"I was going to, but, but, but . . . there wasn't enough time." Todd sniffled and began to pant for breath. "After I put the inhaler in Tony's room, I went down to mine to get the gloves and superglue tubes, but I got sick."

"And by the time you'd finished barfing your guts up, it was too late to finish the job. So you rushed to the hospital, hoping to give yourself an alibi for the murder of the woman you loved and then came back to pin the blame on an innocent man. And let me get this straight: You wanted to be what? A hero?"

"Oh, God, I didn't mean it! I loved her and I'm so sorry!" Todd howled as he slapped his right hand over his eyes. Then, while continuing to clasp the Cheery Cherub Bear to his breast, he slowly slipped to his knees and began rocking back and forth as he wept.

Suddenly, I was aware that Mulvaney, Delcambre, and several uniformed cops were moving past me. The patrol officers handcuffed Todd and half-carried, half-dragged him from the stage as the room exploded with the sound of anxious voices.

"So, it really was a mistake," Mulvaney said.

"That's how it'll play in court, because you'll never be able to prove otherwise, but don't you freaking believe it. That isn't genuine shame and remorse." I jerked my cane in the direction of the cops as they dragged Todd out the door. "He's just upset that his life as a hero is over . . . and fifteen minutes from now, it'll be somebody else's fault."

Twenty-Three

Ash joined us on the stage and I noticed she looked troubled.

I asked, "What's wrong?"

"Honey, you may be used to watching a person tearfully confess to a brutal murder and then go catatonic, but it's still a pretty new experience for me. That was awful." She slipped her hand into mine and gave me a tender smile. "And by the way, I'm so proud of you. How did you figure out why Todd did it?"

"Yeah, and what was that crap you gave us in the car about how you'd rather be with your wife than finish the investigation?" Delcambre demanded.

"Did he really say that?" Ash asked.

Delcambre gave my wife a wary look. "Hi, Mrs. Lyon."

"Hello, Sergeant Delcambre."

"Relax, her sewing supplies are in the exhibit hall," I said. "And I *was* done for the day, right up until I heard him moaning about his missed opportunity to save Jen. That's when it all began to make sense."

"How so?" Ash asked.

"He glossed right over the circumstances of her death, but made a big deal over how devastated he was that *he* couldn't save her. That's when I became convinced that he was your classic emergency service glory junkie. Think of the cop that injures himself in an imaginary life-threatening fight with a suspect, just because he wants to be admired by his peers."

"Oh." Ash's eyes widened and I knew she was remembering a bogus assault-on-a-police-officer case I'd worked on years ago that I'd eventually forwarded to Internal Affairs.

"Or the firefighter who starts an apartment-house blaze so that he can 'discover' it," said Mulvaney.

"Exactly. Anyway, it just seemed to me that as long as Todd was in the mood to wax nostalgic about his devotion to Jennifer, that there was a good chance to roll him. Luckily, I guessed right." I let go of Ash's hand for a moment to grab the trophy from the podium and hand it to Mulvaney. "Here. You'll want this. It'll probably keep him feeling guilty if you have it in the interview room while you talk to him."

"Thank you, Brad. For everything." Mulvaney took the trophy.

"And can you do me a favor? When you get the chance, check on Donna Jordan's status at the hospital. If she's still there, I'd like to go over and talk to her."

"We'll give you a call later," said Delcambre. "Meantime, we've got a prisoner to take to the station."

As I turned to take Ash's hand again, Lisa blindsided me. She threw herself against me, wrapping her arms around my chest, while suffocating me with the overpowering scent of a perfume that probably had some edgy name such as "Crazed" or "Bondage," but smelled like Jordan Almonds. Meanwhile, Ash looked as if she was thinking about winding her right fist up, à la an old Popeye cartoon, and smacking the teddy bear judge across Chesapeake Bay and over to the eastern shore of Maryland. I wouldn't have blamed her if she did, but this was my problem and I had to address it.

"Oh Brad, that was one of the most amazing things I've ever seen in my life," Lisa said breathlessly. "You were so brave and you're so smart."

"Hold that thought," I said, disengaging myself from her grasp. I turned to the microphone and tapped it to make sure it was still on. "Excuse me, before we resume the award ceremony, I'd like to ask the group something."

The hum of low conversation died.

"I have a question about Lisa Parr, or Quesenberry, or whatever her name is this month. I don't know whether she needs glasses or not, but she's been hitting on me like a woodpecker on a suet cake and she's fully aware that I'm happily married to the sweetest and most beautiful woman in the universe." I paused to glance at Ash for a moment and then looked back at the crowd. "I didn't understand what Lisa's major malfunction is. But I've since learned that this is her MO at teddy bear shows. Is that true?"

There were nods and many murmurs of assent.

I'll give Lisa this: she was tough under pressure. She pretended to be surprised and then smirked. "Somebody certainly has a high opinion of himself. Me? Attracted to a flabby old guy like you? Please. That's the most ridiculous thing I've ever heard."

"Maybe so, but can I have a show of hands as to how many of you think that she is the *perfect* artist to design and make a line of stuffed animals called Bimbo Bears?"

Everyone's hand immediately shot skyward and there was about a second's worth of silence before the laughter and applause began.

"Thank you. As always, the teddy bear community has restored my faith in humanity." Stepping away from the microphone, I smiled at Lisa, whose lower lip was trembling. "Was it good for you, honey?"

We needn't have stayed for the rest of the award ceremony. Dirty Beary won an honorable mention, which was a little embarrassing, because I'd always known the bear should never have been nominated in the first place. Unfortunately, Ash's snow tiger didn't do any better than Beary. It, too, was awarded an honorable mention; however, a collector purchased the tiger before we left the room. Another collector offered to buy Beary, but I declined, because I'd already decided to give it to Sheriff Tina when we got back to Remmelkemp Mill.

Still, we had a pretty good time. We met lots of teddy bear artists and fans and I was peppered with dozens of questions. I had to beg off from saying anything about the ongoing murder investigation, but I was happy to answer any and all questions about Lisa. Later over dinner, I had the opportunity to bring Ash up-to-date on everything else that had happened, including the cheering news of Wintle Toys' decision to void their contract with Tony Swift and their interest in coming to some sort of licensing agreement with Donna Jordan.

It was just after seven o'clock when Delcambre telephoned to tell us that Donna was still at Mercy Medical Center. Her blood pressure was so dangerously high that she'd been admitted for observation and would be in the hospital overnight. Thirty-five minutes later, we were outside her room. I didn't think it would be good for Donna's blood pressure if I entered unannounced, so I asked Ash to go in first. She did and after a little while, she opened the door and told me I could come in.

Donna was sitting up in the hospital bed looking twenty years older than when I'd last seen her. There was an IV inserted into her left wrist, a blood pressure cuff around her right bicep, and so many sensor wires attached to her body that she resembled a life-sized marionette. She looked at me and I noticed that the electronic chirping sound marking her heart rate accelerated a little. I decided to stay near the door for now.

"Hello, Brad. Your wife told me a little about what happened." Donna was hoarse and I knew it was from screaming. "I'm sorry for everything I —"

"Donna, you don't have to apologize to me. You had every reason in the world to think I'd double-crossed you."

"You can come a little closer."

"Thanks, I'd like that." I went over and stood next to the bed, slipping my hand over Ash's.

"What will happen to Todd?" Donna asked.

"Probably a plea bargain to the Maryland equivalent of voluntary manslaughter and then prison. It's where he belongs."

"That's sad. He was one of Jen's victims, too."

"He chose to be a victim."

Donna met my gaze and I think she understood the unspoken part of my last statement. Then she looked away and said, "Ashleigh told me that you had something to do with Wintle Toys breaking their contract with Tony to make the Cheery Cherub Bears. Thank you."

"You're welcome. However, Jeffrey Wintle asked me to pass this along to you with a message." I handed Donna the business card. As she studied the engraved printing, I continued, "He said that he'd like to offer you the Cheery Cherub Bears licensing deal, and to call him. He's still here in

Baltimore if you're interested."

There was a small plastic waste receptacle attached to the bed's safety rails. Donna tossed the card into it with the other trash. Then she pulled a tissue from a box sitting on the small table adjoining her bed.

Dabbing her eyes, she said, "No, I couldn't do that. I made those cherub bears for *my* baby and it would dishonor his memory to see them turned into something tawdry."

"That's what I figured you'd say, but I at least wanted to give you the opportunity." Then I leaned my cane against the bed and slowly reached out to touch her hand. "But can I just give you something to think about before we go?"

"What?"

"You loved Benjamin more than anything and you'd have given up your life for him, wouldn't you?"

Donna sniffled and nodded.

"How do you think he'd feel to know that the only thing he represents in your life now is a source of hurt and anger?"

Ash reached out to stroke Donna's shoulder.

"This entire Cheery Cherub Bears torture session is over. You can make a fresh start. So, if you could give up your life for him, think about giving up the rage. You both deserve far better than that."

Donna didn't say anything else, so we sat there a little while longer in silence. When it came time to leave, Ash leaned over to give Donna a hug and a kiss on the cheek. Then we drove back to the Maritime Inn.

Later that night, as we lay in bed in the hotel room, Ash said, "You've been very quiet."

"Just thinking."

"About Jen's murder?"

"Hell, no. The last thing I want to do is give another second's worth of thought to that sleazy mess. No, I was thinking about the next teddy bear I want to make."

"Really?" Ash rolled over and snuggled up next to me. "Tell me more."

"Well, if you can have the Confection Collection, why can't I start a line of fictional cop character bears? Dirty Beary was the first . . ." I leaned over to kiss her. "And the next one is going to be an authentic Sergeant Joe Fur-day from the original *Dragnet* series from the nineteen-fifties. Thank you for showing me a new and wonderful life, my love."

"My pleasure, Inspector Lyon."

And so I lay there in the darkness, listening as Ashleigh's breathing grew slower. Soon, she was asleep. But I was wide awake, wondering just how the hell I was going to make a Fedora hat for a teddy bear.

A TEDDY BEAR ARTISAN PROFILE DOLORES J. AUSTIN

In Chapter Six, Brad Lyon meets a woman named Dolores Austin and tells her how much he admires her *Winnie the Pooh* shadowbox tableau. The artist is a real person and my wife, Joyce, and I met her at a teddy bear show in Timonium, Maryland, in April 2005. Dolores's *Pooh* creation won first prize in her judging category at the prestigious Teddy Bear Artist Invitational (TBAI) held in Binghamton, New York, in August 2005. It was one of the high points of her life as a teddy bear artist.

Dolores lives in Dunmore, in northeast Pennsylvania, and her passion for making stuffed animals evolved from a series of earlier artistic endeavors. Her first creations were Tole painted items that were so well received, one of her handmade ornaments hung on the White House Christmas tree during the Clinton presidency, while another piece is currently housed at the

Smithsonian Institute. This led her to creating rag dolls with hand-painted faces and, finally, teddy bears in 1995.

"After that, I was hooked. I just *knew* that I was great at designing! But, yikes! Looking back, my first bear still scares me," Dolores told me with a laugh.

That may be, but if so, the quality of her work improved both swiftly and tremendously, as is evidenced by her success at TBAI. She's also won awards at many regional teddy bear shows and in 2005 her seventeen-inch bear, Madison T. Bera, was nominated for a Golden Teddy, one of the top artist awards in North America. Madison is a sweet little girl bear wearing white baby shoes, an infant's short-sleeve shirt, and a diaper — one of Dolores's signature items of ursine apparel for her "Bearied Treasure" editions of baby boy and girl bears. And the diapers have been known to provoke some interesting conversations at teddy bear shows.

Dolores said, "Most people are surprised when they push the diaper down a little bit and see the bear has a belly button. Inevitably, someone will ask me if the bears are anatomically correct . . ."

With that said, you'll have to hunt Dolores down at a bear show to get the answer.

As with most artists, Dolores thinks long and hard about how a bear will look before she even begins to draw the pattern. It has to literally "jump" from her head before she's satisfied that the bear is ready to be "born." And she only creates a few at a time. Most of her bears are made as either one-of-a-kind or in extremely small editions. Along with creating bears from mohair, leather, and old fabric, Dolores also works in a medium known as needle-felting. This is a process by which large beds of steel needles are moved in and out through wool to create felt, fabric with designs, or three-dimensional shapes.

"It's almost a lost art form," said Dolores. "It's time consuming, but you have the ability to add features to your sculpted bear that aren't possible with other materials. Your creativity can *really* flow with felting!"

However, her biggest joy is going to teddy bear events where she can show off her furry friends to collectors.

"That's when the real fun begins," Dolores said with a smile.

If you have any questions about Dolores' wonderful bears or her schedule of appearances at events around the country, she can be contacted via e-mail at Dolores@BearMaker.com.

AFTERWORD

If you ever visit Baltimore, I heartily recommend that you explore Fell's Point. I love the district and it's worth noting that the bookshop visited by the fictional Lyons is a real place, a store called Mystery Loves Company. (However, don't go looking for a *Pam and Pom* mystery: the books exist only in my imagination . . . although I'm tempted to write one.)

Similarly, while there is no Har-Bear Expo Teddy Bear Show, Maritime Inn, Basingstoke Township, Dumollard Ani-Media, or Wintle Toy Company, several of the teddy bear artists named in this book are real people: Cindy Malchoff, Marsha Friesen, Penny French, Anne Cranshaw, and Karen Rundlett, among others. Furthermore, the story of how a photograph of Brad holding one of Karen Rundlett's bears ended up in *Smithsonian* magazine is taken from real life. It happened to me while my wife and I attended a San Diego teddy bear show in January 2002. The picture appeared in the August 2002 edition of the magazine.

Finally, the Teddy Bear Artist Invitational event mentioned in the book is a genuine event that teddy bear fans can attend. It's a great show and the proceeds go to help save endangered species. In 2006, I was blessed with the opportunity to do the national launch for *The Mournful Teddy* at TBAI. The show featured a mystery theme (a teddy bear was kidnapped . . . or *cub*napped, I haven't decided which yet) and I was invited to participate as the "Chief of Fur-ensics," a position created by Penny French, one of the event's organizers. The punning title was so deliciously awful, I was compelled to incorporate it into this book, but Penny deserves the credit . . . or blame.

The Invitational is held annually in mid-August in Binghamton, New York, and you can learn more about it by visiting the web site at www.tbai.org.

ABOUT THE AUTHOR

John J. Lamb is a retired homicide detective and hostage negotiator. He and his wife collect teddy bears.

The employees of Thorndike Press hope you have enjoyed this Large Print book. All our Thorndike and Wheeler Large Print titles are designed for easy reading, and all our books are made to last. Other Thorndike Press Large Print books are available at your library, through selected bookstores, or directly from us.

For information about titles, please call:

(800) 223-1244

or visit our Web site at:

www.gale.com/thorndike
www.gale.com/wheeler

To share your comments, please write:

Publisher
Thorndike Press
295 Kennedy Memorial Drive
Waterville, ME 04901